BLEEDING
TREE

OTHER NOVELS BY WENDY MOSER

PRODIGAL SONG
FLOWERS IN GREAT PROFUSION

BLEEDING TREE

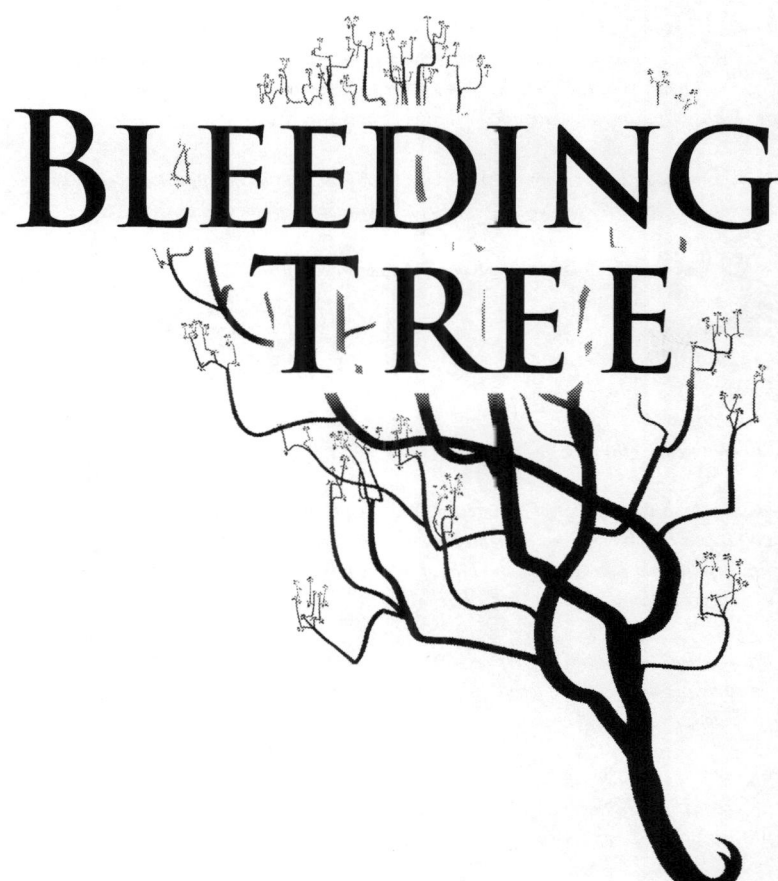

WENDY MOSER

iUniverse®

BLEEDING TREE

This is a work of fiction. All of the characters, names, incidents, organizations, and dialogue in this novel are either the products of the author's imagination or are used fictitiously.

iUniverse books may be ordered through booksellers or by contacting:

iUniverse
1663 Liberty Drive
Bloomington, IN 47403
www.iuniverse.com
1-800-Authors (1-800-288-4677)

ISBN: 978-1-4917-4983-8 (sc)
ISBN: 978-1-4917-4985-2 (hc)
ISBN: 978-1-4917-4984-5 (e)

Library of Congress Control Number: 2014918561

Printed in the United States of America.

iUniverse rev. date: 10/29/2014

Prologue

Hot water splashed against the side of the claw-foot tub, taking the blood down the drain. So much blood. Steam lifted from the edge of the tub and permeated the all-white bathroom. It was a sterile room. He liked that. A no-nonsense room. Clean and sterile. The mirror on the medicine cabinet was low, and he had to bend slightly to see into it. He smeared a small circle on the glass with a washcloth. Wild eyes stared back at him in a face he didn't recognize. The bottle blonde hair, the mustache, and the beard stubble made him look older than his years. They made him feel strong and invincible. He smiled, but his cold eyes didn't.

After he washed his hands thoroughly, he grabbed the last clean towel to dry them and then wiped down the sink. When he bent over the tub to collect the rest of the dirty towels, his arm started bleeding again, blood dripping down his fingers and into the drain. He ran the water slowly until the tub was clean again. The pillow case that he'd taken from the empty bedroom was full of towels that held the evidence against him, all their blood co-mingling with his own.

His footsteps and heartbeat pounded conflicting rhythms as he moved around on the black and white bathroom tiles and bounced down the wide, freshly varnished stairway. He was elated. He came, he saw. He lived, they died. It went just as he had planned it, just as he had envisioned it. Revenge was sweet.

He went into the office under the steps and picked up a bottle of Scotch, downing a few gulps for liquid courage. It helped. He jumped when he heard a noise, a scratching on a door, but it was just a dog on the back porch. Was a dog. Now a dead dog.

In the kitchen, he choked down a few bites of a chicken leg and gobbled up a large cookie. The November winds were howling like a wounded man. He'd heard that sound before, coming from his own throat. Adrenalin surged through him like a jolt of electricity, and he ran out of the front door, locking it behind him.

Chapter One
San Diego, California
October, 1975

Thirty-year-old Jerry Collins stepped out of the shower, slipping on his bathroom floor. The phone was ringing in the living room of his small San Diego apartment. He raced across the burnt-orange, shag carpet, wrapping his towel around his hips and securing it with a thumb and fist. He didn't get many phone calls. It had to be his girlfriend, Peggy, … or her husband, Phil.

"Yeah?" he said, hoping it was Peggy.

"Hi, Jer."

It was his brother. Disappointment mingled with relief. He didn't want to talk to Phil. He really didn't want to talk to Phil.

"Jimmy." He took a deep, long breath. "So what's wrong? You never call me."

"Nothing much. I just wanted to tell you that the old man …." Jimmy stopped, and Jerry waited for his brother to continue, his voice deep and calm, icy cold.

"The old man is dead. It was mysterious circumstances."

Jerry couldn't believe it. He'd waited forever to hear those words. He dropped his towel and raised his fisted left hand victoriously in the air.

"Dead? Mysterious circumstances?"

"Yeah."

"What was mysterious about his death? Did someone finally kill him? Did you?"

"The mystery is, he didn't die years ago. And no one killed him."

Jerry knew exactly what Jimmy meant. It was a miracle that no one had murdered his dad. He had more enemies than a mob boss. Before Jerry could find words, his brother let out a shrill laugh. It cut right through Jerry's brain like a long, thin filet knife. He could feel the cold blade dragging down his throat, as his brother's laugh echoed in his ears and came out of his own mouth. Yeah, he and Jimmy had a lot of pent-up passion for their father, and it was not love.

There were no more words. They'd said all there was to say about their father. "How's Mom?"

"She's Mom. She'll be fine. She'll be better now."

"Yeah," Jerry said. "We'll all be better off."

"Can you make it to the funeral?"

"Sure. Wouldn't miss it. I'll get a plane ticket tomorrow. Be home by Wednesday."

"Okay. Mom will be glad."

"I'll call and let you know what time."

"See you then, Jer."

"Yeah. See you in a couple days, Jimmy."

His brother hung up, but Jerry held the phone for a long, silent moment. He was holding on to the best news he'd had in years. He could breathe again. He finally hung up the phone and started across the room, his towel across his shoulder, his back relaxed. The pain from his childhood beatings and humiliation dripped from his shoulders to his chest, to his thighs, to his knees, to a puddle of bitterness on the floor at his feet. He felt taller and stronger as he walked back into his steaming shower. He felt like a man for the first time in his life.

Now he could make plans. He'd never dared to take control of his life before, but he had just been given his freedom. He felt giddy as he stepped back into the shower, and started to hum, random notes at first, looking for just the right tune. The song that suddenly came to him was the "Deliverance" theme. He could hear the dueling banjos in his mind, as clearly as if he were hearing the song on the radio. Back in the shower, water pelted the tiles, banging out a percussion accompaniment. He put words to the melody. "See you in hell, you stupid old man," he sang over and over again to the tune of his chosen song.

As he towel dried and got ready to go out for the evening, he continued to sing, working himself into a frenzy. He'd dreamed of killing his father so often, he almost felt guilty that the old man was dead. And then he felt disappointment wash over him, that he'd never actually realized the dream. He wished he had just a few minutes face to face with the evil that was his father, to tell him and show him how powerful his hatred was. Maybe he'd get the chance when he stared down into the open coffin at the lifeless form that had been his tormentor. Maybe he'd break the old man's nose like the old man had broken his so many times before. Who would know? It would be sweet revenge.

Chapter Two
Pine Falls, Iowa
October, 1975

"What did Jerry say?" Debbie Collins asked her husband, Jimmy, when he hung up the phone. "Is he coming for the funeral?"

Jimmy stood facing the staircase and didn't answer at first. Debbie could barely hear him when he spoke, his voice almost a whisper. "We ran up and down those steps like jackrabbits every day, Deb. Mostly to jump at Dad's beckoning or run away from one of the bastard's beatings." Jimmy's eyes were glazed over, as if he were watching the scene play out. "Jer got the worst of it."

"Jimmy," Debbie asked louder. "Is Jerry coming?"

Jimmy turned toward Debbie, nodding. "Yeah, he's coming. Said he wouldn't miss it. He's going to call me with his flight schedule." Jimmy finally looked at Debbie. "Mom still insisting she's moving?"

"Yes," Debbie said. "I think she's looking forward to being in town, now that Big Jim is gone."

Jimmy grunted. "Yeah, I bet she was fearing the old man moving close to any respectable people." He shook his head and grimaced. "She'd a been mortified most of the time. Like Jerry said, this is the best of all possibilities for Mom. For all of us."

Debbie nodded, lifting the avocado-green, floral pillows from the threadbare harvest-gold sofa and fluffing them up. "I'm surprised that Jerry thought of that. He's right. She'd have been too embarrassed to enjoy church circle with her friends. Of course, most of them knew Big Jim. They just didn't know how cruel he is ... was to her."

Jimmy glared at Debbie. "Well, she's staying here until after the funeral, and that's settled. I got enough on my plate right now. I don't have time to add any new jobs in the next few days."

"I'll help her. I know she wants to move as soon as possible, and really, Jimmy, I want that, too. I can't seem to please her at all." Debbie punched each pillow.

"You just got raised like a princess, always wearing those pretty clothes and taking dance lessons and piano lessons. That's not the real world, Deb," Jimmy said, waving his arms around the living room. "This is. The cooking, the cleaning, the laundry, the kids. Working hard is the real world. Working your fingers to the bone is the real world. Not all that ballet and painting nonsense."

Jimmy followed Debbie into the kitchen and sat down at the big oak table. "Any leftovers? I know it's late, but talking to Jerry made me hungry. Get me a piece of that chocolate cake and maybe a glass of milk."

Debbie uncovered the cake pan and lifted out a double slice of the two-layer chocolate cake. She poured a large glass of cold milk and set it in front of Jimmy, then sat down beside him. He scooped up a big forkful of cake and shoved it into his mouth, drinking the milk before the cake was swallowed. He left a ring of chocolate goo on the rim of the glass.

"What else did Jerry say?"

"I think he was relieved." Jimmy chewed and thought. "He said he'd been meaning to come back and see Mom." He scooped up another big bite of cake. "Jer said his life was pretty busy, but he thought he'd be able to get away from work for a few days." Jimmy looked at Debbie with a smile, his teeth covered in chocolate. "Jerry kept saying, 'So Big Jim is really dead?' as if he thought I was playing a joke on him."

"Well, you might have tried that, if you'd thought of it."

Jimmy laughed a quick, grunting laugh. "Yeah. Why didn't I? I wish I had thought of it when we were younger. I could have pulled that prank over and over. He'd a fallen for it every time, wouldn't he?"

"No." Debbie shook her head, a subtle smile on her face. "He'd call me to verify. He never trusted you." Debbie stood up and took the milk jug, pouring herself a small glass before returning it to the refrigerator. "I'll bet you my egg money that he calls me tomorrow to check on the story before he buys his plane ticket. He'll probably ask for Dad."

"What will you do for the kids' lunch money if you give up your egg money?"

"I'm not going to lose, Jimmy."

"So, you and Jerry talk often?"

"More than you know."

Jimmy frowned, and Debbie knew that look. She was glad he hadn't been drinking.

"He hates to talk to your mom because he never gets any news. He'd never talk to your dad, and he doesn't trust you, so who's he going to talk to?"

"What does he care about anything around here?"

"It's still his home."

Jimmy's frown turned into a scowl. "It's not his home anymore, Deb. I've worked hard to keep this farm in the family. My family. He'll be a guest here. That's all. This is my home now." Jimmy slammed his fist on the table for emphasis.

"I guess I better get the guest room cleaned up tomorrow then," Debbie said, dunking the chocolate covered plate and glasses into the sudsy water and then in the rinse water. She laid them on a clean, white dish towel to dry.

"Deb, do I look like my dad?"

Jimmy was looking at his reflection in the shiny toaster on the kitchen counter.

Debbie turned to look at him. He was tall and dark like his dad, and he had the same blocky build with thick arms and big hands. The face was a bit different, but probably because of the age difference. Debbie always thought Jimmy looked like his dad, but she was loathe to say it out loud. "No, Jimmy. You are a blend of your parents. You have your mom's blue eyes."

Jimmy smiled. "Yeah. Jerry has Dad's evil eyes."

"Well, I'm tired, Jimmy. I'm going to bed. Don't be too long."

"I'm just gonna go over the prices here a few more times and see what I can get for the corn and the beans, if I sell right now. I won't be long, Deb." He reached for Debbie's hand and squeezed it, his sign that sleep would come long after bedtime.

She turned off the sink light and flipped on the hall light. She was hoping to have a third child, but hadn't expected Jimmy to be in the mood, with his father lying in the Morgan Mortuary, his body still warm. She sighed and looked back at Jimmy as she left the room. Maybe it was the release he was needing. His dad was gone, and in a quick twist of fate, he'd become the man of the house. Now that his dad was dead, he'd have the weight of the world on his shoulders. And she'd vowed on their wedding day to help him in any way that she could.

After pulling down the quilted bedcovers, Debbie went across the hall to the bathroom. Untwisting her bun, she let her long, dark hair fall to her waist. After washing her lightly freckled face, she took an extra moment to smear on a touch of color to her cheeks and draw black liner under her tired, brown eyes. She went back to her bedroom and opened the closet door. Her sheer, black nightgown, the one she'd bought right after Christy was born, hung on the hook at the back, away from prying eyes. Jimmy would give her just enough time to put it on. She was tired, really tired. But she never said no to Jimmy.

Chapter Three

Jerry Collins still felt like a child when he thought of his father, and that made him angry. He tightened both his hands into fists. "I'd kill him right now, with my bare hands," he grunted, "if he wasn't already dead." He took a deep breath. "Wished I'd a done it," he added in a whisper.

His thoughts were more macabre than the words that he could actually speak. His first thought was that his father deserved to die ... a long, painful death, just like the animals that he slaughtered.

And what was his mother thinking, putting up with Big Jim for all those years? "Yes, James. Whatever you want, James. I'll get your slippers, James. Let me wash those overalls, James." There was no way she was going to wash the pig smell out of his dad's clothes. It had become his dad's smell. His dad smelled like a pig, grunted like a pig, and he was a pig. James Collins, a filthy, nasty pig. And a very rich one. If he handed you a dollar bill, it would smell like pig shit.

The call from his brother with the news of his dad's death had brought back many memories, none good. After he hung up, and after his euphoria dissipated, he felt like a kid again, a stupid kid, and Jimmy was playing a joke on him. First thing in the morning, he'd called back to the farmhouse and talk to his sister in-law, Debbie, to find out if it was true. Right after he made a pot of coffee. Right after he took a few deep breaths. Right after he cried, until no tears would fall. It was over. He prayed that his days, and nights, and months, and years of hell were over.

"Yes, Jerry," it's true. Your dad is dead."

Jerry heard relief in Debbie's voice when he called home the next morning. She had been traumatized by the bastard. And probably her kids had, too. He didn't even know their names, he was so removed from the family. The Collins family ties were really ropes, binding and painful, cutting into you so deeply, they made you bleed. Even though the ropes had been severed with his father's death, the feelings would never return. He would be numb all the rest of his life, in his heart and in the part of the mind that lets you give a damn about anything. Now he remembered their names. The girl was Christy, after Great-Grandma Christine. And the boy had his dad's middle name, Douglas. Jimmy's kids … they got to carry on the family DNA … inherited anger, cruelty, and hatred. Lucky kids.

A quick glance at his reflection in the mirror reminded Jerry he was getting older. He'd been trying to stay young, but time was getting the better of him. He held on to the fantasy that someday he'd be a successful lawyer with a loving wife and a couple of kids. He'd worked out, kept his hair blonde with a little help, and had even grown the heavy sideburns that were popular. But his brown eyes, Collins' eyes, were wrinkled and squinty, dull and lifeless, just like his father's eyes. He always hated looking into his own eyes.

Now, when he looked in the mirror, all he saw was a loser. Capital L. The Beatles had even written a song about him, or so he thought. The tune had come to mind every time he'd been passed over for a coveted promotion at the law firm where he worked. The paltry money he was making didn't give him the lifestyle in San Diego that he'd hoped for.

And just to remind him of his place in the family, his mom had called a few weeks earlier to inform him that he was not mentioned until the very last in his dad's will. Even the snot-faced rug-rats were in line before him. His brother would inherit the farm land, nearly 1000 acres, along with the dairy barn, the pig lot, and a small herd of cattle. There was no justice in this world. All he could hope for was that Jimmy would feel generous enough to give him the thirty-five untillable acres near the winding creek-bed. That plot of land was lush with trees and shrubbery, his hiding place. That's where he went to day-dream when he was a kid. If he could talk his mother and brother into giving it to him, he'd build a rustic cabin there, right in the middle of the pines. He'd stake out his claim, hunker down, and become a hermit. They'd never even know he was there. His father wouldn't approve, but his father was dead.

The last time he'd seen his father alive, they'd argued. And he could still hear his dad's hostile voice saying, "If you want something ... anything ... you have to work for it." Jerry had considered picking up the golf club that leaned against the office window frame and taking it to his dad's thick head. But he didn't. His dad continued, his voice becoming louder, "You will never get a penny of my money until you are the last one standing. Your brother does all the work on the farm, and his wife takes care of the chickens, and the hired men, and the paper work. And the young ones will grow up to do the same.

Go, enjoy your place in the sun." The old man had sneered at him then, and Jerry could see his disdain. "Just come back and visit your mom from time to time."

Well, he would go back. He'd go back for the old man's funeral and take a look at the *Last Will and Testament* of James Douglas Collins. Jerry was an attorney. And a good attorney could find a loophole in any legal document. He'd contest it for sure, and he'd break it, but only after schmoozing his mom and getting her on his side. Yeah, Jerry Collins was not going to take any crap, especially from his dead father. And he wasn't going to take it from his dad's clone, Jimmy, either. He could get mom on his side. They were a lot alike. He had her light coloring and frail bone structure. He shared her love of the arts. He had her temperament. He was her son in every way. All but the eyes.

Jerry's family went to the back of his mind, after he made his flight reservations for the next day. Today, he was sticking with his plan to take the day off work, ride his Harley out to Coronado Island, and meet up with his girlfriend, Peggy. His shiny, nearly-new bike was sitting in the far end of the parking garage of his apartment building, all gassed up and ready to go. He loved taking it out just for fun, and today the weather was especially nice. Sometimes he wished he had a car, but the motorcycle was his only mode of transportation. He'd bought it to fit in. Lots of the partners at the law firm had Harleys. And he'd met a few of his best friends at Harley rallies.

Peggy's husband, Phil, was one of them. They had the same bike. In fact, all their gear matched, like they were a team. He'd made the date to meet Peggy when she'd called to tell him she was leaving Phil. Jerry couldn't let that happen, even though he really felt her pain on all the occasions Phil had demoralized her and rubbed her nose in her stupidity and unworthiness.

At first, Jerry considered talking her into staying with the bastard so they could keep seeing each other. Their relationship had been going on now for almost three months, and so far he was sure Phil didn't have a clue. But if Peggy left Phil, Phil might figure it out, and he'd be hoppin' mad.

So today, after much thought and with deep sadness, he was going to tell Peggy good-bye. Even if she stayed in the area, he would not see her again. He would not cross that forbidden line that could lead to his own demise. It was the only thing he could do ... the right thing, the smart thing. She'd never dare tell Phil about them. Phil would never let her live to regret that kind of honesty.

And Jerry did like Phil a little. He was the only one that Jerry could confide in about his deep anger and bitterness towards his family. Phil seemed to understand. He said they were sympatico. Jerry was angry at his father and his brother, but mostly at himself. Phil was angry, too. But his anger was non-specific, general. He was just generally pissed off. After a few beers, he'd loosen up and say the most outrageous stuff. He was a ticking time-bomb of emotion, energy and execution. And he never let anyone forget that he owned Peggy. She was his ... bought and paid for.

Jerry had been attracted to Peggy since their first meeting at a California Dreamin' Rally. Peggy loved riding on the back of Phil's bike, and she looked beautiful straddling the powerful machine in her short shorts, her long hair billowing in the night breeze. The three of them rode together a lot. Sometimes when Jerry followed them, Peggy would lean way out, until he thought she might fall off. He wondered if it was her desire, to commit suicide by tumbling to the road, right in front of Jerry's bike, and letting him put her out of her misery. That would end all her troubles and his.

When she'd called him that very first time, she'd been crying and said Phil had twisted her arm again, and he'd punched her in the stomach. She'd said that she'd lost a baby that way once already, just weeks before they'd met Jerry. She'd called him a second time and asked him to meet her, just to talk. They'd met in the parking lot of a well-known apartment house, and she'd instructed him to drive to the nearby cemetery where she'd assured him that they would be alone.

"Phil is heartless," she whimpered. "And he hates children. He said they just ruin a man's good time." It was obvious that she was afraid of Phil. And she told him she was really afraid of getting pregnant again. Jerry didn't know if the beatings she'd talked about were real. He'd seen a few well-placed slaps that didn't look playful, so it wouldn't surprise him. He really had intended to stay out of it. It was between a man and his wife. And Phil was, after all, his friend.

But Peggy had changed his mind after an hour of talking, crying, comforting, and kissing that first night.

"Phil was wonderful at first," Peggy said. "We were two flower children, forever singing the anthem of the wild and free." She looked off toward a large, stone mausoleum near a creek bed in the distance. "Then he got drafted." She looked into Jerry's eyes, and he could see her fear building like a storm.

"And he was thrilled about going to war," she'd said. "The way he talked made me sick to my stomach. He wanted to kill them all. He wanted to gut them and watch them die slowly. He never talked like that before he was drafted, so I didn't know that Phil, evil Phil."

"When did he go, you know, on his tour of duty?" Jerry asked, stroking Peggy's thick, silky hair.

"He left for Vietnam a few days after our first anniversary. When he came home, he was different. Sorta satisfied but excited. The thrill of killing exploded from his eyes every time he talked about it. If we had a fight, he'd remind me how easy it would be for him to make me disappear."

Jerry nodded. He knew the type. It sounded a little like his brother Jimmy, only with more killer instinct. He'd fallen in love with Peggy that day. He'd felt needed. He'd felt loved. But Phil was always in the picture, even when they were alone. Like today. He would imagine Phil in the shadows when they kissed, spying on them when they made love. Yes, this would have to be their last time together.

Jerry zipped up his worn, brown biker jacket, the same one every guy had, and revved up the bike's engine. He was late meeting his girl for a long, lazy day, their last time together. Peggy would be waiting for him on the far side of the bridge, not too far from the Hotel Del Coronado. She lived on the wealthy side of the bridge. Phil was a hell of a computer salesman, making his way to the company's top salesman. And Jerry lived on the working man's side, with his meager junior attorney status and matching salary.

The sun reflected off the tallest building's glass windows and washed into his eyes as he turned off the bridge and made his way down the island's busy, narrow street. The sidewalks were filled with tourists strolling by quaint little restaurants and specialty shops. Someday, he would be sitting at one of those outdoor tables with his own wife, drinking a bottle of Mateus wine and laughing. But today it would be a ride to the shadows of the hotel, to a small parcel of land there and a tryst with someone else's wife.

Yeah, Peggy was his type, a Debbie look-a-like, and he didn't know if he could give her up. She was bringing a picnic and a transistor radio. They were going to eat, dance and talk. And more. She had a lovely soft mouth and such a pouty smile.

He could see her in the distance, her bright yellow halter top loose above tanned bare skin and tiny, fringed denim shorts. She looked like she was bare foot, jumping up and down like a ballerina and waving her hands. He started to perspire. This was going to be one long, hot good-bye.

Chapter Four

Debbie stepped out of the screen door onto the farmhouse's wide verandah. Buster, the large, yellow retriever nosed the door open and joined her. The dog followed Debbie everywhere when the kids weren't home. He was her golden shadow, his long tail thumping a happy rhythm on everything it hit. Once, the vigorous wagging broke his tail, and for two weeks a splint held it upright at a forty-five degrees angle. The banging continued, only louder, until Jimmy yanked the splint off with one jerk. Buster was a happy dog. A big, old, stupidly happy dog.

The house shivered and rattled in the strong breeze, and Debbie gathered her long sweater tightly around her body. The last of the afternoon sun was wedged between the old oak tree branches, each limb well over a foot wide. The tree was over two hundred years old, standing tall and strong for several decades before the house was built. Debbie had heard the rumors that the tree had been used for hangings in the early days, doling out justice to lawbreakers in the territory. But she couldn't bring herself to believe that. Yet, it wasn't that long ago that the town had gotten a sheriff and a deputy. Sometimes she studied the tree, looking for the branch that might have been used for the hangings. At times, she thought she saw a dark red stain on the gnarled bark, and with an artist's eye, the shadow of a lifeless body swaying like a metronome.

It was going to be a cold October night, temperatures dropping quickly when the sun went down. Some years they had snow by now, but thankfully, this had been a warm autumn. She squinted at the road, watching for the school bus. Taking a seat on the old rocker by the door, Grandma Collins' rocker, she waited. After Jimmy's mom moved to town, she hoped that the house would feel like her house, her home. Jimmy's mom must have felt the same way when she became the lady of the house after Grandma Collins died. She and Jimmy would be the third generation, one overlapping the other in a continuum of life. Dougie would be next, and one of his kids would follow, and so on. Collins' kin would always live in this house and work the land. It was their birthright.

The school bus was late again, so Debbie gave up her vigil and stepped back into the house, into the cool hallway. The straight, wide stairway flanked the left side of the enormous, formal living room. A big country kitchen and dining room swept across the entire back of the house. She'd spent many hours a day in the kitchen, and this day was no exception. She had noodles to make and beef to cube and dredge in corn starch before frying. Jimmy would have none of the easy supper fare that many farm wives prepared ... casseroles, or eggs and bacon. He had to have meat and potatoes every night. And dessert. Tonight's menu would be beef stroganoff, her own mother's recipe, and apple crisp made from the apples in their own orchard.

As she bent over the old kitchen sink to fill the pasta pot for her home-made noodles, she thought about Jimmy. He hadn't even taken a minute to mourn his father, working harder than ever to make sure the crops were harvested before the first snow-fall. He'd told her he only had a few days according to the *Farmer's Almanac*. He'd admitted that he probably shouldn't have fired the hired man. He was right. Tim Buckly had always been a faithful and steady worker. He'd needed the job, and Jimmy needed the help, especially now.

The last time she'd seen Tim, he'd come in from the back porch all angry. The screen door had slammed, announcing his arrival. He'd demanded to know if Jimmy had all the authority to fire him or if Debbie had any say in it.

"I thought we were friends, Deb?" he'd asked in a large voice that was higher pitched than his normal slow, deep tone.

"We are, Tim," Debbie had whispered and then repeated louder. "We are friends."

"Jimmy just fired me and you know about it, don't you?" Tim had been holding his John Deere hat in his hands, and it had twirled like a windmill on a stormy day. "I don't get it. I work around here like a slave, like I own the place, and he fires me." Tim's voice had softened, "And he said it had something to do with you."

Debbie had pouted, bit her lip, and then sighed. "Jimmy doesn't like the way we talk to each other all the time. We're too … friendly. And I made the mistake to tell him that I enjoy talking to you, that you always have new and different things to talk about."

"So … it's just talk, after all. I know you like to hear what books I've been reading, the news from town that you don't get way out here, and well, I know you like me sharing about the lectures I go to. So I say, 'so what?' Something wrong with that?"

"Jimmy, is just so focused on the farm work. He really doesn't think about other things. And he doesn't understand why I do."

"I know why," Tim had said, his dirt stained fingers combing through his thick, black hair, his hat falling to the floor. "You're a thinker, Deb, always have been. That's why Jimmy's brother liked you. You aren't just a housewife. You're more like me. You like chewing on the news and having life experiences. You gave it all up for that dumb farmer you married."

Debbie had stepped forward and lifted her chin to look directly in Tim's eyes. "Jimmy is not dumb. He's taken this farm to the maximum potential, all by himself. His dad was too sickly these last few years. You know that we kept it a secret from the town, so the old man could hold on to his dignity. But he wasn't right in the head. He got on you hard a time or two, and he made Jimmy's life miserable."

"Yeah, and every one he met, too." Tim bent over, picked up his hat from the floor and slipped it back on his head. "Sorry, Deb." He'd walked toward the door, and then he'd turned quickly, nearly bumping into Debbie, who was following him. He'd looked down at her with more than friendship in his eyes. "I'll miss you."

Debbie felt tears building in her tired eyes. "And I'll miss you, too." She'd added, "Now I'll have to come to town more often to find out what's going on. And I'll have to pick out my own books at the library."

Tim had stepped out the back door, and Debbie had gone back to the sink where she'd been skinning some tomatoes to pack in the hot, sterilized jars. From behind her she'd heard Tim's deep, slow voice calling to her.

"It's cause I have all my hair, isn't it?" He'd walked away, and she'd heard his pick-up tear down the gravel drive.

Debbie had laughed softly and wiped at a stray tear. Tim's hair was as thick and wavy as it had been when they'd dated in high school. Yeah, he still had the best hair, and his last comment had made reference to the fact that Jimmy was losing his hair, nearly bald on top with wisps of gray-brown hair sticking out from beneath his ever-present farmer's cap.

The back door slammed and sent shivers up Debbie's spine. She relaxed when she saw it was Christy, and she smiled when the girl yelled a joyous greeting. Christy was always happy to be home. She'd been expecting the kids at any time, yet she'd been lost in a daydream. Dougie followed his sister into the kitchen. He was her boy, waiting with open arms for a hug, the youngest kindergartner in his class. Sometimes, she didn't know if the hug was for him, or for her. She captured him in her arms and lifted him up to plant a kiss on the top of his head. When would he be too big for her kisses?

Debbie gave them both big smiles and large sugar cookies. "Nectar?" she asked, as she poured purple Kool-Aid into bright-colored Tupperware glasses. Both kids dropped their book-bags and grabbed a glass, sitting down at the round oak table by the back window.

"How was school?" Debbie asked, sitting down with them for the only break she'd get in the day. She poured herself a glass of Kool-Aid, too.

"Okay." Christy wiped at her mouth with the back of her hand. "But why did Dad fire Mr. Buckly? Mr. Buckly's son, Randy, said it's because you like each other. He said his dad cried right in front of him."

Debbie shook her head, confused and embarrassed. "Of course, we like each other, but Dad didn't think he was working hard enough. Tim liked to … day dream."

"But now they'll have no money for food. And Randy said his mother needs shots every week. She's very sick."

The door slammed again and Debbie jumped. This time it was Jimmy coming in. He looked sweaty and frazzled, and his cap was dirty with finger prints and a few globs of an unknown substance.

"I need to hire another man," he said, going to the sink and filling up his blue tin cup. "I'm getting too old to do this all alone. You may have to do the milking for a while, Hon," he said to Debbie. She sucked in so much air, the sigh she let loose scattered the school papers the kids had laid on the table to be signed.

That's just what she needed, one more thing to do. She looked at her jagged fingernails with permanent dirt deposits under them from gardening, glanced at the steaming pot on the stove ready for the noodles, and thought of the loads of dirty clothes piled up in the dank, dirt-floor basement. And she cried, small tears, no sound, but in her head she was wailing. She wanted to dance again, or take a book to read under her favorite tree. She wanted to feel pretty again. But those days were over.

And Tim wouldn't be there anymore to make her feel alive. He would be added to the never ending list of people in town who hated them. She looked at her husband and shook her head. Sometimes, she wished she'd never met him. Jimmy was becoming just like his father.

Chapter Five

Jerry met Peggy with his arms wide open. She ran to him in slow, glorious, psychedelic motion. If he hadn't been in love with her before, he was now. She was the picture of his forbidden love, his sister-in-law Debbie, the young Debbie before babies and age had ravished her body and left it soft and pudgy. The Debbie he thought was his soul-mate. Jimmy's kids were supposed to be his kids. He hated both Jimmy and Debbie for taking his dream and making it their own. They both knew that he was in love with Debbie.

But now he'd had a second chance with Peggy. And Peggy was younger and wilder than Debbie could ever be. Peggy was a flower child. Even today, she was wearing a big daisy in her hair. She was playful and encouraged him to explore the limits of all that they did together. In his dreams, she would have his baby, his love child. But his dreams faded, and he reminded himself that she was Phil's wife. She would have Phil's baby.

"Hungry?" she asked, after so much kissing his lips hurt.

"For what?" he asked, their bodies heating up as he made circles in the dust with a long, thin twig.

"I brought some bread, some cheese, some grapes, and Chianti." She rummaged through a small basket, bringing out a little checkered table cloth first and then a little clear bag. "And some pot," she added with a smile.

As she set the makeshift table up on the thick, green grass, Jerry sat down by the pine trees that bordered their little space and looked out at the magnificent view. They'd found this place by accident a few months earlier. It was probably on the Del's property, but it was set apart from the hotel and seemed to be unattended. The grass was always thick, lush, and way too long. But very comfortable for an afternoon of fun on a picnic blanket.

"Oh, no. I forgot the corkscrew." Peggy was fumbling in the bag that was empty.

"Let me have it." Jerry grabbed the bottle sheathed in basket-weave. He took out an elaborate Swiss army knife and jabbed one of the attachments into the center of the cork, deep and hard, and with a few twists, he yanked out the cork. Only a small chunk fell into the dark red wine. "No problem."

Peggy smiled. "There never is a problem with you. You are good at everything you do."

That's why Jerry loved her. She always saw the good in him.

"My dad died," he told her.

"Good. Good for you. How do you feel about it?" Peggy sipped from the wine bottle.

"Great. I feel great. I'm free. My mom's free. We're all free." Jerry nodded and smiled.

"I'm going back for the funeral." He wanted to tell her their time together was over, but he didn't know exactly what to say, so he changed the subject. "How's Phil? Is he getting the picture that you might leave him?" He took a long look at her. "Does he know what he could lose?"

Jerry took a bite of bread and washed it down with a gulp from the bottle. Peggy grabbed the bottle from him and drank deeply, followed by a few grapes that she stuck, one by one into her mouth. She chewed slowly and looked off at the rippling ocean in the distance. Her dark hair shimmered with a golden sheen, and her long, black lashes dragged across her heated cheeks every time she blinked. She turned to look at Jerry.

"I told him. I wrote him a letter." She nodded. "He knows I'm leaving. He's been pretending he didn't get it. But I know he did. His eyes are burning with hatred every time he looks at me. I think he's afraid I'll ask for too much in the divorce."

"You don't have to ask. This is a no-fault state, fifty-fifty. You automatically get half."

Peggy's eyes lit up, and then her lids dropped to brooding. "Then it will be a fight to the finish. He'll never give me anything. He'd rather see me dead. I'll just disappear."

Jerry hadn't thought of that. Phil was one man that could make that happen, and if Phil knew the truth, Jerry was sure he would be next in line for annihilation.

"He's had other girls. I know he has," Jerry offered.

"I think he has, too. But how do you know?" Peggy demanded.

"I've been with him. We go to a bar, and he hits on one pretty girl after another until one agrees to go home with him. He always leaves with someone. I don't know where he goes, but he goes."

"Why didn't you tell me? I've been ready to leave him for a long time, but I wasn't a hundred percent sure. It was just a feeling, a whiff of heavy perfume or a stain on his pants. I just didn't have proof."

Peggy stood, turned away from Jerry, and wrapped her arms around her shoulders. Jerry could see she was crying so he let her. She deserved it. She had a lot to cry about.

"I told him there was someone else. But I didn't tell him about you."

She turned toward Jerry. "There is someone else, right? You'll be there for me, won't you?"

Jerry struggled to his feet. "Of course, Peg. Sure, I'll be there." He said it, but he was pretty sure he wouldn't be there at all. "I'm a bit bummed, thinking Phil might find out about us. Let's not hurry this. Let me see what I can do for you, legally. We need to make sure he can't fight this. We need to make sure you can win."

"Are you scared of Phil, too?" Peggy asked.

Jerry took a deep breath, remembering Phil's nasty temper and his strength when they wrestled a few times. Phil could have hurt him, but he was just playing. Jerry for sure didn't want to meet the end of Phil's fist in a fit of anger. So he'd have to outsmart him. "Give me some time, okay. Stay with him and try to make nice. I just need some time."

Peggy smiled and slid her body into Jerry's arms. She was so warm and beautiful and in some ways so juvenile and silly. They'd never had a meaningful conversation. She was just a temptress and a delight. But in the end, she wasn't Debbie, who was the valedictorian of their class … smart, and creative, and full of energy.

Peggy kissed his chin, his cheek, and then he kissed her back. The grass was so tall that they got lost in the thick, green blades, and the afternoon became evening as they played, and whispered, and cuddled. Jerry hoped he was doing the right thing. He wasn't sure, but it felt right.

He would have become paralyzed if he'd seen cold, driven eyes watching them. But as his energy exploded inside Peggy, he had no cares at all. He heard the echo of a deep guttural engine rev up, the sound becoming a tiny thread of his consciousness. But at that moment, it didn't matter. Everything was good.

Chapter Six

"See to it that the children have their Sunday best on tomorrow." Bernice Collins addressed her son, Jimmy, who was standing next to Debbie in the parlor, late in the afternoon, the day before her husband's funeral. Sun shards slashed Jimmy's face in half, making him look happy and angry at the same time, like he was wearing a theatre mask … half comedy, half tragedy.

"Yeah, Mom. That's Debbie's job." Jimmy glanced at Debbie, who smiled kindly at her mother-in-law. "Mother, I'll take care of it," she promised. "You will be very proud of your grandchildren."

Bernice lifted her upper lip in the way she always did, and Debbie considered that a snub of indifference. Jimmy's mom had never been overly friendly. She'd been all business in the years they had lived together, no time for silliness, or even just sitting down with a cup of coffee after breakfast. Since Big Jim's death, she hadn't shed a tear. Debbie pitied her mother-in-law, so lacking in emotion. Big Jim must have beaten joy and laughter out of her like he had both of his sons. Whatever punishment he doled out to Bernice in the past had made her loyal and cold.

Her Jimmy had never laid a hand on his own kids, but once when he'd had a lot to drink, Scotch and water times ten, he'd lifted his hand to Debbie. It covered her face completely and ended in a push as he stepped back just in time. She'd told him that was the last time he'd strike her. The next time his hand was raised to her, she'd be finding an attorney, and she'd be taking the kids to Illinois to live with her family. He'd acted really sorry the next day and said that only an animal would hit a woman or a child.

The only time Bernice had let Debbie hug her was right after they found Big Jim's body lying in a heap on the barn floor, his skin still clinging to the pitchfork tines in a gruesome draping. He'd gone out to the barn to pitch hay from the loft and had fallen on the pitchfork and then tumbled twenty feet to the floor below, his skin and blood still clinging to the deadly prongs. He must have been there for hours, before Bernice found him and came running into the house to get help. Debbie knew right away when she saw the old man that it was too late. But she called the telephone operator to send help, and then she'd held Bernice for a few minutes, so close that she'd felt the old woman's heart beating two times for each of her own.

"Jimmy, is Jerry's room ready yet?" Bernice glared at her son.

"Mom, Debbie handles that, too." He shook his head and scowled at his mother. "Are you okay?"

"I don't know why Jerry has to come back. He'll just go on about what a terrible Father Big Jim was," Bernice said. She wrung her hands and touched her left eyebrow where Debbie knew her headaches always started. "I know there was bad blood between them. Big Jim didn't seem to notice, but I did. Jerry hated his father." She rubbed her eyebrow again. "Big Jim did the best he could as a Dad, but he just didn't know what to do, so he did just as his dad did, exactly what his dad did."

Bernice picked up the old family picture sitting on the small phone stand by the fireplace. Big Jim, a young man then, stood next to his dad, shoulder to shoulder. His brother Virgil sat with his mother on a settee. Virgil held his mother's hand. None of them were smiling. Bernice put the picture back, laying it face down.

"Jerry reminded Big Jim of his brother Virgil," Bernice said. "He said the man was lazy and spent too much time reading and playing cards. Big Jim had to do all the work, so when your grandpa died, your dad inherited the farm. In the years that followed, your Uncle Virgil visited the farm at least once a month, always with his hand out, needing money for this or that, and Grandma Collins always gave it to him, until he died.

"Jerry's nothing like that, Mother," Debbie said. "He works as a lawyer and hasn't been home for any hand-outs ever, that I can remember. I'll be glad to see him. And you will, too."

"He doesn't need to come back to see me," Bernice said. "But I guess I'm glad he's coming back. It wouldn't look good in town if he didn't. At least he's putting on a show of respect."

Bernice headed toward the back room where she had her sewing machine. She turned at the door with a stern look directed at Jimmy. "Well, is his room ready?"

Debbie smiled and shook her head. She took a pile of folded clothes … a blanket, sheets, and towels … from the bench by the front door and headed toward the steps.

"Right now, Mother. I'll have it dusted and clean sheets on the bed in just a few minutes. But you do know he's not coming until later tonight?"

"Who's coming?"

Debbie smiled. "Jerry's coming."

"I don't know why. He never cared for Big Jim. But I guess I'm glad he's coming."

Debbie trudged up the wide mahogany staircase. At Bernice's insistence, she had polished the dark wood on the banister and along the carpet edges weekly with Old English furniture polish until the wood glistened a shiny black. The dark gray carpet down the center of the steps had seen better days and would be light green after Mother died. There would be no changes until that day. It would still be Mother Collins' house, even after she moved to town.

Debbie walked to the end of the hallway and into Jerry's old room at the back of the house, far away from the family sleeping rooms. She stepped down from the carpet onto the wooden floor. This part of the house had been the servants quarters when the house was new. Grandpa had built the room big enough for two bunk beds. And it had its own small, private bath, nothing fancy. In fact, it still had one of the old style toilets with the water stored in a wooden box on the wall, a pull cord for flushing. In the back corner of the room, there was a narrow door that went up to the attic.

In the early days, the room had been shared by a man servant and two or three farm hands. And decades later, the bunks were removed and a single girl had been given the room. The old trundle bed and dresser that she'd used were still in the attic, under a blanket of ancient dust. She was grandma's hired girl and did the cleaning and washing for room and board. She was also Grandma Collins' companion. After Grandma died, the room had been vacant until Jerry asked for it. He liked the privacy.

When Jerry lived there, he had a few magazine pictures of voluptuous models on the walls, all with great legs. His favorite was Jane Mansfield, who he said was really a brunette. She had to be, he said, with those big brown eyes. And on the inside of the attic door, he had taped a picture of a naked girl, the first one Debbie had ever seen. He'd showed it to Debbie once and then left it there to irritate her, knowing she'd have to look at it every time she went to the attic for something. She was going to ask him to take it down tomorrow. She didn't want Christy or Dougie seeing it. If she'd asked him to remove it, he probably would have made a big production out of it, just to embarrass her.

He didn't have much furniture, a small chest of drawers, an old writing desk, and a double bed that sagged in the middle. Jimmy said it was from all the action in the early days. But Debbie couldn't believe that Jerry had that much action.

Debbie was on the bed only once. One night when Bernice and Big Jim were in town for a church dinner, Jimmy had brought her out to the farm to neck, hoping for more, he said. Jerry had been there, and they'd all hung out in his room. When Jimmy left the room to steal a bottle of his dad's Scotch, Jerry had pushed her down on the bed and laid down on top of her for just a minute, and then he'd let her get up without even trying to kiss her. He's joked that he just wanted to say he laid Debbie in his own bed. Technically, he'd been right. Debbie had been so afraid that she couldn't breathe, with Jerry's face so close to hers. She was terrified that Jimmy would find them and think she was a party to it. And then she'd envisioned Jimmy killing his little brother, and it would be her fault. She knew Jimmy had a temper, and he was strong as a bull. And he had a jealous streak.

But when Jimmy returned, Jerry was reading a poem to her about butterflies, and Jimmy danced into the room like a fairy with elephant feet. "Jer," he'd said. "Don't you even know how to talk to a girl when you're alone?"

Jimmy's eyes had rolled so far back in his head that Debbie had laughed, and to this day, she knew that Jerry thought she'd been laughing at him. He was never very friendly again, and she felt subtle disappointment bordering on hatred seeping from his eyes every time he looked at her. Debbie felt sorry for him. And she understood him. They were a lot alike. She snapped the sheets open and stretched them onto the bed, a task she'd done so many times she didn't have to think about it. So instead, she thought about Jerry and what it might have been like had she made the right choice years ago.

Chapter Seven

The twin engine prop-plane landed at the small airport in Pine Falls after a short flight from Minneapolis. It flew right over the Collins' farm land, acres and acres of gently rolling hills and gutted creek-beds, acres gathered over decades by Jerry's grandfather, Conrad Collins. Some of the local folklore considered him the areas richest land baron in the early days, and none of those who knew him thought too kindly of him. In return for the deeds to their property, he helped all the struggling farm widows by building them a nice little ranch house on their property and taking care of all their worldly needs. Most of them embraced the idea with thankfulness. In that way, he had acquired several hundred acres of property near or adjacent to his own farm, bringing his final total to over one thousand acres.

He became a legend. After acquiring the farms, he would move renters with their growing families into the big farmhouses, and with a heavy hand and a watchful eye, he became a respected businessman as well as a hard-working farmer.

Jerry stepped out onto the tarmac, a runway three times as long as needed for the small plane he'd taken from

Minneapolis. It was so long, that a jumbo jet once landed at the airport for a charter trip to Hawaii. And President Nixon's new Air Force One had made some practice landings there, since the rarely used airport was isolated from large city air traffic. Debbie said that on one of the touchdowns, it nearly shaved off the top of the oak tree in the front of the house. Jerry thought she had been exaggerating.

As Jerry followed in the small line of disembarking passengers, he spotted his brother waiting by the terminal door, tapping his foot and looking at his watch. Always moving, always in a hurry. At one time, he'd thought about asking Jimmy to come visit him. But the slow, easy pace in California would have driven Jimmy insane. Too bad he didn't get that done. An insane brother would be easier to deal with.

"Jimmy," he called from the gate.

"Jer," his brother responded.

The two men shook hands awkwardly, and then both right hands slipped into pants pockets.

"Nice Leather," Jimmy said, touching Jerry's sleeve.

"Thanks. It keeps me warm on my cycle. Thought it might be cool here in October."

"You bike?"

"Harley. It's a great ride."

"Oh, I was thinking you meant bicycle. We have some new trails here, old river beds."

Jerry laughed. "It seems warm today."

"Yeah, Indian Summer. It's changing tonight. Might hit forty degrees before morning."

"Mom, okay?"

"You know Mom. She's cooking and baking like this is a damn family reunion."

"Yeah. That's Mom." Jerry took off his jacket. "Kids okay? Debbie?"

"Yeah. Dougie is getting to be a smart aleck. Reminds me of you. Christy is eleven going on twenty-one. She's so ready in her mind to be an adult, but she's still, you know, a little girl."

Jerry picked up his suitcase and pushed at the door. Jimmy pointed to his pickup ... dusty and muddy from working in the fields after the recent rain.

Jerry frowned as he gave the truck the once-over.

"Yeah," Jimmy said. "It's filthy. We had just enough rain to make a muddy mess but not enough to help the parched fields."

Both brothers were silent as the truck moved slowly down the airport road.

"Beer?" Jimmy asked.

"Sure."

"Where to?"

"Dew Drop Inn still open?" Jerry asked.

"Yup. I guess we can go there."

Jimmy turned onto the highway towards town. Jerry laughed when he saw that Jimmy was guiding the car with just one finger on the lower edge of the steering wheel. "Like the old days."

Jimmy smiled. "I taught you that."

"Yeah, but you didn't tell me that there was no damn power steering fluid. I missed that corner by thirty feet."

"Hit the tree square on. Daddy really gave you hell."

Jerry wasn't smiling now. He remembered all the trouble he got into because his older brother headed him in the wrong direction or just plain lied to him. He'd been too unsuspecting, too gullible. But not anymore. Jimmy would never get the best of him, ever again.

The Dew Drop Inn was just like it had been for years and
years. The door was jammed, so you had to give it a good
push. The old, wooden floor tilted to the left toward the big
mahogany bar. He'd had his first beer there. Kissed his first
girl there. Gotten into trouble there when his brother ratted
him out and said he was under age. He'd watched the girl he'd
just kissed take his brother's hand as he was being escorted out
alone. Jimmy was smiling at him, that gotcha smile.

"How about a pitcher?" Jimmy asked.

"Sounds good. I could use a good cold one. They don't
drink beer in California. It's just Sangria, Lambrusco, or
Chianti. I'd love a good, cold beer."

The waitress smiled at Jimmy and gave him a big hug. She
was a cutie. Jerry wondered if she was old enough to be serving
alcohol.

"Friend of Christy's?" he asked.

"Nope." They both watched the waitress wiggle away.
"Friend of mine. I come here so often she thinks I'm her
boyfriend." Jimmy nodded to her when she looked back.

"Debbie's my girl. But my brain can't get that straight with
my eyes."

The waitress came back, wearing fresh lipstick, hot pink,
and carrying two pitchers of frothy beer. Jimmy wadded up two
ten dollar bills and pressed them into her hand. She kissed his
cheek.

"Does Debbie know?"

"Yeah. She encourages it. She feels sorry for Santha. The
girl's got two little ones at home to feed and no husband. She
and Debbie met at the laundromat when our washer broke
down."

Just like Jimmy to have a sanctioned flirtation. But knowing
Jimmy, that's as close as he'd ever get to real fun. And so Jerry

felt sorry for him. Jerry on the other hand could have a quickie any night of the week, if he wanted to. Peggy was his girl, and she was crazy about him.

The brothers drank in silence. They'd said all they cared to say. They weren't close, and Jerry was still harboring old anger, the depth of it always boiling to the surface of his skin when he was anywhere near Jimmy, until he could feel it showing on his face, the redness making him even angrier.

The ride home after two pitchers was more friendly. After bantering cheerfully about life without Big Jim, Jerry talked about California, and Jimmy talked about the corn crop. "Sweet corn just didn't take off this year. It was a bust for Debbie's Christmas fund. She had big plans for the money, but it looks like she'll have to settle. Looks like the field corn is a might better."

Jerry looked toward the farmyard as they turned into the driveway. The sun was just setting behind the barn, making it glow a deeper crimson as the house was being swallowed in the dusk of a moonless night. Mom was probably cooking potatoes in her big cast-iron pot. There could never be enough potatoes. And for a moment Jerry felt sorry for Jimmy. He had to live all these years with Mom and Dad. Go to sleep with his wife in the room next to his mom's and dad's room, make love to his wife in the same room where he'd slept as a boy. And now, a man, he was still sleeping there.

The back porch smelled a little musty, the big stack of empty bushel baskets waiting for the apple harvest. Jerry hated this time of year. He was always on apple duty while Jimmy was driving the tractor. Jimmy got the man's job, and Jerry got the woman's job. He was always second class to his brother in his dad's eyes. Big Jim and little Jimmy. Bernice and Jerry. Mom.

He couldn't wait to see her and give her the hug she always loved.

He rushed in the door and found his mom just where he knew she would be, stirring a big pot on the gas stove, all the burners lit up.

"Mom." He twirled her around to hug her.

She pulled away. "Jerry. Where have you been? I expected you an hour ago, and the food is getting cold." She frowned at him. "And you smell like beer."

Jerry looked at Jimmy, and Jimmy was smiling, that gotcha smile. Someday Jerry was going to wipe that smile right off Jimmy's face.

Chapter Eight

Jerry lay still as death in the dark room. He thought he heard
something and turned his head with a jerk. His mother stood
at his bedroom door, just looking at him. The hall light was
shining behind her and shed a stream of light onto his wind
up clock. It was five in the morning. It was the day of his dad's
funeral.

"Mom?"

"Sorry, son. I just wanted to check on you and make sure
you were okay. I can't believe you are really here."

"Of course, I'm here. Where else would I be?"

"Anywhere but here." Bernice took a few steps inside the
room. "Can we talk?"

Jerry ran his fingers through his hair. He was tempted to
say no, but he didn't. His mom needed to talk, or she wouldn't
be here.

"Sure, Mom."

"I don't want your brother hearing us." She shut the door
softly and dropped onto the chair by Jerry's bed. "You think
I don't understand, but I do. You boys were not treated right
when you were kids. I tried, really I did, to protect you, but …."
Bernice put her hand over her mouth as if she had said too

much, and Big Jim's anger was about to rain down on her. She closed her eyes and took a deep breath. "I just didn't have the strength. Your father was a brute. And in some ways I feel more alive with him gone. I feel like I can breathe." She sighed and shook her head.

Jerry pulled the covers back and sat up.

"Thanks, Mom. I needed to hear that. I know it was hard to say, but I think you will be okay now."

"And Jimmy ... he's following in your father's footsteps. Oh, he's not as mean, yet..." Bernice stiffened her back. "But he will be."

Jerry had nothing to say to that. He'd been the victim of both Jims. And he hated them both. His mom continued, "I have something I want to tell you. Just in case. There are some gold coins tucked under the rafters in the attic. They're in an old sock, held by twine. Nobody else knows." Her eyes became slits. "That's for you. It's the best I could do. I know you aren't going to get a fair shake. But it's something. You deserve something."

Jerry touched his Mom's hand, and she was trembling. "Thanks, Mom."

I decided you should have something after we gave all that money to the Stoddard family to start over in Wisconsin. If the girl's family had stayed in town, we would have been so ashamed. And it would have killed your dad. He was so proud."

Jerry was curious but decided to let his mom talk. He nodded for her to continue, hoping to reassure her that he knew what she was talking about, although he didn't have a clue. But he was starting to see the picture, and he liked it.

"She was four months pregnant when her folks told your dad and me. She didn't show, well you know, so it was hard to believe at first. Until I took a closer look."

Jerry nodded again.

"I talked your father into helping them out. Your brother didn't know for sure, until we told him. I guess he didn't believe her. But your dad was really helping him out, when he helped them out. You know, to get out of town."

So, all Jimmy's problems went away in the early morning hours of a Sunday morning, when the Stoddards piled into the new Buick station wagon Dad bought them and headed out of town. Now it all made sense.

"Jimmy and Debbie were married by then." His mom snorted, and he saw the curled lip of her pride. "The Stoddards let us know when the baby was born. It was a girl."

For a moment Bernice's shoulders drooped. To Jerry, she looked ancient, and then her back stiffened again. "Just don't forget about the coins in the attic. And keep it to yourself. No sense in anybody else knowing."

"I promise, Mom. No one will find out about the money."

Bernice got up and walked slowly to the door. "You get going back to California as soon as the funeral is over. You get back to your life." His mom stood over him, studying his face for a moment, and in a voice as soft as a whisper added, "I wish I'd had the guts to just up and leave this town."

Jerry watched his mother step out into the hall light and shut the door, leaving the room dark and deathly still, as if she'd never been there. She'd admitted to letting bad things happen to him, and Jerry hated her for that. But she'd redeemed herself a bit by showing him the only mercy he'd ever known in the house. The house of a child's horror. His horror. He'd do what his mom asked. He'd get out of town right after the funeral, on a late flight back to a place where he could breathe.

At one time, his mom had visions of grandeur. She was going to make it big, be someone with her flute-like voice and movie-star looks. Her blonde hair was thick with soft, attractive curls, and her blue eyes sparkled like a million fireflies. And her long, thin fingers poked and weaved through her hair when she was nervous.

Her entire family was going cross country, from Maine to California to pursue her dream of stardom, a young girl's dream. But sadly, on a quick stop in Iowa to visit relatives, her father took sick and died, and the family never left the area, staying with her father's sister until her mother remarried. And soon after, his mom's dreams were dashed in a moment of passion with a young, strapping farm boy named Jim Collins. She never lost her Eastern accent, which made her an alien in farm country, her words still ending in ah or eh. She stubbornly clung to her might-have-beens until her hands were rough and her nails brittle ... her dreams over. It was too late for his mother, but not for him.

Chapter Nine

Jerry sat up. Daylight pushed slowly into the window and
seeped across the floor. Had his mom really been in his room
earlier in the morning, telling him all kinds of secrets, or had
it been a dream? He stood and went to the double window that
looked out over the back of the farm yard. Maple trees that his
mom had planted years ago were peaking a glorious red behind
Debbie's colorful vegetable garden. The dusty, charcoal creek
bed snaked its way between the flaming, copper trees, meeting
up with Mineral Pond. Steam hissed its way across the rippling
water, making the pond look like a cauldron of boiling broth.
This early morning vision could only be seen a few days a year,
when the water was still summer-warm and the air winter-cold.

Jerry had painted the pond once on the back of a small
piece of cardboard. He'd mixed a dark brown from his color
palette to frame the scene along the edges. And when he felt he
had all the colors just right, he gave it to his mother. She was
young and happy then and had been so proud of his efforts.
She hung it in the living room. Finally, his father was going
to know who he was, an artist. When his dad came home, his
mom proudly showed the painting to him.

"Look what our Jerry did," she said, lifting her hand gracefully toward his work, as if in a dance pose.

His dad glanced at it and went to his chair. "He doesn't have anything better to do? I told you he was old enough to help around the farm." His dad picked up the *Farmer's Almanac* and turned to September.

"Take it down. I don't want him to get ideas that he can do that while Jimmy does all the work around here."

"But Jim, he's only seven. And he's good, really good."

"What would you know about that? I know you thought you were going to be something, but turns out you're a just a plain, old farm wife. That's all. And Jerry's going to be a farmer, just like me. Take it down."

Jerry's mom took it down and slipped it under his bed later that night. She told him to keep it there and someday, when he was famous, it would be worth a lot of money.

"You'll get out of here, son. I'm sure of it." She patted his back as he cried. That was one of the last times she was tender with him. His dad forbid it. It would make him a sissy, his dad said.

And now she'd come to his room, telling him there was a stash of gold coins in the attic just for him. Where had that sweet, loving woman gone? Wherever she went, she never came back. Later, after the day was done, before he left this God-forsaken place, Jerry would check the rafters and see if his mom was telling the truth. Debbie said she'd been forgetful lately, and maybe she was delusional.

The day was going to be long, starting with a farm-house breakfast of over-easy eggs, thick slices of ham, fried potatoes, stewed tomatoes, apple strudel, cinnamon rolls, and lots of coffee. Jerry loved the smells mingling into a mélange of hot oils, spice and fruit. The mood was almost festive. The only tears he had seen were from the kids who had never met death face to face. In their minute frame of time, they had no perception of their own demise. Life seemed eternal. And so they cried. Not for the monster who had given them all a reprieve, but for the idea of an end to time.

"Jerry?"

"Yes, Mom."

"Can you help Jimmy today, you know with the cows?"

"Mom, I'm not that sure he wants me to. I was never that good at it."

"Don't worry, Jerry. It's done." The voice was Debbie's. She was standing next to him and touched his arm briefly. She would never have dared doing that if Jimmy were in the room. "I went out early this morning. Couldn't sleep."

Jerry took a deep breath, and his shoulders moved up a few inches. "Thanks, Deb."

Debbie turned to her mother-in-law. "And any way, it's kind of late for that, Mother. It's getting on seven. Jimmy will be in for breakfast, so we might as well start. We have to be at the church by nine."

"Is it going to be a large crowd?" Jerry asked.

Bernice nodded. "We think everyone in town will come. And of course, all the farmers will."

Jerry nodded. "To make sure the old man is really dead."

Bernice stiffened but said nothing. Debbie glanced at Jerry with just a slight nod. So it was still the same around here. The old man ruled with an iron fist, and everyone jumped at his command. A hell of a way to go out of this world. Hated by all, and then he heard a muffled cry coming from Christy, who was wiping at a tear. Except maybe the kids.

It was as Bernice predicted, a county happening. Jerry hadn't seen that many old people all together for a long time. He wondered if they ever thought about the fact that young people didn't stay around. It was like Stepford wives in reverse. All old, all gray, all wrinkled, all stooped, or as his boss often joked, all stoo-ped.

As the family stood together, side by side, everyone stopped to pay homage to the widow and the new Lord of the manor. Jimmy was loving it. He stood taller, and his voice was louder. Jerry became more annoyed with each condolence, until he had a splitting headache. After the bar-maid lifted her tiny hand to Jimmy, almost bowing, Jerry could take no more and went in search of someone to talk to.

He spied Abby Stoddard right away, standing with a cute little teeny bopper, no doubt her daughter. Abby looked old. Phil would have said, 'tired and put away wet.' She saw him, and her eyes moved around the crowd and then back at him.

"Looking for someone, Abby?"

"My husband. I ... wanted you to meet him."

"Daughter?" Jerry asked.

Abby nodded.

"But not the first, right?"

Abby's eyes dropped, and she leaned into her daughter's face, whispering something and the girl hurried off.

"She'll be a great flower-child someday...soon."

"What do you mean, not the first?"

"I know. That's all. And it's okay. I know Jimmy had his fling with you. You and me, we had ours. Only he was more productive than I was. I was painfully aware that I was second fiddle to Jimmy, even though I asked you out first." He'd said too much and scowled at his personal revelation. "I'm surprised you're back here, in these parts."

"My husband got a chance to rent the Johnson place, the farm where I lived when I was young. I believe your brother owns it now."

"My ... family owns it now." He couldn't bring himself to tell her the truth. He wasn't in the will. He didn't own anything.

"That's not what I heard. I heard your brother got it all."

"Sad, eh? A Father would set two brothers up for a duel."

Abby looked confused, and then she appeared to understand.

"I'm not the only loser here, Abby. You are, too. And your first kid, wherever she is."

As Jerry left her, Abby was dabbing a tissue under her eyes, looking every bit the grieving family friend. Well, she probably really was the only mourner here today, Jerry thought. She lost out on a really big inheritance by virtue of no virtue. She could have been the one. She could have pushed the issue, and if she had, she would be the woman standing next to the richest landlord of the county as the mother of all his children, including the daughter she gave up for money.

Instead, Debbie stood next to Jimmy. Poor Debbie, she had no clue. She had no ambition. If she did, she'd be showing off, reminding everyone of her new found status. Debbie probably didn't know how close she'd come to not being Mrs. Jimmy Collins. He had a mind to tell her.

Jerry spotted Debbie at the food table, serving. Always serving. He waved to her, motioning for her to come to him. She obeyed. He liked that. He never knew until now that he could make her jump at his command. She was a jumping fool, trained well.

"You know, Debbie," he said, looking over her head, "As I watch our Jimmy over there, I think how close he came to having Abby by his side. Aren't you the lucky one?"

Debbie smiled. "I guess."

"And you could have been my wife. Coulda, woulda, shoulda, huh?"

"But I fell in love with Jimmy. And if I'd married you ... I wouldn't have my kids."

Jerry's mouth became the curl, the Collins' curl. "But you would have had better kids," he said, walking away before she could respond.

The news he wanted to deliver about Abby's daughter would be better told somewhere more private. Where he could comfort her. All he had to do was motion her to his side. She would come at his beckoning, well taught by his brother, his father and his subservient mother. He almost felt sorry for her. Life was not going to get any better for Debbie than it was today. The leaf doesn't fall far from the tree. And Jerry was convinced that Jimmy didn't fall far from his tree. Jerry just hoped his own tree was his mom, who at one time had had a heart.

So yes, he felt sorry for Debbie. They were a lot alike. Debbie deserved to know the truth. Everyone does.

Abby sought him out this time, defiance on her face, hands on her hips.

"She's my first, Jerry. Sally's my first daughter. And my only daughter."

Now he knew the truth, and it was a doozy. Finding truth in this family was like an Easter egg hunt, with no end to the number of eggs hidden.

Chapter Ten

The large crowd at the funeral became a convoy of rusty pickups and dusty, old sedans as they made their way down the narrow gravel roads to the Collins County cemetery for the graveside service, or as Jimmy called it, the planting.

Jerry pondered Pastor Johnson's sermon for James Douglas Collins. There was no talk of salvation, no room at the mansion with Big Jim's name on the door. So, the pastor had come to know his dad very well. The words were more threatening than Jerry had expected. More ominous about the human spirit, and what God had hoped for from each worldly being during the duration of its earthly visit. God was surely disappointed in Big Jim. Yeah, Pastor knew the old man for sure. It was a tragedy when the departed wasn't beloved and wouldn't be missed. Sighs of relief replaced sobs of sorrow in the overflow crowd.

"Well," Jimmy said boldly, as he sauntered toward his car, "Now it's time for ham sandwiches and cherry Jell-O." That was his dad's legacy. In years to come, all they'd remember about that day was the luncheon served by the ladies in the church basement.

Jerry nodded. "Same old, same old, huh? We couldn't muster up a better feast to send Dad off?"

"Dad's choice would have been Spam. I think it was written in the will, that he wanted Spam sandwiches and lime Jell-O, but Mom said he'd get ham. She seemed pleased to change his plan."

Jerry shook his head. "Yeah, Spam would have been more appropriate. We ate that at nearly every meal." He looked at Jimmy briefly. "I confess, I sorta like fried Spam. I have it sometimes for a quick snack in my place after a late night."

"He and Mom still ate it for most noon meals." Jimmy shook his head and curled his lip. "But thank God Debbie took over for supper."

Jerry took a sweeping view of the crowd. "I noticed Santha seems to stand pretty close to you all the time. In fact, she's right behind you now, holding a baby in her arms."

Jimmy turned and lifted his hand in a friendly greeting. "I'm a rock star now, Jer. Like Bob Dylan."

"Oh, contraire, big brother. You're the new object of hatred now," Jerry said. "Be assured, the town will learn to hate you like they did Dad."

"I hope so," Jimmy said, nodding. "That's a good thing. That means I'm doin' my job."

"It won't be earned hatred, Jimmy. Dad worked for it. He deserved it." Jerry sucked in a deep breath. "They'll hate you even more because you just inherited their hatred. It's not the same. The jealousy will be fierce."

"What do you know about that?" Jimmy hit Jerry on the side of the head as he made his way to Santha's side. He lifted the little girl from her arms and made silly faces to make the baby laugh. And then Jerry got it. Jimmy had had a fling with the young waitress, and the baby girl was his. It had to be. First Abby's kid and then Santha's. Jimbo planted his seed everywhere.

Debbie glanced at Jimmy and then got in the car with the kids. The look on her face as they waited for Jimmy said she knew. She just didn't know that she knew. It would be easy for her to have that eureka moment with a little help. The revelation about the love child with Abby would take more thought. But Jerry was up to speed on his brother's antics, and it wouldn't take Debbie long to climb aboard.

He'd gotten a quick look at the old man's will the night before, when Bernice pulled it out of her purse. They were alone in the dining room waiting for dinner. It was simple and specific. Bernice could live off the income during her life time, which seemed to please her. But Jimmy Jr. would inherit the entire estate, followed by Dougie, Dougie's son and then Christy. As always, his dad was a chauvinist, putting the younger Dougie ahead of his sister. Father to son and so on. But there was no mention of any other progeny of Jimmy's or Jerry's. That was the only thing that could be contested in court. Dougie just needed to grow up quickly and have himself a son.

After the luncheon served by the church ladies, and after every person stopped to pay their respects to Jimmy one last time, the Collins family left the church and headed back to the farm. Jimmy walked in the front door first, the official head of the family, followed by his mother, his wife, his children and his brother.

"Party. My office." Jimmy nodded to Jerry to join him. It felt like a command, and Jerry would be obedient this time. Jimmy had already opened the cupboard door to the private stash of booze before Jerry got into the very private room. The room was smaller than Jerry remembered. He'd never actually been in it, just viewed it from the open door from time to time. It was just big enough for a large, uncluttered desk, a massive, green leather desk chair, and two wooden, straight-back chairs. Jerry took one of them, as Jimmy made himself comfortable in his dad's old chair. One picture hung over the desk, an aerial view of the farm-land taken decades ago by a traveling photographer.

It was obvious that Jimmy was familiar with the set up and had imbibed in his dad's Kentucky whisky on many occasions. He looked comfortable, leaning back with his feet up on the tidy desk.

Jimmy pushed the bottle in Jerry's direction. "Come on, Jer, have a little rot-gut with me. It sure as hell isn't any of your fancy California wines, but it won't hurt you. We deserve a little time together. Just us. Help yourself."

Jerry filled the small glass half full of his dad's booze and joined Jimmy in a toast to the future, and then he filled another glass half full and drank it in three gulps, emptying the glass. "Life is looking pretty darn good for you, Jimmy. Looks like you've already got the Collins' reputation."

"How so, little brother?"

"As you left in Dad's car, people were looking at you with a little fear, a little …."

"You mean respect, don't you? A little respect?"

"If that's what you want to call it."

"Jerry, you oughta stay here. I could find things for you to do. You could take care of the contracts and the finances," Jimmy said, sucking down a third jigger full of whisky and then a fourth.

"Jimmy, I've got a life in California, a great one in the land of never ending sunshine, bikinis and free love." For the first time Jerry smiled, thinking how lucky he was. "And I do have to leave here pretty soon."

"Oh yeah, and I've been thinking, Jer. I'm Jim now. Just Jim. I'd appreciate if you'd call me that. Jimmy is a kid's name. I'm Jim Collins. Someday, maybe a year from now, I'll be Big Jim, just like Dad."

Jerry smiled, poked his brother in the shoulder, and said, "If you live that long … Jimmy."

Chapter Eleven

My plane leaves in an hour." Jerry stood up. "You taking me to the airport?"

Jimmy set his glass down hard on the desk and closed his eyes. "I think I'll let Deb take you. She doesn't have to fix dinner tonight. You know, people brought in so much food, so she'll have time." Jimmy stood and looked out the back window.

"Remember when we made a raft, Jer, with tree limbs that we'd collected for over a year? We measured them to make sure they were the same length and tied them together with some rope Dad had in the barn."

Jerry went to his brother's side and looked out at the pond, almost seeing the raft floating near the dead tree that still laid across the pond's edge. "I remember following you onto the small platform and each of us rowing to get to the other side, and then we came back."

"And you couldn't swim?"

"I was only seven." Jerry remembered it clearly now, and the memory was no longer pleasant. "And you pushed me over, right in the middle, Jimmy. Why did you always do that? Trying to kill me?"

Jimmy's hand went to the top of Jerry's head, and he ruffed up Jerry's hair. "Because I could, Jer. I did to you what was done to me. I was trying to make a man out of you."

"Just like Dad tried to do with you?"

"Yeah, I figured it was my duty, being older. You know, the Collins' peckin' order." Jimmy turned to face Jerry, and he was smiling. "Guess it didn't work, little brother."

Jerry didn't smile, but looked at Jimmy for a long, silent moment. "Worked with you. You're the spitting image of Dad." He turned away. "Someday you'll pay for the crap you give people."

Jimmy shook his head. "Dad never did."

"You aren't Dad." Jerry started out of the room, but stopped at the door and turned back to face his brother. "Did Dad have any illegitimate kids?"

Jimmy lifted his chin to look at Jerry, his eyes becoming slits. "Of course not. And I'd know. This is a little town."

Jerry could see his brother was quickly becoming uncomfortable. "Hmmm. I heard a rumor that there was another kid, a bastard Collins. Just wondering."

Jimmy dropped into the desk chair and leaned back, so hard it bumped the wall. "No. I'm sure, Jer. Just a rumor."

"I thought so. It had something to do with Abby. Her kid. Her first daughter."

Jimmy's face warmed to a perspiring red. He tried to laugh. "She only has one daughter, Jer. She's a friend of Christy's."

"So she's your kid?" Jerry asked, relishing his brother's response.

"No. Absolutely not. No. I'm sure of it." His brother was adamant. And his expression had changed dramatically. He was telling the truth.

Jerry's wheels were spinning. Was it possible that the girl with Abby was Big Jim's? "Wow."

"What, Jer?"

"Nothing. I'm just trying to picture Dad with Little Miss Abby-jail thirteen years ago. She must have been, what, sixteen then, back in the day? If it's true, Dad could have done time."

"Not true. Don't be spreading that around, little brother," Jimmy said, emphatically. And Jerry got his confession, of sorts. He left the room, shutting the door behind him as Jimmy picked up the bottle and poured himself another shot.

At the top of the steps Jerry stopped. One more flight up the narrower steps off his bedroom, and he'd be in the attic. Years ago, he'd rushed up those steps daily. He'd be jumping at the sound of his dad's voice, running to hide from the old man's wrath. He'd almost always been the one that had been bruised and battered at the end of the day, even though it was often Jimmy who deserved it. Jimmy, being older, had been able to recognize his father's tone, and somehow he'd escaped. Jerry had almost always taken the blame. Jimmy had lied to save his own skin, and sometimes he'd lied just for the fun of it.

With just a trace of daylight still left in the sky, Jerry found himself in the attic. It was a long room with narrow, arched windows at both ends. He didn't have to search long before he spotted the black sock filled with gold coins hanging low and out of the eye level of anyone who wasn't looking for it. Jerry took the sock to the window and emptied it onto the dusty floorboards. There were dozens of large gold coins, and some smaller ones. The dollar value would be quite large, since they were all very old.

Mom had come through. Jerry decided not to take the coins and left them for another time. He put the sock back where he found it, where his mom had hidden it safely through the years.

It was his birthright. He had something to show for all the pain and humiliation he had suffered at his father's hand and at his brother's. She'd mentioned other things, but he didn't have time to look through the dusty boxes that were stacked behind the sock. That trip down memory lane would come at another time, after his mother was gone.

He made his way down the stairs and called out to his mom to say good-bye. He would thank her with a kiss on her cheek. She would know without asking what he was saying to her.

"I took her back to her place a half hour ago," Debbie said, slipping on a heavy blue sweater.

So his mom left without saying good-bye. Just as well, Jerry thought. No sentiment here. He held the door for Debbie and followed her to the old family Buick, a classic now by some standards. It was as if he'd never been part of this family, as if he'd never lived here at all. But someday, he'd be back. Back with a vengeance. And then he'd be feared and remembered. And he would be the lord of the land.

They rode silently for a while with only soft rock n' roll music in the background. It surprised him when Debbie turned down the volume and cleared her throat. "Jerry," she started, then turned to him. "I haven't told anyone yet, but I'm pregnant. Jimmy doesn't even know. But I guess I wanted to let you know. I don't know why."

Jerry stiffened. He hadn't expected this, and for some reason it made him angry, but he dared not let on. "Congratulations, Debbie. I thought you looked different, happier." And dumber, he thought. What else could he say? He wanted to scream with rage. Jimmy would now have three kids, maybe four. And he still had zero. Big fat zero.

Debbie hugged him at the airport. "We have a secret now, don't forget." She smiled like she thought they were close. "And come back again, soon, maybe right after we have the baby."

"I will, Deb. Thanks." He stepped away, and as she opened the car door, he called her name.

"Deb?" She looked back at him. "Don't let Jimmy get away with it." She looked confused. "You deserve better. He doesn't need Santha, or Abby, or their kids. You and your kids … that should be enough for him. Don't let him get away with it."

He started walking toward the small terminal building slowly, waiting to hear her car door shut, and the car pull away, but he never heard either sound. She was still standing by the car when he turned to look at her one last time through the glass door.

She hadn't moved.

Eureka.

Chapter Twelve

The airport was nearly empty when Jerry returned to San Diego. He was glad, needing to be alone with his thoughts. He remembered Phil saying maybe a tornado or a fire would take out the family. He wished it would. It had been the worst time he'd ever had at home. His mom hadn't been the same. She was so deeply in mourning, that she'd forgotten she hadn't seen him in almost a year. And right from the beginning, she was mad at him for stopping for a beer, thanks to Jimmy. She'd turned away from him and kept cooking that night, as if her life depended on it.

All Jerry wanted to do was give her a hug, a five-year-old boy in a man's body. She had been the one who'd saved him, or tried to, when his dad blamed him for everything that went wrong. She'd been the one who unlocked the door to the closet where his dad had put him after a glass of milk spilled accidentally on the dining room carpet. It was a night when they'd had the neighbors over for dinner. Jimmy and Jerry were rough-housing at the table, and Jerry spilled his milk. It had been so humiliating, to be dragged from the table in front of the Smith's daughters. The girls had laughed, and Jimmy had encouraged them. His mom had him out in time for dessert, but he hadn't been able to look anyone in the eyes.

And now when his mom needed him, she wouldn't let him help. She wouldn't let him comfort her. She was in her own world, stopping from time to time to take Debbie's hand and squeezing it. Debbie was the one Mom went to for her comfort, and Jerry felt awkward and alone. Everyone seemed lost in their own thoughts. Especially Jimmy, who was no doubt thinking how he was going to be the richest farmer in the entire state.

So now Jerry prayed for a catastrophe.

Jerry stumbled up the apartment steps with his luggage. He was putting the key in the lock when he heard the phone ring. He dropped his suitcase, pushed the door in, and ran to ringing phone, answering after the third ring. The line clicked dead after he said hello.

Whoever it was, they were surely impatient, he thought, as he dragged his suitcase to the bedroom. He laid out his clothes for the morning, putting his dress pants in his back-pack. He never wore his good suit pants on the bike but changed quickly in the bathroom before work. If he'd been stopped and had to take off his coat, he'd be wearing a pressed shirt, tie and suit jacket with a pair of blue jeans.

The phone rang again. This time he was able to get to it after one ring.

"Jerry?" His mother's voice. "You … I forgot to say good-bye to you. Debbie took me home, and I didn't think about it until later."

"Oh, hi Mom. I looked for you and even yelled good-bye before Debbie told me you were gone. I guess Jimmy and I had a lot to talk about."

"Yes, you boys were always conspiring about something."

Jerry hadn't thought about it that way. His mother probably had seen them as co-conspirators since they only communicated in a word or two, and mostly in whispers.

"It's pretty late there, after midnight. Are you okay?"

"Yes, Son. Just can't sleep." He heard her sigh.

"I ... I look forward to coming back again to see you sometime, Mom. I'll try to get back more often."

"You know I'm living in a new house now, Jerry. It's small, and I won't have room for you to stay."

"You might move back to the farm. You'll miss it."

"Dad and I bought the house, and this was our plan. I think it's best for me to stay in town, in my own place. Jimmy and Debbie are all moved into our old bedroom and I don't want to make them move again."

"Mom, Dad just died. They can work around you."

"I want to do this, Jerry. You know how I hate to be a burden."

"You wouldn't be a burden to me, Mom."

"But you aren't here anymore, Jerry. You're gone. So this is what I have to do."

"I'll come back, Mom, if you want me to."

"No. I don't want you to. You made your life out there. You made your choices. There is nothing here for you anymore, Son. Nothing you need to be here for."

"I'm sorry, Mom. You were always there for me."

"Times change. Life changes. Your dad is gone. Your brother will take care of me. Don't you worry about that.

Debbie is real good to me, like a daughter." He could hear her take a slurp of coffee.

"And Jimmy does everything for me," she added, her voice revealing the lie.

"Call Tim Buckly if you need help with anything. You don't need to be relying on Jimmy so much."

"Tim Bucktooth?" his mom asked.

Jerry smiled. Jimmy's nickname for poor Tim. He'd been a good looking kid except for the big buck-teeth. As Tim aged, his body finally grew into his face and his big smile, but the nickname Tim Bucktooth had withstood the test of time.

"Jimmy fired him."

"What? He was Dad's right hand man. He was like one of the family."

"Yes. Dad even had a little piece of land set aside for him since he'd done so much for us. But Jimmy said he flirted with Debbie too much, and she didn't like his attention. It made her uncomfortable."

Jerry forgot about feeling sorry for Tim. All he heard was that Tim had also been in the will. Jerry hadn't read far enough and wished now he had a copy of it.

"Say, Mom, do you think you could send me a copy of the will. I just think it would be a good idea for someone to go through it and that's my area of expertise, you know. I'm an estate lawyer."

"Sure, son. I'll send it along. But Tim isn't in the will any more. Jimmy saw to that right away, if that's what you're worried about."

"No, Mom. Just send the will. I just want to make sure you are taken care of." He knew he was taking a risk to ask her to do something. She'd probably need help, and then Jimmy would be involved."

"Jerry?"

"Yes, Mom?"

"Did you get your ... inheritance?"

"I found the coins, Mom, and thanks. But I left them for my next visit. I really appreciate you thinking of me. It means a lot."

"You can't do much with them, but it's something."

His mother obviously didn't have a clue about their value.

"You are my son, too."

"Thanks, Mom." It seemed wrong to have to thank your mother for recognizing that. He wondered if his father ever thought of him in those terms. Son."

The conversation ended with Jerry promising to be home again soon, maybe even for Christmas.

"You do what you have to do," she said, and then she said, "Good-bye." It sounded like a forever goodbye.

The phone rang again. Jerry answered it in three rings, and it went dead when he said hello. He started to get worried. Was someone playing a trick on him?

The phone rang again. This time Peggy was on the line.

"Jerry, I'm really scared. Phil is going crazy, and I can't stay here. He's out right now, probably drinking. Can I come over? I'll leave tomorrow, I promise. I've already made plans to go live with my mom. I'll get a job and my own place later."

"I didn't know your mom was still alive."

"She lives in Coarsegold, near Yosemite. It's far enough away from here. I don't think he'll come looking for me."

"Yeah, that's a good idea."

"Can I or not?"

"What?"

"Come over tonight?"

"Sure. I guess. Just make sure he doesn't follow you."

"Thanks."

Peggy hung up, and the phone rang again, right away.

"Peggy?"

The phone went dead.

It had to be Phil, and he probably knew about the two of them. Jerry's life was looking a little pitiful now. His dad all but disowned him, his girlfriend was someone else's wife, and his best friend probably wanted him dead. The California dream had turned into a nightmare.

Chapter Thirteen

Jerry paced in front of his apartment door. Perspiration beaded on his forehead, and he felt feverish. Where was Peggy? She said she was leaving an hour ago, and it was no more than a fifteen minute cab ride. The knock was so soft that he didn't hear it the first time. The second knock was strong, hard, rapid, almost like a Morse code SOS. He opened the door slightly and pulled Peggy through the small space, suitcase and all. After securing the deadbolt on the front door, he closed the drapes on all the windows.

"Were you followed?"

Peggy set her suitcase down and dropped into his La-Z-Boy chair. "No." She started to cry.

Jerry unlocked the front door and looked out into the dark night before securing the lock again. He shivered, though it wasn't cold. "Maybe you shouldn't have come here. Phil might have followed you."

"Does he know where you live?" Peggy asked.

"I don't think so. We've always met somewhere."

"He didn't follow me. He passed out after giving me hell."

Jerry looked at Peggy for the first time and winced. She had broken skin everywhere. It looked like Phil had dug into her with a small knife. And there were burns on her arms and one on her chin.

"He wanted to make sure I knew who was boss, and he wanted me to always remember that I am not perfect in any way." Oddly, Peggy stopped crying. Her eyes were glazed over, and she was taking shallow breaths.

"He's right. I'll never be the same."

Jerry looked in his medicine cabinet and found the antiseptic he'd bought when he first learned to ride his bike. He'd taken the bike out wearing shorts and burned his ankle when he leaned into a corner. Peggy didn't flinch when he dabbed the ointment on her wounds.

"Does your mom know you're coming tomorrow?"

"She will. I wanted to call her when I got here. I didn't want him to hear me."

Peggy made her call in his upstairs bedroom while he sat at the small kitchen table and made plans. What if Phil knows about him? What if he comes to find him? What if he tries to hurt him, too? He'd have to move, change his life in almost every way to avoid Phil. He'd probably never see Peggy again. He was surprised at how sad that made him. He really cared for her, but he just didn't know if he loved her. Looking back at all the Collins men, he wondered if love was just missing from their genetic make-up. Love was pounded out of them at an early age. Self-preservation and self-love being foremost in their minds. He liked holding onto someone, kissing, and sleeping together, but that wasn't love.

Peggy came down the steps slowly, her red, puffy eyes meeting his. "She's expecting me tomorrow. She'll meet me at the bus station. Can you get me a cab in the morning?"

Jerry nodded, then changed his mind. "No." He saw her disappointment. "I'll call a cab, and I'll go with you and stay until you are safely on the bus."

Peggy smiled. "You'll have to be careful, Jerry. I promise, I never said anything to Phil about you, but he's smart. He might figure it out."

"I'll be careful. I'm going to do my usual routine for a while, but I'll just go places that are in the open, safe places. I'll change my routine slowly, so he won't notice."

Peggy closed her eyes and tears started to flow. He held her until her sobs became hiccups. "You sleep upstairs in my bed," he said. "I'll stay here on the couch and keep watch, just in case." He took her suitcase up the steps to his bedroom. She gave him a kiss on the cheek and then shut the door.

As he went down the steps, he became aware of noises, lots of them, coming from every part of the apartment. Noises he'd never heard before. It was as if his apartment was alive with his fear. And he was afraid. He pulled a flashlight from his kitchen drawer. After inspecting the kitchen and basement door and checking on both the front and back door locks again, he was quite sure they were alone.

When the phone rang, he jumped. He let it ring several times, but it kept ringing. Finally, he picked it up. There was a dial tone. Someone was playing with him, and he could almost see Phil's evil smile at the other end of the line. It had to be Phil. Who else could it be? Unless it was his brother, giving him a hard time. Jimmy would do that, too. Two of a kind. And he'd had the bad luck of knowing both of them.

Chapter Fourteen

When Jerry awoke, someone was standing over him. He could just make out a form through the loose weave of the blanket he'd used to cover his head. The black of the night sky had faded to a dull gray, so the form was only a shadow. Bolting upright, he reached out and pulled at an arm. Right away, he recognized Peggy's scream. When he pulled the blanket off his head, she was kneeling next to an over-turned lamp at the side of the couch, holding onto a spatula.

"Sorry," Jerry said. "You took me by surprise."

"Welcome to my world," Peggy said, dropping onto the couch beside him. "I can't wait to get out of here. The bus leaves at eight, but you can take me sooner so you can get to work."

Jerry looked at the small clock behind the television. It was six o'clock, and daylight was edging the top of the trees across the street in Riverside Park. "Yeah. Let's get you to the bus depot. But, like I said, I'm going to wait until you are safely on the bus, and the bus is moving."

"Thanks, Jerry." Peggy kissed him, but the kiss was void of any real passion. She'd had that kicked out of her for good, he was afraid. She was wearing blue jeans and a dark blue sweater, as if she wanted to blend in with the surroundings. No more flash and peek. She'd become serious in the few days he'd been gone.

"I'm going to get a job in Coarsegold. Mom says they need a cleaning lady at her apartment complex, and she thinks we can be a team ... work together."

"That's great. A good place to start. But don't sell yourself short. You're smart. Go to Junior College, get a skill." Their eyes met. "You can take care of yourself."

Peggy looked doubtful.

"Hey, you're still alive, right?"

Peggy nodded and then smiled. "I'm a survivor."

Jerry grabbed the spatula. "Let's put this thing to good use. I'll make you the best flapjacks you've ever had."

"What?"

"Flapjacks. That's what my mom called 'em. Pancakes where you come from. It's all the same." Jerry went to the refrigerator. No milk. He opened the back door and lifted the lid on the metal milk box on the stoop. "Fresh milk, delivered today." He stooped down and pulled the plastic carton up, nearly dropping it when he saw the large spider crawling in the corner of the box. There was no way that thing got in the milk box by itself. Someone had been there after the milk was delivered. Jerry looked around. No one. He didn't tell Peggy. She had enough to worry about. This was his cross to bear.

After eating the pancakes and bacon, Jerry tidied up the kitchen and took a quick shower. The cab arrived on time, and they both settled into the back seat. The ride was long and silent as they both contemplated their fate. Peggy was starting a new life, and Jerry was hoping to do the same.

The bus was waiting at the depot, and Peggy climbed aboard after another kiss, a more passionate one, followed by one on his cheek. "Good-bye, Jerry," she said. She stepped onto the bus and never looked back. He knew he'd never see her again.

The cab took him to work, where he found several messages on his desk, one of them from Phil. It said, 'Peggy left. Good riddance. We need to celebrate. Meet me at the Boot Heel at eight.' Phil's favorite biker bar. Great.

It was a long day at work, and Jerry couldn't concentrate. Would he go, or wouldn't he? That was the sixty-four-thousand dollar question. He didn't think he should, but he knew he must. It was not a suggestion. It was a request, a command. It would probably be the best place to find out where he stood with Phil. To see if he needed a restraining order. The Boot Heel was a public place, and he would be able to get help there, if he needed it.

After a cab ride home and a quick change of clothes, Jerry went to the garage for his bike, then decided against it. He'd take a cab and say his bike needed some work. A cabbie would know where he was and get him home safely. If he was still alive.

Chapter Fifteen

"I'm meeting a friend at the Boot Heel ... a bar just across the bridge." Jerry said, in his trial voice. "My Harley broke down ... having it repaired."

The cabbie nodded, but Jerry could tell he wasn't listening.

"This friend. He might try to kill me."

The cabbie turned down the Reggae music, and tilted his head slightly, keeping one eye on the road. "Do you want me to call the police, Mon?"

Jerry took a deep breath. "No, but could you pick me up there at ten? Same place you drop me off?"

"I'll try, Mon. But I don't like gettin' in thee middle." The cabbie adjusted his mirror to see Jerry more clearly. "You look okay, Mon. I'll be there as close to ten as possible. If I have to come a little early, that be okay? You'll have to pay, Mon."

"Yeah. Sure. I will probably stay put until ten, but you be there first. If you can. I'll pay for your time."

Jerry stepped out of the cab and handed the cabbie the fare plus a nice tip.

Show time. This would be the defining moment in his future. Would it go okay, or did he need to move ... far, far away? It would be hard, getting a different job and apartment in a new place. But he wasn't happy with his life here, and he wasn't happy with his stupid choice to see Phil's wife. It just seemed like the thing to do at the time, but it was oh so wrong. Everybody was doing it. His brother was doing it. So the whole country was a mess.

Free love. Love, Love, Love… and then there is tomorrow and the next day when you realize that it's a stupid way to live.

"Jer." Phil was calling to him from his favorite table by the window. Bright, colorful t-shirts from gangs and concerts hung over the window. The air was filled with blue smoke from legal and illegal methods of imbibing. Pipes were everywhere, and cigarettes were small and damp. And there was a lot of sharing. Peggy always said she left there high and never smoked anything.

Jerry couldn't stop sighing. It was as if he were suffocating. Phil might as well just thrust a dagger into his chest now. Then jump up and down on him until the deed was done. He deserved it. He dropped onto the stool next to Phil and took the joint Phil offered him. After a long, deep drag on it and then another, he felt better.

"She's gone."

"Yeah. I got your message."

"I made sure she'd think about me. I'll go after her later. She can decide how it … ends."

Phil took a quick puff and held the joint between his fingers and examined it as if it were a precious jewel. Rolling Stone's music filled the air. After 'Good-bye Ruby Tuesday', Janis Joplin started singing 'Take a Little Piece of my Heart.'

"Pick the music, Phil?" Jerry asked, in a voice he did not recognize. He sounded like a little kid on helium.

Phil laughed. "Next up, Tony Bennett's, 'I Lost My Wife in San Diego'."

Jerry loosened his shirt, took it down a few buttons so he could breathe. "I can't say it's good to be back," he said, mostly to himself.

"Oh yeah, right. You've been to a funeral. Better get used to it."

Jerry tried not to react, but looked around the room to see who he could grab if it got bloody. Beer came in pitchers, and Jerry downed two glasses while they watched two young girls make their way slowly into the room. Some girls always attracted attention. They were wearing small, blue-jean cutoffs, cut up the sides all the way to their waists, and polka-dot bras. They had bare feet, toenails painted bright red. Daisies twisted into crowns haloed their bleach-blond heads. Jerry forgot his plight for a moment and took time to admire the twin angels, as Phil nick-named them. Phil said he'd christen them both later.

"Going home with those two," Phil said. "Takin' them to my place. No wife to stop me."

Jerry didn't doubt it. Phil grabbed each girl by the wrist, pulling them into his arms. They giggled when he tucked five-dollar bills into their bras. They smiled and waved at Jerry when they left the table. They probably thought he was part of the deal.

"They're getting drunk on me and then meeting me at the back door in a couple hours. Good thing I brought the Shelby five-oh-oh." Phil finished off his beer and poured another. "So what happened at the ranch? Did your dad really bite the bullet? Did you get to see him all waxy and gray, his lids sewn down over nickels?" Phil smiled as if he liked the visual of the old man's corpse, laying lifeless in a casket.

Jerry downed another beer, thankful that the cabbie was coming, and the girls were waiting.

"Yeah, dead as a doornail."

"Anything new? Was your hot sister-in-law all over you?"

"No. She's pregnant again. Just couldn't wait to tell me when she took me to the airport. She hasn't even told Jimmy." Jerry met Phil's eyes for the first time, and it took his breath away. They were slits filled with rage that made his face shine crimson. If Jerry made it out alive tonight, it would be sheer luck. He pitied the silly, little girls who were doing their best to follow Phil's instructions so they could go happily home with him. They were drinking martinis and dancing around all the tables like ballerinas. Soon they would be punching bags.

"And Jimmy has two kids I didn't know about. One from years ago, and a baby from a bar-maid he just met," Jerry shared, hoping to redirect Phil's death stare.

"My kind of guy," Phil nodded, finally blinking. "He's a real man. But he can be obliterated."

That word scared Jerry. It wasn't 'removed,' or 'killed,' or 'brought to his knees.' Obliterated was a much darker and more terrifying word.

"Tell me more," Phil asked, moving closer to Jerry. "What's it like, living so far out of town? Anything could happen, and no one would know."

Jerry could feel Phil's eyes going from him to the girls as if he were watching a tennis match. So he babbled. He babbled about everything and anything. He babbled for his life.

"It's not so far, really. The old homestead is just two miles north of town on Collins Road. Someday, the place will probably be in town." Phil was staring at him. "The old man wanted everyone to know it was his kingdom so he stuck an old Ford pick-up out by the mail box, painted it bright yellow, and had Collins printed on the doors in large black letters. If anyone wanted to get even with the bastard, they wouldn't have any trouble finding him."

Phil wasn't really paying attention now, he could tell. The girls were winning the tennis match, and he was coming in a distant second. He told Phil about the coins his mom had saved for him. Phil glanced at him, his interest piqued. "Yeah, she tied them up in one of my dad's old socks and hung it under the rafters by the window. Any dummy could find it." Phil looked at him as if he were an idiot. Telling Phil the sock story was stupid. It made him look weak and insignificant. Well, that shoe fit him pretty good these days. Finally, his watch said ten o'clock. He wanted to flee but he had to be careful.

"Gotta go, Phil. Have a meeting tomorrow. Big trial. Family trust thing."

Phil nodded. "Let's do this again, Jer. Maybe we can come up with a plan for a tornado, or fire, or something back at the ranch."

"Yeah. I'd just rather forget I ever knew any of them."

"Well, you have your coins, that'll buy you a new life. Where are they anyway? You keepin' them in your pocket?"

"No. Left them in the rafters. Didn't want to appear too needy."

"She's ballsy, your mom."

Jerry had to agree. It was brave of her to keep something from his dad.

Jerry walked slowly to the door. He didn't want Phil to know he was running hard and fast in his mind. He'd always be scared of Phil. But when Jerry reached the door, his safe haven, Phil was engaged in a battle for the girls' attention with a much heavier guy, a real Hell's Angel, not the pretend variety. Phil had the man twisted over a bar stool, and the room got quiet, so quiet you could hear a pin drop. But instead, it was the sound of a crack and a pitiful wail as the pinned man gripped his dangling arm and dropped to the floor. Phil had pulled the man's shoulder out of the socket and the lower arm looked broken. Phil smiled and then turned to take each girl by the wrist, escorting them to the dance floor. Soon he was dancing with both girls, a dance of pent-up rage.

Chapter Sixteen

The cabbie dropped Jerry off at his townhouse door and offered to check on him during the night, between fares. Jerry's new best friend. The only one in the world that knew he was in mortal danger.

"Thanks, really, buddy, but I'll be okay."

He felt anything but okay when he let himself in the house. The only thing he knew for sure was that Phil was not there. He kept the lights on and slept in the living room, on the floor behind his La-Z-Boy.

The phone started ringing around four o'clock. Every time he picked it up, it went dead, the connection broken. It kept him on edge, just where Phil wanted him. After several days of middle of the night phone calls, someone finally answered him when he said hello.

"Jerry?"

"Peggy? You okay?"

"No."

"Where are you?"

"With my mom. She's in the hospital. She just came out of surgery. It doesn't look good. She might not ... make it."

"What are you going to do?"

"Stay here till, well, I'll stay for a while and help her."

"That's a good idea. You don't want to come back here for sure."

"I might have to."

"He'll kill you."

"I don't have any place else to go."

"I'll help you."

"You can't."

"I can get you some money."

"I'm pregnant."

Jerry felt all the air go out of him. He couldn't speak or think.

"Jerry, are you still there?"

"Yes," he said. No, he thought. Not for Phil's baby.

"Take a few days. Think about it. You'll never be safe living with Phil. You know that."

He could hear her crying even with her hand covering the mouthpiece. And then a muffled voice, a man's voice, said something to her.

"Gotta go. Mom needs me." And she hung up.

Jerry was sure that she would go back to Phil. And she would suffer all the days of her life until he mercifully killed her or found someone else.

Every morning, Jerry left his apartment at a different time. He put a match between both front and back screen doors and their frames, knowing that if either one of them dropped, someone had entered or at least tried to enter the townhouse. At the end of the week he was exhausted.

The phone rang at least five times every night with no one on the other end. He expected to hear from Peggy, but he didn't. And thankfully, he hadn't had to talk to Phil either.

He was planning on sleeping in his bed for the first time that night, finally too exhausted to care if Phil might come to kill him. As he was making his way up the stairs to his bedroom after the ten o'clock news, the phone rang again. He slowly picked it up. It felt like a hundred pound weight. He readied himself yet again for Phil's deep, demonic voice telling him he was going to die.

"Jerry?"

It was his mom's voice. He felt relieved.

"Yeah, Mom. How are you?"

"I'm well."

She never asked him how he was. "You don't sound good, Mom. And why are you calling so late?"

She was silent for a moment. "Well, things are not good out at the farm. I can't sleep, so I called you."

"What's wrong?"

"Debbie is pregnant."

"Yeah, I knew that. Something wrong? Is she okay?"

"Well, she was going to leave your brother, Jimmy."

She always mentioned Jimmy as if he didn't know the guy. It made him laugh sometimes, but not this time.

"Why, Mom?"

Another long moment of silence. "Well ...." She took a deep breath. "Apparently, your brother, Jimmy, has another child. The mother has asked for child support."

Jerry wasn't surprised to hear his mother tell him about the bar-maid's baby, since he'd guessed that already when he was home. But he was surprised that Jimmy confessed his sin to Debbie.

"He told me it isn't true. Swears it isn't his."

"Yeah, sure, Mom." Jerry felt a sense of elation. "Why didn't he just help her out, keep this on the quiet?"

"You know your brother. That would have been an admission of guilt."

Yeah, he knew Jimmy. Jimmy always got away with everything. But not this time. It was his turn to pay. Jerry had warned him. He felt vindicated for all the times Jimmy had made him the scapegoat. It was the first time that he could think of when he didn't feel like the black sheep in the family. This time he was the good son.

"What's Debbie going to do? Kick Jimmy out?"

"No. She went full circle, from hating him after the woman admitted it was true, to accepting it as 'Jimmy being Jimmy.' She's going to let Jimmy help raise the baby. I guess the woman, the mother, is, or was, a friend of hers."

Jerry stiffened like an ironing board, and he'd taken in so much air he felt like he was going to burst. Rage hit him like a cold blast of icy air, and he could see it in the face reflected off the television screen. He looked just like Phil.

Life would never be the same again for Jerry. After he said good-bye to his mom and hung up the phone, he opened up the bottle of scotch he'd been saving and downed half of it in a few quick swallows. Several diabolical plans swirled around in his head, each one ending in his brother's demise, bringing some solace. And finally, he was able to get a few hours of sleep after deciding to get away for the weekend for a much-needed trip.

Chapter Seventeen

"Hey, Jer."

Jerry turned around awkwardly in the narrow hall. He was waiting in a line of hundreds of people, all crowding toward a small window to get tickets for the Rolling Stone's Final World Tour coming up the next weekend in San Francisco. He felt a stabbing pain in his shoulder as his eyes settled on the face of the voice.

"Phil, how are ya?" Phil had made his way to Jerry's side with a few well-placed shoves. "Not good, man. Not all that good."

Jerry was almost at the ticket window. "Want me to get you a ticket?"

"Sure. But I might not get to go. I've got to do some personal stuff next weekend."

"Like what?" Jerry asked before he thought. He knew he'd probably have to talk to Phil about Peggy, but he was hoping to avoid a crowd. Then again, a crowd could save him if it got ugly. "Meet me out front." Jerry glanced toward the wall of doors at the other end of the corridor.

Phil nodded and turned to leave. Jerry could hear a trail of angry voices following in his wake. He got three tickets, general seating, hoping that Peggy and Phil would work out their problems, and he'd be home free, bowing out of the friendship quietly. And the concert.

Phil was waiting outside in the parking area. Jerry handed him the tickets. "Got you two, just in case. So what's happening?"

"Peggy's gone for good, coming back in a couple weeks to get some of her things. I'll change her mind, one way or another. I think she might have a lover. You got any ideas who?"

"Don't think so," Jerry lied.

"I'd like to kill him. That'd be the best way to get things back to normal with Peg. She's mine. I've paid for her over and over again. Who does she think she is?"

Jerry shook his head. "Who can figure. You can do better."

Phil reached out and patted Jerry on the back. "Thanks, Pal. It's not her, I could live without her. It's that she'll take everything I've worked for. It's my money, but she'll get half of it. I'll have to start over, and I'm not going to do that. I won't let her leave. After I'm done with her, nobody will want her."

"You don't mean that."

"Sure do. And I'll take care of the bastard, too." Again Phil grabbed Jerry's shoulder in a gentle grip.

"You understand. I know you do. Your dad took your future away. Your stupid brother, the farmer, is going to get everything you deserve. He doesn't deserve all of it, man. You're a Collins. You worked on that damn farm. You put in your time in that hell-hole, Pine Falls. The loot belongs to you, too."

Jerry pursed his lips. "Yeah." Phil was right. All his life, it was Jimmy this and Jimmy that. Jimmy played a saxophone in the school band, Jimmy was the football captain, Jimmy got married, Jimmy had a son. Jerry looked at Phil. "You don't even know the half of it."

Phil snapped his jacket shut to the cool evening air. "Come on, Pal. I'll buy you a beer, and we can commiserate. I'll blow off my steam, and you can blow off yours. I'm glad I never had a brother. Just two dumb sisters that did things my way. I learned a lot by terrifying those bitches. I had to break a few arms, but they never told. They never dared."

Jerry sighed. Phil was right. Someone has to be the boss. Someone has to be the driver of the sibling bus. And he'd lost out by virtue of birth order.

Jerry followed Phil out of the parking lot, and both bikes hit numbers well above the speed limit as they rode west toward the ocean to another one of Phil's favorite bars, just a hole-in-the-wall, a real beer joint. No name, unless *Budweiser* flashing over the door was the name. It seemed that in some ways Phil had become Jerry's older brother. Everything they did was Phil's idea, or his way. Jerry had substituted Phil for Jimmy. And Phil had a Debbie look-a-like wife, who Jerry had been romancing. Maybe he was getting even with Jimmy while using Phil. His psychology teacher would have called it a text-book case of resentment and pay-back. That concerned him and excited him. For once he had taken a chance, taken a stand.

They parked the bikes in a busy back lot behind the bar and strode in together, wearing twin leather jackets and boots and carrying the same gloves. Yeah, brothers, Jerry thought. Just like brothers. Phil bought Jerry beer after beer as they talked. Like brothers.

As Phil listened, Jerry told him about the Collins family, right down to the bigger bedroom for Jimmy. The nicer car for Jimmy. The better clothes for Jimmy. How the dairy barn was down the drive, a long walk on a winter's morning, and Jerry had to trek there day after day. But Jimmy got to sleep in on cold winter days, since his duties were over after the harvest. He found out how cold the back porch was when Jimmy locked him out one night, and he'd had to sleep on the settee by the screen door in the dead of winter. His father had beaten him with a leather belt for missing the milking that morning, his hands so cold he could barely move his fingers. Some of the cows had gotten sick, and his dad had to take them out of service. Some of them went to the butcher shop. His stories went on and on, until he'd stopped, exhausted. He knew he'd said too much when he mentioned the oil painting he'd done as a kid and how his mom had hidden it under his bed. "It's still there, I think."

He finished with, "And now with Dad gone, Jimmy has moved into the master bedroom."

"Yeah, nothing new, Jer. I've heard this all before. I think I know your family better than they do. I could write a book on how badly you've been treated, how you're in love with your sister-in-law, and how your dad was an ass."

Phil looked at Jerry and shook his head. "Well, good for you. One down, five to go."

Jerry smiled. "You're right. It's not impossible for me to get an inheritance. One simple catastrophe could make me a millionaire, and the most important person in Pine Falls."

Phil laughed with him. "It could be done. A fire, a tornado, an airplane dropping from the sky." He moved to face Jerry. They were almost exactly the same height, so he could look him eye to eye. "What are the odds of any of those things happening?"

Jerry felt uncomfortable being that close to Phil, who already said he'd like to kill the guy who was sleeping with his wife. The look in Phil's eyes said he knew about his tryst

with Peggy. The friendly voice, the smile, the gentle grip
again on the shoulder said otherwise. Jerry could feel beads of
perspiration forming on his upper lip. He was crazy confused.

"Gotta go," Phil said, still looking deeply into Jerry's eyes.
"Got some milking to do in my own barn tonight, after I find a
cow to take home."

Jerry was glad Peggy was gone. He pitied any woman who
found Phil attractive tonight. Phil was really angry. If he could
get to a phone, he'd call Peggy and tell her to stay the hell away
from Phil forever, to divorce him and let him have everything.
But it was probably too late for Peggy. Like his dad always said,
"You made your bed, now you gotta lie in it."

Jerry was relieved after Phil left, his bike's engine growl
resonating in the bar's back doorway long after the bike had
disappeared. It seemed that all was still well with the two of
them, and Jerry convinced himself that Phil didn't know he was
the bastard who was sleeping with his wife … yet.

After a few minutes, Jerry left the bar's back door and
headed out to his own bike, settling on the seat and revving
up the engine. He started down the alley slowly, watching for
Phil, who he feared might be lurking in the shadows near the
dumpster. He wouldn't be surprised if Phil followed him home
and killed him while he slept. As he turned from the alley into
the busy street, he thought he heard another bike behind him
but didn't see one when he looked in his mirror. He was getting
paranoid, but that didn't mean he didn't have a reason to be.
He had a damn good one. Phil was heartless, mean and a little
crazy. Jerry decided he needed to be more like Phil.

Chapter Eighteen

Debbie pushed Buster out the screen door. She'd been going through the bushel baskets of picked fruit on the back porch, looking for a few perfect apples to use for a Halloween centerpiece, and Buster was making the task impossible. He loved apples and wanted a bite out of each one.

"Jimmy," she called to her husband, as he came around the barn. "Buster needs some exercise. Can you take him with you?"

Jimmy pulled off his John Deere cap and swiped a weathered hand across his brow. He frowned, looked at Buster, then shook his head with a hint of a smile. Buster was carrying his own leash, and his tail was wagging.

"Yup, I guess," he said. "He can come with me to get some firewood. It's gonna rain tomorrow, maybe even snow, they say. This time the weather man'll probably guess right, and I sure don't want to have to root through the mud." He slapped his hat back on his head and pulled at the bill to snug it on.

"Anything else? Mom comin' for dinner?"

Debbie smiled sadly. "Yes. She wants you to pick her up, and she has to be back at seven for *The Lawrence Welk Show*. Do you think she's okay? It's only been a few weeks since Dad's death."

Jimmy wiped his nose with a dirt-stained handkerchief.

"Are you kidding? Mom seems as happy as I've ever seen her," Jimmy said, adding, "And she's out of our hair." He blew his nose and closed his eyes. Blood spotted his dingy handkerchief.

"Jimmy. Are you okay?"

"Yeah, I guess I have a cold or something. It's the dusty fields."

"Christy's friend, Sally Stoddard, is coming for a sleepover." Debbie looked at Jimmy to see if he was listening. He was studying a bill that she'd left on the table and looked up when she was quiet.

"Her dad is renting the old Johnson place. Remember Abby Munson? That's her mom."

Debbie watched for Jimmy's reaction. Nothing. "Sally and Christy are a few months apart in age."

Jimmy tucked loose strands of hair under his John Deere cap. "Can't say as I remember him. He must be a good renter, no late payments. But I do remember her from school. She came to Dad's funeral."

"Yeah, she was there," Debbie said, nodding. "She moved away the last year of high school, just before graduation, and I heard she had a baby that she gave up for adoption. But I guess she decided to keep her." Debbie sat down on the kitchen chair. She wanted to ask Jimmy about Abby, but it probably wasn't a good time, with Sally coming over. She thought she'd get him thinking, though, for another time, when they'd have to talk about it. "You always liked her, I remember. You teased me that it was her or me."

"Yeah, she was a looker, a real flirt. But not as pretty as you, Miss Butter Valley."

Jimmy hadn't called her that in years. Her one and only claim to fame. She still found herself embarrassed that she'd won the contest. Her mother entered her in it, and she had to do a tap dance for the talent contest. She won that portion, but had taken third place in the bathing suit competition. Her legs were so thin, Jimmy called them bird legs. He told her he fell in love with her when he saw her draped across the back of the big white Cadillac, wearing only a pale blue bathing suit and white high heels.

When he found out that Jerry had taken her out on a date, her fate was sealed. Whatever Jerry wanted, Jimmy got. The date, the marriage, and the kids. It was always a competition for Jimmy. And Jimmy always won.

"I remember now, something, a rumor about a pregnancy. They say it's always best to give the baby up. Who knows." Jimmy shrugged his shoulders, and Debbie thought that was that. And then he spoke again, surprising her. "I sure never expected Abby to come back with the kid and live on one of our rental farms." He looked back at the bill in his hand. "She should have stayed away."

Debbie lifted apples from her basket into the big earthen bowl, arranging them from side to side and top to bottom while Jimmy got himself a glass of water. They spent many hours a day together now, not talking. She wondered if he remembered their anniversary celebration planned for the next day at church. He'd promised her something really nice, and she dreamed about a pearl necklace to wear with her black dress. But he broke most of his promises, so she wasn't going to hold her breath.

Life had never changed for Jimmy. He did what his dad and grandpa did. Debbie did what his mom and grandma did. She thought about how different Jerry's life must be and wondered what she'd be doing if she'd married him and lived in California. They'd be talking. They'd go to museums and art galleries and concerts. They had so much in common ... the arts, music, literature. Jerry must be thriving, she thought, since he never came back and rarely called home.

She and Jerry had become friends in high school, where they met in art class. He still mentioned her art work every time he came home, and last time was no exception. After dinner, the first time they were alone in the kitchen, he'd asked her if she was still painting, and he shook his head when she told him no.

"You were an artist, Deb, a good one," he said, lifting her hands to look at her dirty fingernails. "Now look at you, doing labor, hard labor around here. You should be painting. Your work should be hanging in studios and art centers. Whatever happened to that great portrait of Elvis?"

"It's in the basement, in a box."

"It doesn't belong there. It belongs up here, on a wall. You should be proud of it. Jimmy should be proud of it."

He'd looked Debbie in the eyes. "You're a stupid girl. So smart, and you threw it all away."

Jerry had been right. She'd given up a lot for Jimmy. Life would have been very different with Jerry. But he was still a Collins man. And he would probably be just like Jimmy, if he were in Jimmy's shoes. Debbie sighed deeply several times, until her lungs hurt.

Jimmy finished a second glass of water. "C'mon Buster. You look like you need some fresh air, big boy," he said, with little enthusiasm.

Debbie nodded. "Always does."

As she chopped the stew meat for dinner, she wondered if Jimmy really was the Father of baby Raina, Santha's little girl. Did Jimmy know Santha before Debbie did? Did Santha seek her out at the laundromat to make friends with her because of Jimmy? How could he do this to all of them?.

She'd been thinking about Santha's baby constantly since Jerry had suggested the idea in the car on the way to the airport his last evening. He didn't say anything for certain, just hinted at the possibility. But it made her suspicious, and then a few days later, Jimmy's revelation confirmed it.

He'd come to her with the news that Santha wanted him to accept responsibility for his child, his daughter. And she wanted money every month for expenses. Jimmy had acknowledged to Debbie without emotion that it was a possibility, that he might be the Father of Santha's youngest child. Debbie had nearly broken down, tossing a vase onto the floor with an anger that she didn't know she could feel. It shattered into several pieces, just like her heart had been shattered. The truth always hurts the wrong person.

Finally, After much thought, Debbie had suggested a divorce and offered to leave Jimmy so that he could marry Santha. But Jimmy and Bernice wouldn't hear of it.

"We need to stay united," Bernice said. "We've weathered worse storms."

Bernice had taken Jimmy's side, with the old adage that men will be men. But Jimmy's mother seemed older after the news, as if she had been deeply disappointed in her son. Her perfect world was eroding. She would have seen more imperfection in her life had she looked, Debbie thought, but she refused to see the truth.

That evening, after they all talked about Santha's request, Jimmy went out to the barn. Bernice fidgeted in the kitchen while Debbie did the dishes. And when Debbie hung the cotton towel to dry, Bernice admitted to Debbie for the first time that life had been hard with the Collins men.

"I didn't fit in," she said. "I was just the cook and housekeeper for all of them." Debbie hugged her. "Mom, I know. I feel the same way. You just watch the goings on like it is someone else's life."

"Yes, Bernice had said, tears glistening in her eyes. "That's how you survive. You don't have to look for flaws in this family. You just have to keep from tripping over 'em."

So here she was, taking Bernice's place, making dinner for the family, folding clothes, and cleaning floors, all the while her world was crumbling. There were two children who could be her husband's and two children who were his for sure. Debbie was going to look closer at Sally tonight and see if there was any resemblance to her own kids.

She had to stay with Jimmy, no matter what, for the kid's sake. In a few years the farm would belong to them free and clear, when Jimmy's mom passed away. And Dougie would be standing here long after they were both gone. Poor Jerry would get nothing. Debbie shook her head. Jerry always came in last, always lost out. Jimmy always got the girl, Jerry always got the fantasy. And now Jimmy got the farm. And Jerry got the boot.

Debbie was finishing the potatoes when Jimmy walked in the door. "Smells good."

"Just stew meat in the pan with the onions."

Jimmy reached into the bushel basket by the kitchen table and tossed Debbie a nice, big red apple, and she caught it. "Pie, too, Hon?" he asked.

"Sure. It's already baking."

"We're heading to the barn to stack the wood, right Buster? Be back in about an hour, and dinner best be ready."

Debbie watched Jimmy and Buster walk toward the barn with a wheel barrow full of twigs and small logs. Buster ran across Jimmy's path from side to side, playfully. Jimmy tried to run him down with the front wheel. If he could only be that good to the kids or even to her, life would be perfect. Yet he didn't seem to have any affection for a human being, just a dog. He was his dad's son. Debbie had had a good life, though, until Santha and her baby disrupted it, devastated it. A beautiful home, a handsome husband, two great kids, and the pretense of love. Pretense was almost as good as the real thing.

She wished for just a moment that she could go back in time, forget about Santha. But Raina would always be a part of their lives because she was a part of Jimmy's. And so life was not so great anymore, and there was nothing she could do about it. She felt tired and used. All used up. And her news would wait. Her news about her own baby would be anticlimactic now. She'd wait until he asked, she thought, see if he noticed. And then she'd tell him, as if it didn't matter much to her.

Debbie sat looking out the side window while the stew simmered. She watched Dougie play ball by himself in the yard and was about to join him when a young girl on a bike turned off the gravel road and came up the drive. She had long, flowing mousy brown hair with tiny side-braids crowning her head. It looked like she was wearing new jeans and a name-brand jacket. Nice clothes for a farmer's kid. Her mom was trying to impress them. The bike looked new, too.

"Christy, Sally's here," Debbie called, and then watched the two girls meet at the front door.

"Let's take your bike out back to the barn," Christy said. "It'll be safe there." Yes, Debbie thought. Life had been good. Safe. Happy. And then the illusion was exposed for all the world to see, with the conception and birth of a baby named Raina. And life, as she knew it, was over.

Chapter Nineteen

Sally and Christy came out of the barn, their arms and hands
moving expressively, their eyes flashing with excitement.
Debbie pulled the kitchen curtain back to get a better view, as
the girls came toward the house together. In the dimming light
of a nice October day, they looked and sounded like sisters,
almost identical. They were about the same height. Sally's
hair was thin and mousy brown, a little darker than Christy's,
which had blonde highlights. And Sally had an odd gate that
reminded Debbie of someone. It was awkward, yet steady,
almost rhythmic. Debbie thought for a moment, then nodded.
It was Jerry's walk. And the hair was Jerry's. Sally and Christy
could definitely be related. Sally could be Jimmy's kid, like Jerry
had implied.

"Anyone want some Kool-Aid?"

Christy looked at Sally, and they both nodded. "I made
orange for Halloween. I can't believe it's tomorrow night
already. It just comes earlier and earlier."

"Mom," Christy said. "It comes the very same day every
year."

Debbie ignored her daughter's tone, so like Jimmy's. She turned to Sally. "How long did it take you to ride your bike out here?"

"I left my house at four, stopped at the Midland grocery for a ... break, then I came right here." Sally seemed anxious to connect to Debbie. "I love your house. It's so big."

Debbie did the mental math. About an hour all together, so maybe forty minutes of riding. She'd often considered getting a bicycle. Pine Falls had just finished a hard surface bike trail through the park by the river. It would be fun to do, and good exercise. Her other friends were doing the new aerobics classes, but she was too busy in the mornings for that. All totaled, she had saved nearly a hundred dollars in the last two years, her secret savings. Next time she was in town, she'd go to the bicycle store and have a look.

Debbie opened the ceramic rooster cookie jar and offered the girls and Dougie a big, round chocolate-chip cookie. Melted chocolate morsels dripped down their mouths and chins as they ate, until they all looked like bums from the trains, with five-o-clock shadows. Dougie tongued most of his away, his eyes crossing to see his efforts. The girls laughed and took the washcloth Debbie gave them, wiping chocolate traces away in lady-like fashion.

"Dinner will be ready in about an hour," she said, shooing the children to the back door. Go out and collect some Indian Corn for Halloween wreaths. We'll put a few together tonight."

Debbie went to the sewing room to check on the costumes again. Halloween was one of her favorite holidays, no pressure, just fun. It was fun to be someone else for a night, play a part, like an actress in a movie. This year, Christy was going to be a flower child. It was a new costume Debbie had designed, recreated from an old dress she'd worn to a wedding. The dress was shapeless on Christy and hung several inches above the girl's ankles, until Debbie did her magic. Debbie found a wide ribbon that she would tie around Christy to help bring up some of the skirt. With the cut off fabric from the hem, she made fabric flowers and sewed them into a small wreath for Christy's head. A peace sign and sparkly shoes finished the ensemble.

Dougie was going to be a Beatle. His costume would be an altered church suit he'd outgrown. After removing the collar, she added a black turtle neck shirt to finish the look. The Beatle wig that Christy had worn a few years ago was still in good shape and fit him. Dougie always got hand-me-downs when Debbie could make them work. He was her Jerry, the one who always got second-hand. Dougie didn't seem to mind yet, but someday, she knew he would resist. That's when she would do things differently than Bernice. That's when she would listen to his needs and take care of him. She would be fair and see his point of view.

The next day was Halloween. Usually, she had her Autumn wreath finished and Halloween decorations up, but Big Jim's death upset the routine in more ways than one. Even dead, he controlled the world, her world. After dinner, she'd get the place decorated with the kids help. And on Monday, she planned a trip into town to make her first big purchase without Jimmy's consent. She hoped the store had a red girl's bike.

Debbie served dinner, discreetly watching Sally's every move and watching Jimmy's interest or lack of it. She noted that Bernice seemed very observant, too. Sally had the Collins' hair for sure, fine and mousy brown. Bernice still had it, her hair staying brown all these years, with just a tinge of gray. The girl tilted her head the same way Jimmy did. She had Jimmy's eyes and thick, dark eyebrows.

"Do you have any hobbies, Sally?" Debbie asked.

"I like to paint. My mom says it's a family talent."

"Which side?"

The girl giggled. "Not mom's. She has trouble holding a pencil. Dad says she can't do much of anything with her hands. He says she just likes to lay around." The girl grinned and added, "And she's good at it."

Bernice scowled, and Debbie grimaced. "Much more than I need to know." Art Linkletter was right, kids do say the darndest things.

Debbie looked at Jimmy to see if he was listening, maybe watching Sally. He didn't seem to be, and then she caught him staring at the girl briefly, right after she mentioned her grandparents.

"They say I'm just like my dad, stubborn and carefree. And bossy," she added. The girl seemed proud of those attributes. She had to be Jimmy's daughter.

"You look just like your mom," Jimmy said, before stuffing a fork of potatoes into his mouth. "You're tall and skinny like she was. How old are you?"

"I'm almost twelve, just a few weeks older than Christy. Mom said we could have been womb mates." Sally laughed, but Debbie was convinced she didn't know what that meant. It meant something to Jimmy, though, and he frowned. "You'd have to be in the same mother," he said, in a near whisper. Or have the same Father, Debbie thought. Jimmy started to look uncomfortable, and that's when Debbie knew that he knew. If Sally was just a few weeks older than Christy, then Jimmy had to have been intimate with Sally's mom at the same time he was intimate with her. Debbie suddenly felt disgusted and called the dinner over. Bernice seemed relieved when Jimmy picked up the keys to the car and lifted her coat off the hook by the kitchen door.

Debbie started clearing the table, her mind elsewhere, interrogating Jimmy silently. Who was first, Jimmy? We know who you got pregnant first, but who did you start with? She looked at Jimmy at just the moment he glanced at her, just before leaving the house. He look confused, angry, and a little scared. Debbie would not confront him now, but she planned to have a talk with him soon. It was clear that Sally was a Collins, and the two girls were more than friends. They were sisters.

Chapter Twenty

The motorcycle hummed along at a deadly speed, the leather seat getting harder as the miles flew by, over a thousand now. The stop in Albuquerque helped a little. The rest-stop was decent with a picnic area and a wide bench, just long enough to stretch out on. He never needed much sleep, so he felt refreshed after a few hours of rest.

The heavy Denver traffic thinned and became countryside again, as the cycle made its way to the eastern border of Colorado. There was nothing to see in the early afternoon hours of a warm, late October. The pungent smell of moldy, smoldering leaves burning in piles scattered across the farmland hovered over him like a smog, and he was thankful he was wearing goggles.

It was an ironic fact that four people were meeting their maker this night, due to unseasonably good weather. If it had been more predictably cold, it might be a different matter. But now it was a sure thing, fate.

He raced through Nebraska, to his destination, Iowa. The estimated time of arrival would be well after midnight but before dawn, just when the sleeper becomes comatose, when the body does not respond to peril, fear … terror.

The state roads were in bad shape, rutted and patched until the patches were patched, and it was difficult at times to keep the bike steady. The ride was becoming more of an effort, more of a challenge, than he'd anticipated. Maybe he was getting old. He laughed out loud at that thought. He'd never grow old.

Sleep fingers pulled on his eyelids and poked into his mind. What was he doing? As sleep swept over him, he reminded himself that this was his fate, too, pre-determined at the time of his birth. This was the final act that would complete him. No one would ever doubt his control again. He was the creation of evil, and Satan was his master. It was his destiny to culminate his life's purpose with an act of pure evil. The thought energized him, and he became fully awake. He had a window of opportunity, and he was not going to back down now.

A gas station in Brady, Nebraska, was still open well after ten p.m. He slowed down and pulled in. If he filled up here, he could make it back at least this far by early morning. He stopped near the pump, and put his kickstand down. No credit card this time. He would use the card on his way back, when he felt safer. He would definitely take advantage of the credit card when it felt right. That was the plan.

A quick stop meant he could leave his helmet and goggles on, keeping a sharp eye from identifying him. The attendant hurried out to fill his tank, and he went into the small, dusty station to pay. One single light bulb hung over the counter. The attendant, a beefy, older guy took his twenty.

"Where are the candy bars?"

"In the freezer. Help yourself."

"I'll have a Coke, too. Love the taste of Coke and frozen Milky Ways."

The attendant dropped the twenty on the counter and opened the old coke machine, moving bottles around to the front.

"Me, too," he said, as he took two frosty bottles out, one for himself. "The damn cooler is freezin' up on me. I might have to get one of the new vending machines." He stuck the top of the first bottle under the edge of the cooler and popped the cap before setting it on the counter.

"Late night, eh?" the attendant asked, wiping his wrinkled brow. His hands were oil stained, a real grease monkey. He made change from the cash register with one hand and picked up a hunk of salami with the other, taking a big bite and munching on it viciously.

"Yeah. Came from California. Glad you're open."

"That's a long ride. Yeah, I'm open till I get done with my work. I'm divorced, after twenty years of marital bliss. All of a sudden, I don't have anywhere else to be." He swept his hand across the room. "This is why … I've been married to this place for years. It's serviced me well. The wife failed."

They both laughed.

"Needin' anything else, buddy?"

"Naw, keep the change."

"Thanks."

"Oh, there is one more thing."

A look of fear snapped into the attendant's eyes. It said, 'this is it. This is what my Ex warned me about.' It was almost Halloween after all.

"Do you have a phone? I need to make a long distance call … collect."

The attendant nodded, relief written all over his face.

"Sure, buddy." He pulled out a black phone that had been tucked under the counter and then went back to the coke machine. He busied himself rearranging the bottles, pretending not to pay attention to the phone call being made.

"Collect."

A short pause.

"The name's ... Jerry."

A long silence followed. Then he placed the phone back in the cradle.

"Sorry, man. No one answered. Guess they didn't want to talk to me. Have a good night."

A few minutes later, he was back on his bike and moving down the road. In less than an hour, he was in the state of Iowa. His heart was thumping. He was pumped up. He was ready.

Chapter Twenty-One

Sally turned over for the tenth time in the double bed. Christy's breathing was soft and rhythmic. Her friend was deeply asleep, clinging to the edge of the bed. Sally could never fall asleep at anyone else's house. She rarely fell asleep at her own house, in her own bed, keeping one eye open for monsters, ghosts, or strangers. She probably watched too many scary shows on television, mostly re-runs of old movies. Godzilla could look in her second story window at any time, and she'd be watching, ready to scream.

Her robe was draped over the bedside chair, and she grabbed it and tiptoed out of the room. The bathroom light was on, the door partially closed, but it shed enough light on the steps for her to make her way down to the landing. A small light coming from the kitchen area guided her the rest of the way, where she hoped there might be an extra cookie in the big rooster cookie jar or even just some crumbs. Eating in the middle of the night was a bad habit that she'd gotten into when she couldn't sleep. Her mom warned her that her habit would not be kind to her in the future, and she could tell it already. Her waist was thick and pudgy, not smooth and tiny like Christy's. And it had been a struggle to ride her bike the seven miles to Christy's house on the gravel road. She probably shouldn't have stopped for the candy bar. When Christy's mom had asked about the ride, she'd been ashamed to tell her the truth. Someday she'd stop snacking. What was it called? Cold turkey. Cold turkey sounded good. Maybe there was some chicken left from dinner.

As she drank milk from the glass by the sink, she munched on her cookie, almost breathing it in. Crumbs dropped on her robe sash, and she brushed them off. Her big dog, Quincey, would have eaten them as they fell, leaving no trace of her nighttime eating binge. But their dog Buster was kenneled on the back porch for the night. He'd barked softly when she opened the refrigerator, so after she finished her cookie and rinsed her glass, she went out to the porch to settle him down. That's when she noticed the back door slightly open. She shut it with her hip and locked it. Her tummy was full, and her eyes were tired. Now she could sleep.

Chapter Twenty-Two

The motorcycle moved slowly along the gravel road, purring like a big yellow cat in the dark, starless night. The rider coaxed and babied the machine to keep it from growling. His whole mission would be in jeopardy if someone spotted him now.

The bike's mirror was aimed at him to keep it from reflecting light to another car or farmer gazing out his window. He took a glance at himself and wondered if he'd gone crazy. Yeah, he'd gone cuckoo a long time ago. He appeared normal to acquaintances, but those closest to him knew the truth. He was full of rage and hatred. The few hairs that escaped the helmet were wispy blonde. He liked the lighter hair and planned on keeping it that way for a while. It was exhilarating to think that in a few short minutes, he'd be on his way out of this place, a different person, fulfilled, his anger spent. But for now, he had to gather up all his hatred to perform. A knife stuck out of his boot, and the wooden handle scraped his leg from time to time. It was a cold reminder of what he was about to do.

Just a hundred feet from the farm's drive he stopped, leaning the bike behind a strong, scraggly bush near the old pick-up that told him he had arrived. The mailbox was empty as he suspected it would be, but he checked it anyway. With a deep sigh and a shiver, he was on his way, walking slowly toward the old farmhouse. He stopped near the big, oak tree that tented the front porch and most of the house. Unzipping his leather coat, he pulled a nearly full pack of Marlboros out of his pocket. Smoking a few cigarettes would give him the edge that he needed. And he had to make sure that no one was awake and watching. One, two, three, four, five cigarettes tossed on the gravel, the pointed tip of his boot kicking them into a neat pile.

It was time ... show-time. Time to go in, do what he came cross-country to do, and get out fast. He wanted to make it back to California by early Monday morning. His plan was to be at work as usual, maybe just a little late. No one would suspect him, but he wanted his alibi to be iron-clad. He would be guiltless to the world.

The door was unlocked, as he knew it would be. The knob was old brass, nearly black from decades of use. So many hands had gripped it and turned it. Jimmy, Debbie, Christy, and Dougie all had used the handle, over and over. Coming and going. In and out. But not anymore. The little family was going on a long journey to the world beyond. He'd heard the story many times about how Debbie had led them all to salvation. He knew Jimmy wasn't a believer as a kid, but turned to religion for a short time after Debbie had a miscarriage. Well, they'd all be together now, forever. He'd see to that.

Chapter Twenty-Three

Sally lifted the rooster head and steadied it on top of the cookie jar. She was about to leave the kitchen when she heard a noise from outside, from somewhere in the front of the house. Buster heard it, too, and whined softly. It had to be Christy's dad coming home late. Sally's dad stayed out late some Saturday nights, and when he returned there was always a loud fight. Her mother waited up for him to catch him in the act, her dad said.

Sally hid in the corner of the darkened dining room and closed her eyes as the front door opened.

Inside, the house was nearly dark, a soft light coming from upstairs and another light shone from the back of the house. He could smell spices and the left over odors of an earlier family dinner. A last supper. How fitting. In a few blinks, his eyes adjusted to the darkness. The staircase was close to the front door. He took a few steps into the living room but changed his mind and turned around. He'd go right up, no detours. If he stopped now, he might lose his courage. He kicked a baseball glove across the threshold. Now it looked more like a home. These people had too much order in their lives, no chaos. They just went about their day to day living in a comfortable routine. The hatred he needed, building with each step up, exploded as he hit the landing on the second floor. Life was too simple for the perfect little family. Life was too easy. That life was going to be short-lived.

Sally didn't remember hearing anyone leave the house after they went to bed, but Christy's dad must have gone out. Who else could it be? She'd been holding her breath since she heard the front door open and close. Footsteps had come toward the dining room, but stopped and turned before Sally could see anyone. She wouldn't have anyway, her eyes tightly shut. The feet shuffled back to the front hall and then up the steps, slowly, so slowly it seemed to take forever. Sally was still holding her breath, her cheeks puffing out.

At the top of the steps, a glance to the closed door on the right told him that Jimmy and Debbie were sound asleep, the snoring loud and rhythmic. He looked to the left. Two bedroom doors were slightly open, the kid's rooms. Kids always leave doors open. It didn't matter which one went first. They were both going. He pulled out the knife. It would be quiet. Left hand on mouth, right hand doing the deed. It was over. The same in the second room. Done.

The linen closet was next to the master bedroom door. He slipped his hand under the pile of sheets until he found the gun. With expert effort, he had it fully loaded with the bullets he'd brought from California. He opened the door to Jimmy and Debbie's room, the master bedroom. A few steps and he had them in sight. One shot in the forehead for Debbie and a second shot in the right temple for Jimmy, as Jimmy lifted up to look at Debbie. Jimmy slumped atop his wife. Her lifeless eyes were staring out, wide and knowing. He studied them for a moment, relieved. He picked up a picture on the dresser, adjusting it so the bathroom light would fall on the faces. He smiled, then laid the picture face down. He left the room, leaving the door open. Debbie's eyes had been beautiful.

Sally tried to comprehend the sound that she'd heard. She knew it. It was a gunshot, no two. Bang, … bang. She mustered up all the courage she had and dropped to the floor, rolling under the library table next to the dining room window. The table was covered with a fine crocheted cloth, and that gave her cover. She prayed she was invisible as she took quick silent breaths. She leaned against the wall and waited, trembling. After several minutes, someone started down the stairs.

This time the footsteps were not slow or silent but thundering and bouncy. She could make out a dark figure standing in the dining room door and then moving into a room under the steps. Through it all, she kept silent, motionless. And then she saw boots take slow, easy steps through the dining room, right by her, and into the kitchen. She squeezed her eyes shut and bit her upper lip to keep from screaming. When she opened one eye just a slit, the figure started toward her again, a big cookie in his hand. She kept her eyes down, hoping if she didn't see anything, she wouldn't be seen. That's when she noticed her toes were sticking out from under the table cloth. She was sorry to death now that she'd let Christy polish her toenails bright red. She held a scream deeply inside her as the shadow stopped at the dining room door and didn't move.

Chapter Twenty-Four

He felt oddly at peace as he stood in the kitchen, eating a cookie, his first reward. The floor boards creaked when he walked to the dining room door. No matter. No one would hear. A lamp on the back porch washed the kitchen floor in a dim light, just enough for him to rinse his hand again, and get a closer look at his self-inflicted wound. He'd gotten shaky when he took the knife from the sheath in his boot, and he scraped his wrist, nicking a good size vein. With a small dish towel, he blotted the blood that continued to seep from the narrow wound, tossing it on the pile of towels he'd used in the bathroom to clean up his mess. No one here would be complaining.

He remembered the pleasant smell of apples and chicken, when he'd first entered the farmhouse and dug around the refrigerator until he found a Tupperware container filled with chicken pieces tucked in the back. He opened it and pulled out a big, meaty leg. After he finished the leg, he lifted a thigh to his lips but dropped it back in the container when he heard a sound. He twirled around to see where it was coming from. His eyes focused first in the dining room. Was someone there? He started toward the darkened room when he heard the sound

again. This time it was clearer, louder, coming from the back
porch. He panicked and went to the door with his knife ready.
A large golden dog lurched up at him when he opened the
door. It dropped instantly on the kitchen floor with a deep
thrust of his knife. He felt a lump in his throat and tried to
swallow. He hadn't thought about Buster. He hated killing a
dog. He stared at Buster for a long, quiet moment, thinking
how beautiful the animal was and how peaceful he looked, like
he was sleeping. He patted the dog's head, said a soft good-bye,
then picked up the pillow case full of towels and left the house
from the front door, locking it on the way out.

After hiding the towels in the barn, he ran down the
driveway, anxious to make his get-away. The gravel drive
was twice as long as he remembered it being when he walked
toward the house less than an hour ago. His motorcycle had
fallen into the bushes, and he had to use extraordinary strength
to get it upright, strength he was quickly losing. He was
terrified now. Afraid of the dark, afraid of the night sounds,
afraid of the howling of the sudden winds. He dropped his keys
and rooted into the thick grass to find them, his eyes blinded
by the dust that was stirring and swirling around him. His bike
fought him as he worked to keep it upright, and he lost his
footing when he tried to lift onto the seat. The bike almost fell.
He righted it again, and managed to get the engine running.

He felt ethereal spirits chasing him as he gunned the
engine, and the bike hurtled full-power toward the highway.
Four newly conceived ghosts were following him now, perhaps
forever. As he goosed the engine, he looked into the rear
view mirror and stared death in the face. His face. A killer's
face. The whine of his bike's engine became a shriek. He took
several deep breaths as he rode onto the black-top road heading
west and out of Iowa as fast as he could go.

Killing four people had been so easy. He'd expected fear, maybe even hesitation, but he was a strong, cold and skillful assassin. It felt right. It made up for all the wrongs he'd endured throughout his life. And the best part? No one would catch him. No one would suspect him. He would be home free, as soon as he got back to California. And then, life would be good.

Chapter Twenty-Five

Sheriff Ron Pierce woke with a sudden urgency. His phone was ringing. He wondered how many times it rang before he'd heard it, he was so deeply asleep. There was trouble in the country. A distraught neighbor was calling, worried about a farm family. Probably nothing. But it was the Collins family, and he didn't take the call lightly. He might need back-up. It was almost dawn, yet still dark, when he pulled the curtain back as he waited for Deputy Neal to answer his own phone. It was an ungodly hour to wake up on any day, but especially on a Sunday. The deputy met him at the Sheriff's office, and they went directly to the Collins' farm, where the caller, Mrs. Victor, sat on the front porch steps, waiting for them.

The two uniformed men stepped out of the patrol car, each putting on official caps ... one, an old and tattered sheriff's cap atop a balding and graying head ... and the other, a new and bright blue deputy's hat pulled down over long, brown bangs.

"Morning ma'am," Sheriff Pierce said.

"Ron," she said, then turned toward the other officer. "Deputy Neal. Glad to have you in Pine Falls." She nodded to the younger man, then turned back to the sheriff.

"Something is terribly wrong, Ron. I came to bring some flowers for the anniversary celebration at church today, and nobody answered the door. I knocked several times." She shook her head and looked deeply perplexed. "And the door is locked. They never lock their door. Usually, I just open it and yell in when I come by."

Missus Victor, could you wait in the patrol car? Listen to the police radio, in case another call comes in? Could you do that for me?" The older woman headed to the car without answering, and the officers took a few steps toward the house.

"When the pastor called right after Mrs. Victor, I knew something was wrong, Neally. He said Jimmy and Debbie should have been there an hour ago, since they were greeters for the early service."

It was a crisp autumn morning. The day was just beginning, yet it looked like night, with rain clouds inching towards them. The last of the night sky was hanging like a silk-draped hammock just beyond the barn.

"If the rains come now, sheriff, evidence will be lost."

"Yeah, Neally, I already found something." Sheriff Pierce picked up a broken twig. "It's got what appears to be blood on it."

"Yeah, I saw a few leaves with dark spots over there." The young deputy pointed toward the gravel drive.

"And there's no movement in the house," the sheriff noted. "Debbie or Buster usually come out to greet me."

"Who's Buster? I thought it was a family of four...Mom, Dad, and two kids?"

Sheriff Pierce did a full circle to face the deputy. "Oh, he'd be the dog. Big, old Golden, a good watch dog."

The younger man pointed to the base of the large, oak tree near the front of the house. Dry leaves were scattered like a thick blanket, with an odd path scraped through them. "Lots of cigarette butts, barely smoked, in a small, neat pile by the tree trunk. Marlboros."

The Sheriff pulled his cap off and scratched his head, his eyes pensive. "Someone was here a spell, maybe waiting for something, or watching." He set the cap back on his head and pulled his shoulders back. "Guess we better go in, see if we have a crime scene."

"Two calls, almost simultaneously, means trouble, with a capital T. Think there was domestic trouble?" Deputy Neal asked, as he walked along-side the sheriff.

"Jimmy's as steady as she goes, Neally. There's never been a call of that sort, you know, domestic trouble." The older officer swiped at his damp brow. He always sweat buckets when something really bad was about to happen, a forewarning. "I hate this job. I shoulda quit a few years ago. I've done my time, by a long shot."

"What would Pine Falls do without you, Boss? I hear you always catch the bad guy."

"Yeah, cause I think like 'em. What does that make me?"

"A criminal's worst nightmare, I'd say," the deputy said.

They continued slowly toward the house. It was a big old farmhouse, the kind a wealthy and generous farmer would have built for his beloved wife. Most of the old farmhouses were big, but not this big and not this nice. Jimmy's grandpa went all out for Jimmy's grandma. This one was painted in the Victorian colors of its day, golden brown with green and red ginger-breading, all dressed up for a Christmas spectacular. It stood alone now against the backdrop of the big red barn, like the last tree standing after a forest fire.

Both men charged up the steps with new determination, a job to do. The sheriff hoped that the family had gone to town, maybe to the hospital or to a friend in need, not thinking to tell someone at the church.

Sheriff Pierce stopped Deputy Neal at the top step.

"The door looks like usual," the sheriff said. "Debbie always keeps a big wreath just under the glass window. She changes it with the season ... so this looks normal." He touched the corn husks and straightened the Indian corn with the tips of his fingers. He tried the door.

"It's locked, like Missus Victor said. They always leave the door unlocked, so anybody can just walk in." He was relieved and anxious at the same time. "Nobody locks their door in Pine Falls." He turned and rubbed his chin. Acid was gurgling in his empty stomach.

"Yeah," the deputy agreed. "It ain't Des Moines, or Chicago, or New York."

"Let's go to the backdoor, since we can't get in here." Sheriff Pierce took the lead. The deputy followed him on the flagstone path at the side of the house, around to the back.

"The porch is in need of some painting," the deputy noted.

"Farmers never have time for that kind of work, Neally." A porch light was on, shining against the drawn shades. The door was locked.

"Odder and odder still," the sheriff said, reaching above the door frame for the key that was always there. It fit just fine, but it needed some coaxing to turn the lock. Both were a bit rusty. And then they were in. The back porch was dark, the air heavy with the perfume of ripened apples and something else. Sheriff Pierce knew right away what it was. He slid a small flashlight from his left pocket, and breathed in the scent of fresh blood. With a sweep of the finger stream of light, they both saw bushels of red and yellow apples lined up against the house wall.

"Debbie makes the best apple pies," he said, to keep his fear at bay. "Love to be sitting at the kitchen table right now, digging into one."

"Me, too," Deputy Neal said, his voice dropping into his throat.

The kitchen door was slightly ajar, and it appeared that something was on the other side. When the young deputy pushed with his hip, he couldn't budge the door open, even a little. He gripped the flashlight in his left hand, his right hand resting like a slab of ice on his holster. The door was stuck. Both men sucked in deep breaths. The deputy tried again, pushing harder. The door finally moved, and the stream of light from the small flashlight landed right between the open eyes of a big old retriever, his days of watch-dogging and barking over.

"They should have been usin' the locks," Deputy Neal whispered.

Chapter Twenty-Six

The deputy stumbled down the steps and sat on the last one with a thud. Nothing at the Academy had prepared him for this. Two young kids dead in bed, the youngest carried back after being murdered in his bedroom doorway, a trail of blood weaving toward his bed and up his bedspread. He was tucked neatly under the covers, like a sleeping angel. The older girl never knew what happened, her eyes shut in eternal slumber now. And the parents, one on top of the other in the safety of their bed, both shot in the head ... one in the forehead, the other in the temple. The gun lay near the husband's right hand. The bastard, the deputy thought. He killed his family and then took the coward's way out.

Sheriff Pierce was taking another look around inside after sending the younger officer out for some fresh air. Deputy Neal had turned a pale shade of green as he moved out of the last room, the bile bubbling as it lifted into his throat. And right outside the front door, he'd made a deposit in some nearby bushes. He was wiping his mouth with his crisp, clean handkerchief when Mrs. Victor opened the car door. Deputy Neal could see she was anxious. He'd have to placate her for a little while longer, until they could tell her something concrete.

He took the front steps slowly, afraid he'd faint. She joined him by the tree.

"Not looking good, ma'am. Not at all good," he said, trying to recall from his recent training what he should and shouldn't say. It was all lost to him now. The sight of all the blood had reduced him to nothing more than a young man who had seen too much this early in his career. "They're all dead, ma'am."

He hadn't been prepared for Mrs. Victor to collapse, but that's what she did, and he mustered up all his strength to take control. He carried her to the steps and held her head until she regained consciousness. "I'm sorry, ma'am, to have been so blunt."

Mrs. Victor was taking deep breaths. "What will I do?" she kept repeating. "Bernice needs to know. She needs to be here."

"No ma'am, she does not. We need you to focus now. This is a crime scene, and we need you to stay calm. We might need your expertise here. You knew the family. You knew the house. Could you wait in the car again for just a few minutes, until the coroner gets here? He'll probably have some questions." The deputy ran out of steam and took a deep breath. "Anybody home at your place that might be worrying about you?"

Mrs. Victor shook her head. "I live alone. Robert's been gone nearly a decade now. No, I'm all alone."

"I have to go back in the house now, ma'am, but I'll come for you as soon as I can."

Mrs. Victor let the young officer guide her back to the patrol car. She sat in the front seat this time and leaned on the door after he shut it. She was crying.

The sheriff joined his deputy on the front porch. He sucked in the cold morning air as if his life depended on it. Neither of them spoke for a while.

"What do we know?"

Deputy Neal shook his head. "We know the world isn't safe for anyone. It isn't safe anywhere. That's what we know."

The sheriff nodded. "I would have been a happy man if I'd never learned that. In all my years in the Sheriff's department, I never saw anything … I mean anything like this."

The younger officer felt tears stinging in his eyes. They never told you in classes what to do when you were suddenly thrown into a gut-wrenching situation. They were always called situations, but he'd never expected to be first on the scene. No one ever talked about the pain, the fear, the heart-ache that he'd feel. Maybe nobody could. It was unexplainable.

Sheriff Pierce glanced at him, tears in his own eyes. "It's okay, Neally. It's okay to feel what you're feeling. It's a good thing, son." He patted the deputy's leg. "You've been thrown into hell, deep and far." He took a few deep breaths and blew the air out of his puffed cheeks. "The scene inside is secure. I checked the attic and the basement. There is no life in that house."

"Maybe I should check the barn?" Deputy Neal said, getting on his feet.

"You do that, Neally. I'll stay watch for the coroner. But be careful, son. Have your weapon ready. I really don't think we have anything to fear. Looks like Jimmy did it, but be ready, just in case."

"Yes, sir. I'll be careful."

Deputy Neal walked toward the barn in steady motion with an easy, steady gait. That's what he was taught. Sudden movement could be dangerous, even deadly. Steady walk, steady breath, steady hand. Two out of three wasn't bad. It would take both his hands to hold the gun, if he needed to use it.

The deputy touched the handle of his gun lightly, ready for anything. He'd really tried to stop doing that after the call had come in to the Academy that a policeman had just taken down a crazed suspect in her own backyard, a small, middle-aged woman toting a weapon. The officer had shot her twice ... the first was a shoulder hit that knocked her down ... the second hit her dead square in the chest. Later it was determined that her gun was not loaded, and she wanted to die. They'd called it suicide by cop. That story had slapped the young trainee in the face like a bag of ice. He decided he'd never use his weapon first, but try to feel out the situation, even at his own peril.

Chapter Twenty-Seven

The barn looked old and needed paint, like the back porch. The deputy took a deep breath before touching the door grip. He'd never been in a barn. The door moaned as he pulled it open with his left hand. It was heavier than he thought it would be. The inside of the barn was nearly void of all light, except for a shard of early daylight that poked through a loose roof board, falling across the loft and drizzling down to his feet. He stumbled against something after taking a few tentative steps. Moving his gun just beyond his feet, he took wild aim. It was just an object, a gleaming, silvery object. He felt tears stinging in his eyes, as he let them adjust, and the object became clear. It was a bicycle. A small red bicycle laying against a haystack. Then a voice in his head, his instructor's voice said, "Take out your flashlight, Neally. Use all the tools available. Stop. Listen. Stay steady."

He made a note that the bicycle appeared to be out of place, since there were no other bikes around it. Then he lifted his flashlight from his pants pocket and turned it on. All the day's light had seeped into the barn, yet it was dark, a gray, earthy daylight. He kept his flashlight on, its shaky beam moving slowly across the rough-hewn walls like a paint brush. No one was in the barn. He finally took a deep breath, and for the first time that morning, he smiled. Not a visible, happy smile. A smile of fearlessness. He had just passed the first real-world test. He had faced his fears, and he had gone full steam ahead anyway, to do his duty.

As he moved around the barn, his flashlight's beam dug deep into the dark, musty corners and skimmed across bales of hay. He discovered a pillow case stuffed with towels hidden behind some leaning farm tools ... rakes, hoes, and shovels. The towels didn't look old, like rags. When he dug into the pillowcase, he discovered they were wet and blood stained.

The deputy grabbed the evidence and hurried out of the barn just as the coroner stepped out of his Buick station wagon. The doctor was carrying his medical bag, which he wouldn't be needing. The man was old, too old for this job, like the sheriff said, but he'd been a doctor in the area since before most of the residents had been born. And there was no replacing experience, as Deputy Neal had learned in a deeply personal way. He hoped he'd never know that first time fear again.

"Dr. Davis," Sheriff Pierce called from the front porch. "It's a mess. We'll be needing a team for this. Did you notify Bernice, er the next of kin?"

The doctor shook his head. "I like to see what they're going to see before I bring them in. But you know who they all are, so we probably don't need her to identify the bodies. If she saw the crime scene, we'd just have one more victim."

Sheriff Pierce nodded. "It could kill her, for sure, since she just lost her husband." He looked off toward the patrol car, remembering Mrs. Victor. "I'm going to have the neighbor come in and have a look around the first floor. See if she notices anything gone, or out of place. Tell-tale signs, you know. But I think this was murder-suicide. The gun laying on the floor next to Jimmy's right hand and all. He must have gone completely out of his ...." The sheriff shook his head and bit his lip, trying to control his emotions. "Got the girl first in her bed. Little guy must have heard a noise and came to his bedroom door. Got him there and then put him back to bed. Shot Debbie between the eyes as she slept on her back, then laid down on top of her, ever so comfy and pointed the gun at his right ear and pulled the trigger. Nice and easy. All found in their beds."

The doctor came closer to the sheriff and patted his shoulder. He nodded, tears filling his old, tired eyes. "It never gets easier, Ron. Never." He sighed. "Show me what we got."

They walked toward the front door, waiting while the deputy helped Mrs. Victor out of the patrol car. She looked like they all felt. Beyond terrified. Numb. She hesitated on the porch.

"Bernice is my dear friend. Does she know yet?"

The young officer shook his head. "Trying to get all the facts before we tell her that she's lost her whole family." He just couldn't say anymore. His voice would fail him, betray his terrible sinking feeling.

Mrs. Victor took a deep breath and entered the darkened hallway. She almost stumbled on a baseball glove near the closet. "This for sure is out of place. Jimmy wouldn't allow anything like this. He was just like his dad, a taskmaster. Everything has a place. Everything in its place. No, he wouldn't let Dougie go to bed with this laying here."

"Sounds ... difficult to live with," Deputy Neal said, realizing immediately the irony of his words.

"Yes. Difficult. Impossible. Whatever you say. I begged Bernice to take her boys away. Let them have a normal life. But she always shook her head and said this was her lot in life. I think she was afraid of both of them. Father and son."

"Wow," the deputy said, under his breath. The poor, old, dear woman living with two monsters. He couldn't imagine it, having himself been brought up in a loving, Irish-Catholic home. His mom was the taskmaster but always with love. And his dad was just the best guy … funny and happy, always smiling.

"Deputy Neal, take Mrs. Victor into the kitchen. I'll take doc up to the crime scene." The deputy nodded, and they split up in the living room, where Mrs. Victor found nothing out of place, a picture-perfect room with family portraits displayed above an old, upright piano. It looked like a sad room, never used and enjoyed … a lonely room. It had history, though, and if it could speak, it would tell of family drama played out between the walls through the years, the carpet stained with many tears, most of them Bernice's.

In the kitchen, Mrs. Victor just shook her head. A glass half full of milk stood near the sink. The cookie jar was open, crumbs everywhere. "This might be enough to make the man lose his temper. It didn't take much."

Mrs. Victor looked toward the back door and started toward the dog. "Why Buster, get up, boy."

"He can't ma'am. He's dead, too."

Mrs. Victor dropped in the nearest kitchen chair. "The monster." Her tears fell then, as she realized the gravity of the situation. Now it was all real to her, and she cried. Dead children, dead parents, dead dog. Deputy Neal let her cry, turning away to wipe his own tears. He couldn't do anything for the people, but he'd see to the dog as soon as he could.

"Any other place we need to look, ma'am?" he asked Mrs. Victor.

"Big Jim's office. It's tucked under the stairway. I've never been in it, but it might give up some motive, I don't know." She lifted to her feet and steadied herself before she led the deputy to the hidden office that was no secret. The door had no visible handle, but Bernice had told her once how to get in. It was Big Jim's idea of maintaining his power over the family, to have his own space. And he warned them all that he'd know if they'd been in there. Bernice had never dared. Once the boys had gone in. But only once.

There was a small latch, just under the heavy wood molding that hugged the steps. You only had to loosen it and push in. That's all. Deputy Neal opened the door, and they both went in. It was a bigger room than either of them expected, long and narrow, from the staircase all the way to the back of the house. It even had a picture window that looked out over the back yard and the pond. Thin, long curtains framed the window that was covered with blinds, pulled to narrow slits. A large oak desk sat in the corner with a comfortable desk chair tucked into it. Two small chairs sat on the opposite wall next to a tall cupboard, the doors open. Mrs. Victor went to the desk and pointed out that a drop of liquid, still wet, had stained the blotter, probably from the bottle of expensive Scotch that stood near it, empty. Three silver flasks lined the bottom shelf, a space empty between two of them.

"He must have taken the flask to his room," she noted. "One is missing. See?" She put her fingers into the empty slot. He would never have left this ... mess. Not ordinarily."

"This was not an ordinary night for them, ma'am."

Mrs. Victor nodded. "I must go home." Her frail voice revealed all of her seventy years. They started for the front door, but she stopped.

"I forgot the dining room." She turned, and the young deputy followed her. That's when she screamed, a piercing, ear busting scream, and pointed down at floor near the library table. It looked like drops of blood in two distinct spots. But when the deputy bent down to look closer, he saw two small feet sticking out from under the table.

Chapter Twenty-Eight

Sheriff Pierce came rushing into the dining room before the screams had ended. The sheriff nodded for Deputy Neal to tend to the swooning Mrs. Victor, while he investigated the new evidence. He hated to think what he might find, so he said a quick prayer and knelt down by the library table. Before he could lift the cloth, the table came alive with shrieks and motion, toppling all the family pictures. The young deputy came to the rescue and lifted the table up as high as he could, setting it down awkwardly. It fell toward the kitchen door. His efforts revealed a very much alive, living pre-teen girl child with wild eyes and fists full of fine, light brown hair.

"We have ourselves a witness," Sheriff Pierce said, softly to the doctor, who'd just come into the room. "But I doubt she'll be of any real help. She appears to have lost her mind."

"Abby Munson's girl," the doctor said. "I have Bible study with her parents. I'll see to her. You get hold of her parents. I'll meet them at the hospital. But first, we need to sedate her."

The sheriff looked deeply into the girl's eyes. "You are safe. We will take care of you. Everything will be okay, sweetie." The last word struck a cord and the girl went limp. It was probably what her mom called her. Sweetie.

After the doctor administered a small amount of sedation, the sheriff carried the girl out to the coroner's car.

The doctor came out of the house after quickly examining the four victims. "I can't do anything more right now." He jotted a few notes in an old, black leather notebook. "It looks like you were right, Sheriff. Murder-suicide. But we might get more insight from the girl after she calms down, if she ever does." He shook his head. "I've only seen this once before. The whole family. It's the absolute worst. Such a shame. Did you get hold of her parents?"

"Yeah, the Father," Sheriff Pierce said. "He's in a panic, and he doesn't know the half of it. I really don't know how much we should say yet. I'm gonna stay at the crime scene until the Des Moines folks get here, keep searching for more evidence."

The doctor nodded. "It's possible .. you might find something else."

"Yes, I'm sure we will, Doc." The older officer shook his head.

Mrs. Victor sat slumped in the nearby recliner. She let out a soft cry when Sheriff Pierce helped her to her feet. "We'll need you as a witness, Viola. Deputy Neal will take you to the precinct for a statement and then home. Try to remember every little detail. It could all be relevant. You were the first person on the scene." He patted her shoulder. "And keep this to yourself until I give you the 'all clear.'"

Mrs. Victor nodded and followed the deputy to the car. "I'll have doc come by later with a sedative, Vi." She turned and nodded again, looking very much like a lost child, her hand in the hand of the young officer.

Sheriff Pierce looked up at the sky, at a beautiful pink haze on the horizon. That frosting pink sky this early in the morning only meant trouble … rain, possibly winds that would threaten or destroy any visuals. He heard a siren in the distance, and then another, ambulances coming to take away the bodies. So first things first. He rushed up the front steps to the porch and continued on to the second floor, to Debbie and Jimmy's bedroom. The image of them laying in a pool of their mixed blood was embedded in his mind. She looked like she was sleeping until the sheriff lifted Jimmy's upper body off of her. Jimmy had been slumped over her, the gun within inches of his right hand. She looked startled, her eyes not just open, but open as wide as could be. A tear stain ran down one of her cheeks. Her eyes were filled with anguish. She probably didn't die instantly, but couldn't move due to Jimmy's weight. She might have died relatively slowly and maybe even heard the screams or last words of her children. Yeah, it looked like murder-suicide. But why? Jimmy had everything to live for. He'd just gotten his freedom from that tyrant, Big Jim. And he'd inherited great wealth at the same time.

Sheriff Pierce looked at the gun again, an odd brand he'd only seen in pictures. Later, he'd have the lab in Waterloo check it for prints, but he was certain they would be Jimmy's. As he left the master bedroom, he met the paramedics coming up the steps. He directed them into Jimmy's room.

"Look for any evidence under the bodies or around them, and just drop what you find into the box. But leave Jimmy and Debbie for the Des Moines investigators." They nodded and moved quickly into the bedroom. The sheriff stood outside the next bedroom door, nearly paralyzed.

Blood spattered over the edge of the doorframe, waist high, and pooled at the threshold. On closer inspection, he could see a small handprint, little fingers that touched the wood lightly. There was a thick line of blood woven into a grotesque web …

a path, that led to the narrow bed where he found the little boy, Dougie, tucked neatly under the covers. His eyes were closed. The boy must have heard something and left his bed to investigate, or to run and hide. Jimmy settled him back into bed, even tucking him in with his teddy bear.

Without warning, the sheriff's stomach contents lurched upward toward his mouth. He turned his head and let it fall on the wood floor. And then his eyes flooded with tears. He had a son, a toddler, a boy who would soon be Dougie's age. He couldn't comprehend anyone killing a child, but especially a Father killing his own child.

After emptying his stomach, he stood in the hall for a while, taking in deep breaths. To his relief, he could smell the deep, sweet odors of apples and chocolate. Debbie was a great baker, and the house always smelled of fresh, sweet baking. What a strange turn of events. The house was alive with the smells of good food, and the people were all dead.

Christy's room was next to Dougie's. He touched the doorknob like it was on fire. He could barely turn it. Christy was a clever, sassy girl. Sometimes, she babysat for his little guy when he had him for the weekend. She was a delight, and you could see the beauty she was going to be … was going to be. Never would be. Never.

He opened the door. A dash of happy, bright sunlight filtered into the room for just a moment, belying the gruesome scene a few feet away. Christy had been awake, too. She was probably sitting on the edge of her bed. The lamp on her nightstand was still turned on. She was slumped to the side, her head resting awkwardly on the brass footboard.

What caught his eye was the crown she was wearing, a crown of aqua flowers, like a halo. Her body laid atop an aqua dress, a dark stain of her own dried blood on the shoulder. She must have been holding up the dress. It was probably going to be her costume for trick-or-treating. Gold ballerina slippers peaked out from under her bed. Sheriff Pierce recognized the dress as a smaller, reduced version of Debbie's bridesmaid dress worn at his own wedding, when he married his second wife.

He sat down next to the girl and held her hand, her stiff, cold, tiny hand. He didn't even move when the paramedics came into the room. He couldn't let go of her hand. If he did, she would be dead. Her death would be certain when they slipped her body into the plastic bag and zipped it up. Her death would be certain when they hauled her body off to the hospital and placed it on a metal slab. Her sweet, short life would be over for certain when they laid her in a taffeta lined coffin. So he just wouldn't let that happen. The paramedics left him alone, taking an early break. There was no hurry. It was too late to make any difference.

If Jimmy wasn't dead already, Sheriff Pierce would have killed him with his bare hands. And then he'd do it again, and then again … three times for three, innocent people whose lives he'd taken. He'd never felt so much hatred for any human being.

Chapter Twenty-Nine

After a fifteen-minute-break, the paramedics returned, and Sheriff Pierce reluctantly left Christy's room. He went out to the yard and wandered around, his emotions bringing him to a near panic. He paced up and down the driveway. There were ruts in the road just beyond the gravel drive, probably from Jimmy's truck, but they didn't look like truck tracks, so he studied them, committing them to memory.

He pulled a pack of cigarettes from his shirt pocket and lit one up. A few long strides brought him to the oak tree, close enough to touch the bark. The old folks around town called it the bleeding tree. The rumor had lived on for generations. People of all color and all walks of life were hung to death on that big branch that was now forty feet off the ground. Lots of guilty folks and some innocent. The state was still a territory then, and mob action was the rule ... the judge, the jury, and the hangman. The tree still gave him the willies. He could never look at it without thinking of the bodies hanging lifeless from the tree. When they were boys, Jimmy loved teasing him about it. He'd make the sign of the noose around his head, stretch his neck and make a face with his tongue out, and then laugh as if it were hysterical. Jimmy always had a mean streak in him.

The sheriff dropped his cigarette butt on the ground and twisted his toe atop it. It wasn't the only butt there, but he'd forgotten until now about the small pile that Deputy Neal had found near the tree. He picked up a couple, checking the brand. Not Camels like he smoked. They were Marlboros, like the deputy said. They were evidence, so he pulled out a baggie and bent to scoop them up. He didn't want to leave any stone unturned. The cigarettes seemed to be fresh, the mouth end still damp. One single cigarette laid a few feet away from the pile. When the sheriff bent to retrieve it, it was laying in a small pool of dried blood, the tip dark red. More evidence.

The outside seemed to be clear of any other curious items, so Sheriff Pierce went back into the house. The paramedics were just bringing down the children's bodies, but they were leaving Debbie and Jimmy until the Des Moines investigators could come and concur that cause of death was murder-suicide. The sheriff asked them to wait outside for him while he took one last look around, one last glance for evidence, before they all headed back to town.

The house was quiet, the shadows of a brewing storm making everything look gray, dismal, and very sad. He hated to be alone in the house with two corpses, but he did his best thinking when he was alone. So he made his way up the steps to the porch and opened the front door. He hesitated before going in, mustering much needed courage. He marched straight up to the second floor.

The master bedroom was still bright with overhead lighting, all the lamps turned on. After taking a seat at the dressing table, he turned slightly and made himself look at Debbie briefly, look away, and then look back at her. From this angle, he could see her eyes, her lifeless eyes. When she was alive, life burst from her sparkling, lovely brown eyes. She was gone. Her eyes said so. Her blank stare told a story that he struggled to hear. She had so much to say, and he planned to sit in the room and listen until he heard her.

Then he turned his attention to Jimmy. Jimmy lying face down atop Debbie, the gun just inches from his right hand, the arm extended toward the floor. He tried to imagine how Jimmy could shoot Debbie and end up in that position. He laid down on the floor and pretended to be leaning over someone. Jimmy hadn't been on his knees, his body had been flat, like he was leaning on his left arm to look at Debbie. Why would he do that? Why not just kneel over her and shoot?

It wasn't making sense, none of it, and the murder-suicide was looking less likely to him. He stood up and went closer to Jimmy, studying his face, what he could see of it, and he thought he saw concern. Yes, concern was screaming from his brow, not anger or hatred. It was love. He thought he could see love. As he looked at them, Debbie and Jimmy, their eyes nearly even, eyeball to eyeball, he could swear he saw a shared thought, a mutual expression of acceptance, as if they both knew that they were dying. It was eerie. It was frightening.

If he was right, if they both knew what fate they'd met at the precise same time, then there was another party to this scene, someone far more sinister, far more terrifying. And that person was at large. That person was roaming the early morning streets of Pine Falls, perhaps taking in a Sunday morning church service or waiting in Hasse's parking lot for the noon meal to be available, maybe a hamburger wingding meal. That person might be at the movie this afternoon, or walking in the park tomorrow.

Sheriff Pierce hurried out of the bedroom and down the steps. He was about to lock the doors, when he remembered he hadn't looked in all the rooms. The bathroom and the guest room hadn't been searched and cleared, so back he went. He found the guestroom neat and clean, the only thing missing was a pillowcase from the bed, no doubt, the one deputy Neal found in the barn. The drawers were filled with men's underwear, pajamas and some heavy sweaters. Men's pants and shirts hung in the closet. He checked the nightstand drawers. He found some ink pens and paper, some old pamphlets on colleges, and under some hankies and sox, he found an old playboy magazine. Nothing more. It must have been Jerry's room at one time.

The bathroom was at the end of the hall ... big and airy. White tiles covered the walls. Black and white tiles covered the floor. The white shower curtain was wrapped completely around the claw-foot tub. The room looked perfectly clean ... too clean. He learned early on that people don't live in clean. He opened the cupboard under the sink. Clean as a whistle, with just a few towels in the back, not enough for a family. The toilet was clean, but the seat was up. Odd? Maybe.

He pulled the shower curtain open slowly, thinking of *Psycho*. He could almost hear the stabbing music that terrified him as a child. He'd been holding his breath, but let it out when the shower was clean, really clean. And then he lifted the plug. As the plug came out, so did a few drops of watered down blood. He captured them on a small cloth that he carried in his pocket for just that purpose. That blood told him everything. Now he knew the truth. Jimmy was also a victim.

Chapter Thirty

Night shadows played tag with the hazy glow from the street lights in front of the brick building that housed the sheriff's office and jail. Sheriff Pierce stepped slowly into the building, into the reception room. He was exhausted. His deputy was staring into his office at someone in the side chair. "Neally, who's in there?"

"Bernice Collins. Doc went over to her house and gave her the news. He sat with her for a while and gave her some sedation. She's a tough old bird. Wanted to come in now and talk. Are you ready to ask her a few questions? Like, why her son would kill his family?"

"The truth is, Neally, I'm almost sure he didn't do it." Sheriff Pierce went to the empty interrogating room and opened the door. "Come 'ere. I wanna show you something." He took his young deputy into the room and pulled down the shades. Then he laid down on the linoleum floor and patted for the younger man to join him. "I'm Jimmy, and you're Debbie, on my left."

Deputy Neal walked over to the window. "Ya sure?" He looked toward the door. "No other way to show me?"

"Naw. It's hard to perceive, if you don't do it this way. We could go back to the house, but I think you'll see it right away and agree with me."

"Now lay flat. I'm going to raise my right hand with a pretend gun and see if I can shoot you and then myself. See if I can land like Jimmy did."

The deputy laid down beside his boss, arms at his sides.

The sheriff lifted up on his elbow. "Remember his legs weren't bent and he flopped, straight legged on top of Debbie. He had to be in this position."

The deputy nodded agreement.

"Let's say he shot Debbie from ... anywhere. He could have been standing beside the bed, looking down at her. Then he crawled into bed with her."

Deputy Neal nodded. "Sure."

Sheriff Pierce lifted his right hand and put the pretend gun to his head, as he leaned over Deputy Neal. "See, I can't do it and land flat on top of you. My arm and the gun would probably still be on the bed. It was all too tidy. Too staged. The bodies were perfectly aligned, eye to eye. He on top of her, his arm down on the floor with the gun by his hand. It just doesn't work." The sheriff got up and helped his deputy to his feet. "Aw heck. Let's just go out there. The bodies will be there for another hour, until Des Moines gets there. I want you to look at their eyes. See what you think."

Deputy Neal nodded. "But first, you have to say something to Bernice. She thinks her son killed his family. I agree that it would be impossible, given the body positions. Let's go with that for now and clear it up later, after we investigate."

"Good," Sheriff Pierce smiled for the first time. "Nobody wants to hear that their progeny is a murderer. I'll just talk to her briefly, let her digest the news."

"Doc's still here, waiting to take her home."

The sheriff tapped on the doorframe of the room where Bernice Collins sat, rigid, on the edge of the wooden chair. She did not turn around, but her hands moved into her lap.

"Mrs. Collins, I'm so very sorry about Jimmy, Deb, and the kids."

He took a seat in the chair next to her.

"Yes, Ronnie. It's been a shock." She turned her face to look towards him, but her eyes focused over his head. "Are you … is it possible … could you be wrong? My Jimmy is still alive. Christy, Dougie?" Her eyes held a small shred of hope, and when he shook his head, they went dull. She pulled her chin up and pursed her lips.

"Bernice, after I looked the scene over again, I'm almost fully convinced that Jimmy did not do this to his family, to himself." He watched for her response. He'd known her all his life. She would not shed a tear. She would not falter. She would not look at him again.

"Can you think of anyone who might do this? Did Jimmy have a quarrel with anyone, or do you know anything that we can use to take this investigation ahead?"

Bernice Collins sat still for some time, finally opening her mouth as if to speak, but changed her mind and shook her head. "They were very happy. Everything was fine, just fine. In fact, they were going to … have a baby."

Bernice would never reveal anything of a personal nature to him. Not yet.

"I must call Jerald. I believe I'd like to go home now and make that phone call."

"Of course. Doc is waiting. He'll take you home. Do you have someone who can come stay with you?"

"Yes, my neighbor."

"I'll get back to you as soon as I know anything."

Bernice nodded.

"And Bernice, I am truly sorry. If there's anything I can do ...."

Mrs. Collins did look at him this time. Her eyes were fluid, and then she squinted. "You were the best child when you visited. Big Jim always commented on how proud he'd be to have you for a son." She stood, patted Sheriff Pierce's shoulder, and left the room in short, quick steps.

Deputy Neal waited in the hall, but his boss did not turn around for a few minutes. When he did, he was wiping at tears.

"Nice old lady. Tough." He picked up a Polaroid camera, and the two officers headed back to the crime scene.

Chapter Thirty-One

The drive out to the Collins' farm seemed longer than Ron Pierce remembered. He'd come out here so many times ... on a bike, in a jalopy, and once he even ran away from home and ended up at the Collins' place on foot. The anger was completely wrung out of him after the long, cold walk.

"Bernice was good to the boys in the early years," he told his deputy. "She'd make them special treats, and they'd do things together. She laughed a lot then. She had a beautiful laugh." He smiled, just thinking of her in those early days. He'd always tell his mom how pretty Bernice looked, all fixed up like June Cleaver, or Harriet Nelson. And then something happened. "She lost her joy when Jimmy was maybe in the fifth grade. I think Big Jim told her the boy's childhood days were over, and it crushed her spirit. Jerry got gypped. He was probably seven or eight when the curtain came down on his childhood."

The officers stepped out of the patrol car, each taking in the murder scene again, hoping to see something that had eluded them earlier. The sheriff took dozens of Polaroid pictures. Pictures of the tree and the place where the partially smoked cigarette butts had been piled. Pictures of the front door. Pictures of the dog. Pictures of the cookie crumbs and milk glass. Pictures of the turned over table. Pictures in Big Jim's office. Then they went up the stairs.

Sheriff Pierce knew that it's always hardest to look around a crime scene the first time, when you don't know what you're going to find. But there was nothing easier about seeing it again. Each time, it became more frightening. Inexplicable.

Jimmy still lay atop Debbie. "See how their eyes meet, and they look as if they were seeing each other, really seeing each other?"

Deputy Neal nodded.

"It looks like they both knew the same thing at the same time. Both victims. Debbie doesn't look scared, she looks ... like she's saying good-bye." The young officer felt a sting of tears, the whole scene so moving. He went to the dresser and picked up the family picture that had fallen over. Sheriff Pierce stood behind him and looked at the picture that the deputy held. Jimmy was sitting in a leather chair, Debbie perched on one of the chair's arms. The boy was behind his dad, his hand on his dad's shoulder. The girl sat at her dad's feet, the skirt of her dress spread out like a flower petal. They were all dressed in navy and red. Jimmy wore a navy blue sweater and Debbie had on a red skirt and white blouse. The boy was wearing a red and navy plaid shirt and navy corduroy pants, and the girl had on a velvet red dress with white lace trim.

"Careful with the fingerprints," the sheriff warned. "That picture might be evidence. Since it was placed face down, perhaps the ... killer looked at it, like you did, to see who he'd just murdered." Killer ... a mean, gruesome word that denotes a horrible monster, not human. He hadn't used the word or even thought of it until he said it out loud. Now that his deputy agreed with him, he could quit thinking in terms of Jimmy, the murderer, to Jimmy, the victim. Jimmy, his old school friend. When had their friendship changed? Well, when was the last time the two of them argued? That would be the time. Ron remembered it well.

They were sixteen or seventeen, and they spent endless hours talking about girls. Ron finally confessed his love for Trudy Beck. The very next day when he arrived at school, Trudy was standing with a few girls and showing off Jimmy's class ring. She had it on a piece of ribbon and wore it around her neck. She made a point of loosening a button on her blouse and dropping the ring down between her breasts. Jimmy came by then and slung his arm over her shoulder. He looked right at Ron and smiled. His eyebrows lifted slightly and his head turned a little, his chin jutted out. Just for good measure, he slid his hand down the front of Trudy's blouse and brought out the ring. Ron Pierce never spoke to him again, unless it was official business as sheriff.

And here he was, on official business. The business of Jimmy's death. The business of finding Jimmy's killer. There would be no more talking between the two of them in this lifetime. He'd never be able to ask Jimmy the one burning question. Why? Why did he throw away their friendship for a few weeks of romancing Trudy? For just a minute he thought about excusing himself from the case, his anger at Jimmy so real again he didn't care who'd done it, and he wasn't sure if he wanted to make a real effort to find out. But above all else, he was an officer of the law. He'd do his duty.

He did end up with Trudy. He married her. But she never got over Jimmy, and the sheriff couldn't look at his wife without seeing Jimmy's fingerprints all over her. So they moved apart, divorced, and she finally moved out of town. Their daughter, Cheryl, was Christy's age.

"So, we agree that Jimmy in all likelihood did not murder his family?" Sheriff Pierce said, his official voice not betraying his born-again bitterness.

"Yup, as far as I can tell."

The sheriff snapped a photo of Jimmy and Debbie from every angle. He tried to be discreet and not get any of Debbie's naked body parts in the picture. She deserved respect. Next, he took a picture of the family portrait, face down, like deputy Neal found it in. And then he took pictures of the gun from every angle. He dropped the gun and the photo in the evidence box.

"Let me show you the bathtub plug, where I found the blood. Maybe your fresh eyes will see more than mine did."

They went into the bathroom, the light still on. Deputy Neal looked around, finding nothing out of place. He agreed that a family with two children and a guest child visiting would not have such a clean bathroom. It was highly suspicious. When the sheriff put the plug in and then pulled it out, blood came with it. They took another small cloth and wiped the drain. The blood was darker now and had dried a little.

"Let's wait outside for the Des Moines team. They should be here soon. Then we can get the bodies down to the funeral home. If we have to, we can come back here for more evidence. There'll probably be something new each time, as we become more focused, know what we're looking for."

When the officers stepped out of the house, the state investigator was pulling into the drive, followed by two hearses. The sheriff knew him from a few other cases. This guy, Bob Green, had a perfect record in town. He had solved all three Pine Falls' murders.

146

"Guy murdered his wife and kids, eh?" The investigator asked while shaking the sheriff's hand. He nodded to the deputy.

"No. We're thinking … four homicides. You go get your take on it. When you bring the bodies in, we'll compare notes."

Sheriff Pierce walked slowly to the patrol car. He took a quick look at the large, oak tree leaning slightly toward the house. Four more deaths to add to all the rest on this condemned land.

Chapter Thirty-Two

When Sheriff Pierce and his deputy arrived back at the station, Bernice was waiting for them in the sheriff's office. She was sitting in the visitor's chair again, her back to them. She did not turn around when they entered the room and spoke before she saw them.

"I have some names. Let's see, there's Tim, the farmhand. Tim Buckly hated Jimmy, but I think he liked Debbie." She took a deep breath. "And there was Abby, Abby Munson, Abby Stoddard now. She was in love with Jimmy, and her husband knew about it. Their daughter might be Jimmy's." That was a real revelation. It almost took their breath away. "And then there's the waitress at the diner, Santha something ... Thomas. Santha Thomas. Jimmy's been helping her out a lot with finances. Her daughter is Jimmy's." She took a few more deep breaths. "And then there's Dick Patrick. He was in a bit of a bind financially, and Jimmy made him an offer for his farm, fifty cents on the dollar. Dick took it, he had to, but Jimmy really stole that property."

Bernice was silent, her ideas spent or so they thought. "Perry Fulbright got into some gambling trouble. Jimmy lent him some money, and I think he's been paying Jimmy back with the use of his daughter. She'll do anything for her dad. That could make her husband, Mitch Cuttler, unhappy."

"Hold on Mrs. Collins," Deputy Neal said. "I need to get a tablet. Take some notes."

He looked at the sheriff and shook his head. He whispered, "For real?"

Sheriff Pierce nodded. "Should be even more names. We'll be at this investigation for a few weeks, if we can find all the suspects."

"Judas Priest," the young deputy said, and then turned back to smile at Bernice.

He grabbed a brand-new tablet and started writing. Bernice gave up a few more people, but they seemed less likely to the sheriff, so he had the deputy put an x by their names.

"Did you get hold of Jerry? Is he coming?" The sheriff was deeply concerned about the older woman being alone in this tragedy. If it were his mother, she'd be a basket case and need him right away. Like, yesterday.

Bernice shook her head. "I've been phoning all day, but I haven't been able to reach him. He probably went out to a concert or something. He's always going out, having fun. His father, Big Jim hated that. He said the boy never worked, not like Jimmy. Jimmy toed the line, and his father respected him for that. They were birds of a feather. But Jerry … Big Jim was embarrassed by Jerry's life. He didn't want to hear about him. So I kept Jerry's calls to myself."

"Sorry, Bernice." Sheriff Pierce dropped his pen and patted her hand. "I mean, Mrs. Collins."

Bernice looked him in the eye, and her own eyes watered just a little. "You were Jimmy's friend until he did something to hurt you years ago. I missed you coming out."

Sheriff Pierce nodded. "Yes, Bernice. I guess I could be a suspect, too."

"No. You're more like Jerry. You take it quietly and don't have to get even. You're a good boy."

Bernice got up and walked out of the office without another word.

"Should I put you on the list?" Deputy Neal asked, his eyebrows tucked under the bill of his cap, as he looked at his boss.

"If I didn't know I didn't do it, I would put me on the list. I really did hate that guy. This is going to be a very difficult investigation. I hope Bob Green has some insight."

"What about Jerry? Do we need to put him on the list?"

The sheriff thought about it for a moment. "Naw. Like his mom said, he's a gentle guy. That's why he left. Anyway, he's too far away."

"Where do you think he is? His mom didn't get hold of him yet."

"She will tonight. I'll check in with her tomorrow. We'll interrogate him for sure, but just for information that he can give us. Who knows? There might be a few more leads. I'm afraid there will be even more people to consider, as we move this investigation along. There could be a hundred when we're through."

"Wow. I'm glad I didn't know this guy." Deputy Neal put down the tablet. "Where do we start?"

"Good question. Who was the first name on the list?"

"Tim. The fired hired-man."

"Let's start with him. Tim Buckly. He's a good guy, and his wife is sick. I think we can rule him out right away, but we need to talk to him. I'll give him a call tomorrow. I think we need to take our time. Sleep on it. We both need fresh eyes."

The deputy nodded. That was another thing he learned at the academy. Don't get so invested in solving the crime that you lose your perspective.

A tap at the door brought the two officers back to the moment. Bob Green stood there with the evidence box. And he was smiling.

Chapter Thirty-Three

The small, tacky diner lit up like a beacon on the side road near Jerry's apartment, and it was calling his name. It was the only place open this time of night, so Jerry parked his bike near the front door and walked in. He sat in the back booth, and the waitress tossed a menu at him. She did not look happy to see him. No one ever did. He slumped over a thin slice of apple pie and scooped it into his mouth with effort. After each bite, he slurped on the day-old, lukewarm coffee the sneering waitress slammed in front of him.

His mind wandered gladly away from her and zeroed in on his long ride back to San Diego. The traffic had been snarled most of the last few hours. He hated California highways. It was never an easy drive, always a stop-start-stop kind of ride. He had to weave in and out of the endless stream of cars and trucks that jammed the highways. Exhaust fumes glazed his nostrils in layers, until he could taste them. But he had to get home. He had to be ready for work in the morning. They'd only given him Friday afternoon off, though he'd asked for Monday morning, too.

The waitress unplugged the diner's neon sign. Her toe tapping and pursed lips told him it was time for him to leave.

He swallowed the last of his pie in one big bite. It was dry and slightly burned, a perfect ending to a really crazy weekend. It didn't go exactly as he had planned it to, but nothing ever did. He'd left San Diego Friday night high with expectations and now, in the early morning hours of Monday morning, he was returning in the lowest of lows. He hadn't really talked to anyone. He felt invisible the whole time. Even the two girls he'd seen earlier in the day refused his offer of a free breakfast. They were all caught up in girl talk about nails, and rings, and hairstyles, and just shook their heads no. They had to be at least thirty, two middle-aged women alone, and yet neither of them could even give him a smile.

He glanced at his reflection in the plate-glass window as he paid for his pie and coffee. He looked tired, old. He looked like life had passed him by. The waitress took his three dollars, turned away, and stepped outside to the parking lot. He was going to tell her to keep the change, but she'd already put all the money in her apron pocket. Good thing she was wearing an apron. Her white hot pants were burning up her thighs. She definitely did not have the body for the out-of-fashion style. Her legs looked like sausages in white, shiny go-go boots that stopped just above her thick knees. But she didn't seem to care and neither did the good looking, young man she was staring at. He looked very excited.

Jerry watched them flirt for a while and wondered what the kid saw in her. She was shameless in her teasing. The kid was holding a small package, a condom-size package, his intent so obvious that Jerry smiled for the first time that day. He bumped into the kid, and the package dropped to the ground. Jerry picked it up and stuffed it in his jacket pocket. He gave the kid a thumbs down, as he put on his goggles and helmet.

And he mouthed the words, "You can do better." The kid was still gaping at him when he started his bike. Dumb kid.

The traffic had thinned out in the early morning hours. It was the first time Jerry had seen the roads so desolate. But he'd never been out that late, or early, on a Monday. He rode his bike down the narrow road … no weaving, no stopping. His neighborhood was quiet. A television set was still turned on in one of the neighbor's apartments, but most windows were dark. Sleeping with the television turned on intrigued him. It might be worth a try. Maybe he could catch a few hours sleep before his alarm went off, and life started up again.

He opened his back door and flipped on the light, surprised to see a note laying on his kitchen floor. His neighbor must have slipped it under the door. It said that his mother called earlier, and that she'd tried him several times before giving up and calling the number he'd given her for emergencies. He couldn't talk to her now, so he'd get back to her later, after work. He was bummed, really bummed. He knew she'd ask him a lot of questions. Where had he been? Why didn't he call her right back? She was always on his case about something, but this time it would be different. He'd be ready with answers.

No matter what he did, he couldn't shake the past. Maybe his mother could help him out with a bit of good news. He could use some good news. In the morning.

Chapter Thirty-Four

Tim Buckly sat in the Sheriff's waiting room in a cold, brown, naugahyde chair. It was an even colder, bleak Iowa November day. Monday, November first. Nothing good ever came of Mondays. He pulled his fingers through his thick, black hair. His mustache was too long, and he wished he'd trimmed it before coming into town at the sheriff's request. He knew it made him look guilty. Guilty of what, he didn't know yet. But his luck was so bad, he'd definitely be going to jail. Just what his wife needed in her condition. It was only weeks, maybe a month or two, and she'd be gone. Dead. Whatever it was that he was supposed to have done would be of no concern to her. She wouldn't have to suffer his shame. But his boys would.

He'd left the boys in charge of their mom after getting the call from Sheriff Pierce to stop by his office, answer a few questions. They were happy to stay home from school with her and had done it often these last few months, since she'd taken to her bed. He promised to take them for hamburgers at Big Boy later in the day. Then he'd called his mom in Des Moines to give her heads up, that he needed her again for a few days. His left hand itched, and he scratched it vigorously with his right hand. He itched everywhere. He was scared.

"Tim?"

Sheriff Pierce motioned for him to come into the office. It seemed a friendly gesture. Yet he was still really scared. The office was lit by one large, brass lamp on the desk, no lamp-shade. Tim sat down opposite the sheriff, across a wide, scratched maple desk. Tim knew his wood. He was originally a cabinet maker, but he hadn't found a job in that field for years. So he took a lot of odd jobs, the last one being farm-hand, Jimmy's hired-man, and he'd been pretty good at that until he was fired.

Tim scratched his forehead, then his knee.

"How's your wife?"

Tim shook his head. "Not good, Ron, er ... Sheriff. She's taken a turn for the worse. They say she may rebound, but right now, well, we're just waiting out her time."

"Sorry to hear that. Janie was in the class after me. She sure didn't deserve this."

Tim nodded. "Sure didn't."

"I have some bad news for you."

Tim knew it. It was always bad news, never good.

"Happened yesterday, er the night before." The sheriff pushed his chair back a few feet and got up. He stepped toward the window, looked out, and then looked back at Tim. "We haven't told anyone yet, and I'm asking you to please keep this to yourself."

He took a seat again and leaned in toward Tim, his voice just above a whisper. "Jim Collins is dead."

Tim stood up with a lurch. His whole body itched. He scratched unmercifully at his head. "What? Jimmy is dead?"

"Yeah. We were out there most of the day yesterday."

"How? What happened?"

"Murdered."

"How's Debbie taking it? Is she okay?"

"Not so good, I'm sorry to say. Dead, too. And the kids."

Tim dropped onto the chair. Tears filled his eyes and his lips tightened. "Oh my God. Oh my God."

"Des Moines investigator found one of your work shirts there, from when you worked in the gas station. Had your name on it. And some blood. What can you tell me, Tim?"

"I ...." Tim covered his eyes. "I don't remember. I ... let me think." He took a few deep breaths. Jimmy was dead. Debbie was dead. The kids were dead. Did they think he did it? That he would murder an entire family because he was fired?

"I usually wore the work shirts to the farm because they weren't good for anything else." He shrugged. "I, I knew I wouldn't be needing them again at the gas station. I was a lousy mechanic."

He swallowed hard a few times. "I was working on the tractor when Dougie came up to me. He'd taken a spill on Christy's bike, and he was bleeding. His knee was pretty banged up, so I carried him to the house. Debbie noticed how much blood was on my shirt. She brought me one of Jimmy's old shirts and took mine to launder. She said she'd wash it and get it back to me, but I told her it was old and not worth the effort. I never saw it again. Maybe she kept it for rags or something. I can't tell you anymore."

"Where were you Friday night?"

Tim thought back. Was he home with Janie? Yeah, he was always home with Janie when he wasn't working. No. That was the night he took a drive into town. He was going to have a beer with the boys, just one, a quick one, but he felt guilty when he got to Main Street, so he drove a few more miles and turned into the park. He just needed some time to think. Think about his future alone. He did think about Debbie, too, and wondered what it would be like if he could rescue her from Jimmy. He loved her. He'd never kill her. Never.

"I took a drive after I got the boys to bed. I was gone for maybe an hour."

"Anyone see you?"

"No." He wasn't sure about that, but he hadn't seen anyone.

"Do you smoke, Tim?"

"Yeah, a few cigarettes a day. Trying to cut back. Trying to quit."

"Brand?"

"Camels, Marlboros, Winstons. Whatever is cheapest at the gas station."

Sheriff Pierce took a deep breath. "I have to be honest. You are on a list of suspects, but it's a long list. Right now, I'm going to let you go. I'll check around and see if anyone can verify your story, just for the record."

He patted Tim's shoulder. "I've got a lot of people to interview, so this could take some time. The news about the murders won't make the paper until later today. I'm hoping to talk to several suspects first. Can you keep this under wraps?"

Tim nodded, his shoulders drooping. "Sure, Ron."

"Thanks for coming in, Tim."

Tim got up and shuffled his feet across the floor to the door.

"You're pretty bummed."

Tim blinked a few times. "I am. I worked for Debbie for three years. I was very fond of her … and the kids."

"But not Jim so much?"

Tim shook his head. "He was a bastard. No offense to Mrs. Collins. He was a chip off the old bastard block." Tim turned to look at the sheriff. "But I didn't hate him. Hate takes too much out of you. I've already got enough on my plate." He

blinked a few times and swiped at his eyes. "Debbie, she ...
Debbie was ...."

"I know. She was special."

Sheriff Pierce watched Tim walk to his truck ... a beat up,
old, red Ford. He opened the driver's door and got in like an
old man. After, slamming the door hard, he dropped his head
onto the steering wheel. The sheriff could tell he was sobbing.
He was pretty sure Tim was not their man. But Bob Green was
zeroing in on him. Well, he didn't know Tim.

So, if it wasn't Tim, then who was it? Who would be
capable of such a monstrous crime?

Chapter Thirty-Five

Deputy Neal bent down to check the suspect list again. He'd gone over Bernice's list, the sheriff's list, and a few other add-ons, combining them into one. It amazed him how Jimmy Collins had lived this long. It looked like everyone in town had a score to settle with him.

The second person on Bernice's list was Abby Stoddard. When she'd mentioned Abby's name, there was definite disdain. She'd told them that Abby's daughter, the one living witness to this crime, could be Jimmy's daughter. That would be motive, for Abby or her husband, Gary. The daughter would be an heir to the Collins' estate, if they could prove it. And then Bernice had mentioned Perry Fulbright, who may have been using his daughter as pay-back for a loan Jimmy had made him. That would be motive, too, if you think about it. And that was all he'd done since they'd discovered the grisly murders yesterday. Think about it. He couldn't get the images out of his mind. Officer training had pictures of scenes like that, blown up on the slide screen. They were pretty bad, but had not prepared him for the real thing ... the once living, breathing, still warm bodies of a small, young family laying there stone dead, their bodies moving quickly into rigormortis. The strongest, most lasting memory for him was the smell of a very clean house, baking odors permeating the walls and furnishings. Once the smells of love to him, were now the smells of death.

Sheriff Pierce came into the office and took the list of suspects from his deputy. He sat down at the desk that they shared.

"Calling Abby next," he said. "I asked her to keep Sally home from school today, when I called to check on our witness, er, her daughter. She agreed. Said her daughter was too distraught to go anywhere. And I figured it will be easier that way, for them to keep the murders under wraps."

He picked up the phone, then set it down. "Anything I should know, Neally before I call? Did you make any other discoveries, or did something pop into your mind?"

"Just thinking about how the town is going to react when the newspapers are delivered." The deputy handed the sheriff a copy of the *Pine Falls Sun*, the one he picked up at the printers, hot off the press. The delivery kids hadn't even seen them. He'd skimmed the article, accurate as far as he could tell, and there were some nice pictures of the family. The article had talked about a pretty open-ended investigation to proceed, with several leads. That would scare the crap out of Jimmy's most benign enemy.

Thirty minutes after the sheriff had called Abby, she walked in the door. She looked petrified, a step beyond terrified. She'd been crying, and wiped at her tears while she explained to Nelda, the dispatch officer, that she was a little late because she'd had to wait for her husband to come in from the field to take care of their daughter.

Sheriff Pierce liked to let the suspects sit for a moment, to watch their actions and reactions. Almost everyone he'd brought in to interrogate looked guilty as they waited, probably going over their story in their minds, so they wouldn't make a mistake. They rarely even heard Nelda offer them a cup of coffee. If they only knew ... the truth is the truth. Unless you have something to hide, it's always the best response to any question.

It never paid to try to out think the interrogator. Almost never. He had a keen ear for a man's deception, but women still baffled him. They were all actresses, like they were trying out for a part in the local theatre. He usually bought everything they said, until he had time to think about it. Quite often, he brought women in a second and maybe even a third time.

Abby had long, bottle-gold hair, and as she waited, she twisted a strand of it into a little knot. Her lips were moving as if she were talking to someone. She knew what was going on and why she was here. That made her actions more important.

"Abby." The sheriff pulled his shoulders back. He'd always liked Abby, maybe a little too much, so he knew he had to be very professional. Considering what her daughter had just gone through, he had to be very careful not to be too aggressive, but being overly sympathetic could be a serious problem in the investigation. He felt sure that she was innocent, but she might know something that would help. Apparently, Gary Stoddard had a bone to pick with Jimmy. When they made the plan to move to Pine Falls, did he know that he would be renting farmland from his step-daughter's blood family? That was the rumor. Abby would know the truth, and Sheriff Pierce hoped to dig it out of her.

"So, how long did you live in Wisconsin?" The sheriff smiled, and Abby took a deep breath. She pulled at a piece of her hair and started twisting again. She did have great hair but maybe a little too much make-up. It made her look hard and older than her age. Just two years younger than he was.

"We moved my senior year." She dropped her eyes, trying to decide how much to say. "Dad got a great job opportunity in Ripon, at a company that makes washers and dryers." She looked up, her eyes curious, searching. He could tell she was trying to figure out what he wanted to hear.

Now the sheriff dropped his eyes, but kept her in his vision. "Did Big Jim have anything to do with the move?"

Abby nodded. "He got my dad the job."

"Who is Sally's Father?" Sheriff Pierce looked up now to watch Abby's reaction. "Is it Jim Collins?"

"Probably." Abby studied the hem on her mini skirt. "I was crazy about Jimmy. The only way I could get to Jimmy was through Jerry. I started dating Jerry, and that brought his older brother right to me, like a magnet. He came to my house one night after Jerry dropped me off. We got, well, a little physical. I was so excited ... and I didn't want to lose him. Jerry was mortified the next day when I told him at school that it was over, we were over. He went on about me being his first girlfriend. He told me how he loved me and how he hated his brother. I remember seeing them fight in the parking lot later that day when Jimmy came to pick me up. Jerry's fists were flying, and Jimmy was holding him off with one hand, no effort at all, laughing his head off. I felt bad for Jerry, but I was in love with Jimmy."

"So you got pregnant right away?"

Abby started to tear up. "Yeah, pretty much."

"And you think Jim is the Father?"

Abby nodded.

"Does Gary know?"

Wendy Moser

"Most of it."

"Any chance …." Sheriff Pierce stopped. This would be a difficult question and could stop the interview. "Do you think it's possible that Gary decided to get even?"

Abby looked up, shaking her head vigorously. "Jim died of natural causes. Gary didn't have anything to do with his death."

Sheriff Pierce squinted, confused. "Jim was murdered. Shot in the head."

"No," Abby said. "I'm talking about Jimmy's dad."

"Big Jim is Sally's Father?"

Abby shrugged her shoulders. "Yeah. I'm pretty sure."

The sheriff didn't see that coming. "How did that happen?" It really wasn't any of his business, but he was curious.

"One night I hitched a ride out to the farm with a Collins' neighbor. I was ready, you know, and didn't want to make Jimmy wait any longer." Abby looked embarrassed. "Jimmy wasn't there. He and Jerry had taken their mom into town for a church function. But Jimmy's dad was there and invited me in … to talk." Abby's expression changed to sadness. "He teased me, and joked around, and got me laughing. I wanted him to like me." Abby closed her eyes as if to see the scene again. "He gave me little shots of some clear booze, I think it was straight vodka. I got silly, giddy, and then suddenly, he had me in a compromising position." Abby sighed deeply. "It just happened, and I didn't know how to stop him, without making him angry. So, I pretended it was Jimmy. He took me home … and did it again on a gravel road outside of town." Abby's voice cracked. "I never had another period."

She cried for several moments, taking tissue after tissue from Sheriff Pierce. "I never told this to anyone, except Gary." She dabbed at her eyes one last time. "That's why Mr. Collins was so generous to my family. He wanted me out of town. He

164

told my dad, if we left, they wouldn't have to deal with the shame. He got my dad a job, and he even gave us a new car. He wanted me to put my baby up for adoption as soon as I gave birth, but I didn't."

"Why did you come back?"

"Gary wanted to farm. I told him that the Collins had farms they rented, and he could try calling Big Jim. He did, and they talked real friendly, and it ended with us coming to Iowa. Big Jim didn't know Gary was married to me." Abby shrugged her shoulders again. "I suppose Gary was a little curious, just wanted to see who this guy was. Sally's dad."

"And Big Jim wouldn't have known the name."

Abby nodded. "I met Gary a few months after I had Sally. I was working at an Insurance company and he came in for an auto plan. He asked me out right away." She dabbed a tissue at her nose. "He wasn't afraid to take on a ready-made family. He's the only father Sally has ever known."

"Do you think he was putting the squeeze on Big Jim?"

"No. I'm sure he wasn't. He loves Sally, and he likes farming. No, he really isn't that kind of person."

"So, he's not the kind of person who would kill either, I suppose."

"No." Abby smiled, and it was obvious to the sheriff that she loved her husband. He felt relief.

Abby looked thoughtful for a moment. "Anyway, Gary was in the hospital till Sunday. He had a kidney stone bothering him. He passed it Sunday morning. They were going to do surgery, but they didn't have to."

Sheriff Pierce checked Gary off his mental list. "I may have to talk to Sally again. Maybe Gary could bring her in?"

Abby nodded, heaving a big sigh of relief. She got up and moved toward the door.

"I'm really sorry that Jimmy and Debbie are dead. Sally will really miss Christy." She shook her head, tears building in her eyes. "She'll never get over this." The sheriff held her while she cried, comfortable in their friendship. "If there is anything I can do …."

Abby nodded into his pressed uniform shirt, and a tear fell on his neck.

"Thanks for coming, Abby. Time will heal."

She stood a little taller. "I doubt it, but, maybe."

Sheriff Pierce watched his friend get into her car. So Big Jim had planted his seed in her. She wasn't absolutely sure it was him. It could have been him, or Jimmy, or maybe even Jerry. But for sure, she had a Collins' heir. He wondered if she'd thought of that yet.

Chapter Thirty-Six

Bob Green didn't have much dirt on Perry Fulbright. The guy spent a lot of time on junkets to Las Vegas, and he'd owed money to everyone in town, until Jimmy saved his butt. When Sheriff Pierce went to the trailer park to check out the story, he found Perry looking years older without his toupee. He was grieving, slumped in a threadbare La-Z-Boy chair. His friendly, easy banker, Jimmy Collins, had just died, and life had changed for him forever.

"Jimmy did make me a few loan," he said. But that was public knowledge. Then he admitted that his daughter, Karen, did do her part to pay Jimmy back. He praised Jimmy for his kindness.

Karen stood along her father as they spoke, her eyes never leaving her father's face. She'd probably do anything for her father, but would she kill? Karen's paraplegic husband, Mitch, sat in his wheelchair near the window, gazing at the big snowflakes that were falling.

The sheriff studied Perry's daughter again briefly as the older man talked. She wasn't a pretty girl. In fact, she was quite manly, and Sheriff Pierce couldn't fathom what she could do for Jimmy that Debbie couldn't. But she appeared to be genuinely saddened by Jimmy's death. They all did. So for now, Perry, Karen, and Mitch, for obvious reasons, were penciled off the list.

Dick Patrick was the next suspect. Mrs. Collins said Patrick's farm was the last one seized by Jimmy, to push their land holdings well over the thousand-acre mark. It was the first acquisition that Jimmy had arranged on his own, without his father, and he was proud of his accomplishment. So proud, he couldn't stop bragging. If he wanted to follow in his father's footsteps, this proved to one and all that he could fill the shoes that made them. Maybe all the bragging got him killed.

The sheriff sent Deputy Neal to the Patrick farmhouse to investigate, have a chat with the old farmer. "The property was abandoned," he said, in his official voice when he returned. "I drove to the neighboring farm, where I learned that Dick's family was grown and gone, and Dick and his wife had taken a room at Pine Fall's newest nursing home. His wife has Alzheimer's, according to the neighbor," the deputy read from his notes. "So I went to the care center, to the Patrick's room." He looked up at the sheriff and his voice changed, became softer and sympathetic. "Well, I checked the old couple off the list of suspects. Dick Patrick could barely walk, using one of those walkers with tennis balls for wheels. And his wife was bed-ridden. The old guy did grumble about Jimmy's cold heart, but then said, 'Thank God Jimmy made this decision for us.'" The deputy shook his head and handed the marked up list to the sheriff. "No, I'm certain he didn't do it."

The sheriff studied the shrinking list, turning it over to see both sides. They were down to Bernice's last two entries, the first being Billy Nelson. The Iowa Bureau of Investigation had a lot on Billy, according to Bob Green. 'He has filled a file cabinet with his antics ... law breaking, and just plain orneriness,' the investigator's report said. 'He hasn't murdered anyone … yet. But he has been arrested several times for domestic abuse and jailed for fights that resulted in injuries … all at the Dew Drop Inn, the bar he owned until recently.' Bob Green's file on Billy Nelson was extensive, putting him at the top of the suspect list. 'Billy Nelson is an angry man, and he hated Jimmy Collins. The hatred ratcheted up when financial woes forced him to sell the bar to Jimmy, and Jimmy told him to scram. Billy didn't take that lightly.' The investigator concluded. 'As soon as we put Billy's name in the system, it slung mud in every direction. I'd circle this guy's name with indelible ink.''

The sheriff folded up the report and tucked it under his doodle pad. Yes, Billy could be the one … motive, physical strength, and lack of common sense. It was time to talk to Billy Nelson. Right after he visited with Santha Mason, Dew Drop's favorite bar-maid.

Chapter Thirty-Seven

Santha Mason walked slowly down the street and turned into the darkened ally. She was two blocks from the Dew Drop Inn where she worked long hours as bartender, or barmaid, or both on slow nights. She was two blocks from the big, black hole that she'd been drowning in for the last few days. The jig was up, her secret becoming her undoing. She was done here. She had to get away, had to start over.

The town of Pine Falls was always quiet in the late afternoon. Women were home with their children, making supper, their husbands still at work. In an hour or so, most of the men would be at the bar. Each one had a story, but it all ended with, "I need liquid courage to go home, Santha," or "I need you, Santha."

Santha always nodded and patted them on the knee as if she understood. She didn't. Her own kids were at her neighbor's house while she was at work. Lucy did the best she could with the two little ones, but they were a handful. Sometimes when Santha picked them up, they were dirty and bruised. Bruises made a line on their little wrists, or ankles, as if they'd been restrained. Lucy was too old to be babysitting, but she was available, and she needed the money. And Santha needed a babysitter.

Santha had come to hate her job. Some nights when she got home late, she felt like a poorly paid prostitute. Sometimes the really drunk men would pull her onto their knee and nuzzle her throat while slowly tucking a dollar bill into her bra. Every dollar helped, so she didn't stop them. But it hurt. The manhandling broke her spirit. She felt ashamed. They sometimes tugged at her long, reddish- blonde hair to bring her face closer to theirs. She never wore her glasses to work because she didn't want to see the customers closely. Their greasy hair, dirty fingernails and glazed over eyes made her uncomfortable, and her attempt to squirm away seemed to turn them on.

Then she met Jimmy. He was really friendly, always smiling from the far end of the bar. He treated her with respect when she served him, and he expected all the bar flies to do the same when he was around. He yelled at the men who tried to become too familiar with her, and sometimes he knocked them off their stools, or their feet if they were standing. He was her hero long before he was her lover.

He rescued her many-a-time when a customer would just pick her up and head out the door with her, as if she were an object, bought and paid for. That's how the drunks saw her, an object of their fantasy. The tiny woman who waited on them, made them feel strong and manly. None of them ever asked about her life, her hum-drum life. They didn't want to know her emotionally. They only wanted to know her physically.

Jimmy was different. He knew her story because he asked. He knew she came from Missouri, a run-away when she was only seventeen. He knew her son's name. Brady. He always asked about Brady by name. He brought a toy for the little boy from time to time and always left her a big tip. "To help her out," he said.

So, no one became suspicious when he started leaving her bigger tips, twenty dollar bills, sometimes more. She accepted the money gladly. She had to, for Raina's sake. Little Raina, conceived in the women's restroom one rainy night in April, a night when life had gotten too hard for Santha. She had been groped, her skirt torn, and she had screamed.

The assailant had rushed out the back door before doing his deed, along with the other two drunks who were look-outs, and the bar was suddenly empty, accept for Jimmy. He'd heard her sobs and burst into the restroom. He'd taken her in his arms that night and comforted her. She'd been the one who had initiated the petting, touching him lightly through his clothes, unzipping his pants. He had whispered his love and admiration for her as he reached into her blouse. He'd kissed her with real passion, not lust.

And before she or Jimmy came to their senses, Raina had been conceived. She was hoping with all her heart that her baby girl was Jimmy's baby. She'd hidden her pregnancy as long as she could, but it was soon brought to light by a guy whose wife was having his sixth child. The guy knew without a doubt that she was pregnant and had made it known to all the barflies after he'd downed three scotches. He'd announced both impending births, saluting her with his fourth drink.

"To my wife, and little Santha here. May your baby and mine be born healthy!" He'd lifted his glass and Jimmy dropped his.

They'd all looked closely at her, and those with kids nodded. Her breasts were growing before their eyes. They'd all smiled but not in a kind way. All of them except Jimmy. He'd looked terrified, his eyes as big as saucers. He'd studied her body and then looked into her eyes for an answer. She nodded.

They'd only been close a few times, all of their passion spent in the women's restroom, their love nest when the bar was empty. After he bought the bar, he'd stay late some nights and helped her clean up. Then he'd helped himself to her on the thick, green blanket she kept for them under the bathroom sink.

Following each act of loving, he'd promised he'd take care of her and never let her down. And he didn't until a week ago. He'd come into the bar early and pulled her aside. He'd handed her an envelope with a check in it for ten thousand dollars. He'd kissed her, held her in a bear hug, then told her to leave town. He'd said his wife was on to him, and he didn't want a messy divorce. And he surely didn't want to lose his drinking hole. This was his bar, and as long as she was barmaid at the Dew Drop, he would never be able to patronize the place. He'd said he would never be able to look at her without wanting her.

She'd considered going back home to Missouri, to her mom's place, take the children and start over. But she could never leave Jimmy. She was addicted to him. He made her feel soft and small, weak and strong at the same time. She held out hope that one day she would be Mrs. Jimmy Collins, her Raina James the legitimate daughter of the richest man in town. Her Jimmy, not Debbie's.

He didn't love Debbie. He couldn't. She did not doubt that he loved only her. It flashed in his love-sick eyes at the exact moment he was expressing that love with such deep passion. He belonged to her. She'd never start over anywhere but in Jimmy's life, Jimmy's house, Jimmy's bed. That was her dream.

And she was dreaming it right up to the time the red spinning lights brought her back to reality. The patrol car was coming right at her. It screeched to a halt at the back door of the Dew Drop Inn. An officer stepped out and squinted into the setting sun to look at her. It was Sheriff Pierce. He'd helped her out a few times when she was walking home late at night.

"Santha."

"Ronnie."

Even though he was almost old enough to be her father, he had an ageless sensuality. He was Lucy's nephew, so she knew him pretty well. They'd had a few meals together at Lucy's.

"What's wrong, Ronnie? Why are you here?"

"We need to talk."

Santha felt her body shudder, like ice had been dropped down her back. Something was wrong. Terribly wrong.

"I need to take you back to the station. I have some bad news."

"Tell me now! What's wrong?"

Sheriff Pierce pulled out a rabbit's foot from his breast pocket. He moved it around nimbly between his fingers. He hesitated before speaking, making her ever more anxious. "It's Jimmy Collins."

Santha felt her eyes bursting, her passion … love, need … but mostly raw fear, exploding from them in painful spurts of agony.

"He's … he's, well, he's dead."

The sheriff watched Santha's legs go out from under her as she slithered down toward the gravel covered alley. He caught her just before she hit the ground. The name 'Jimmy' came out with her last breath before she lost consciousness. As he lifted her into the back seat of the patrol car, he looked at her face briefly. She couldn't be twenty years old, and yet this Mother of two was managing all on her own.

She couldn't possibly be guilty. And yet Bob Green considered her one of the prime suspects. He'd found a love letter she'd written on a Dew Drop Inn receipt tucked away in Jimmy's desk, along with a check stub for ten-thousand dollars made out to her. She wasn't all that innocent either.

Chapter Thirty-Eight

Sheriff Pierce stood outside the patrol car in the back parking lot, an unlit cigarette between his fingers. Inside, Santha lay prone on the backseat, out like a light. He studied the cigarette, wondering why he'd started smoking again. He'd been trying to give up the nasty habit for the last couple years, for his young son. It was the first time in his life he really cared to make a sacrifice. His second wife didn't smoke which made it easier. His young son said "icky" once when he pulled out a cigarette from the pack in his breast pocket. And he stopped for a few months. But habit got the better of him when his second wife left him for a better provider, and a non-smoker. Their little boy was just two. Now his ciggies were his best friends. He lit one up.

He paced back and forth by the patrol car and looked in the open car door at every turn, waiting for Santha to regain consciousness. He was getting concerned that maybe she bumped her head when she fell. He thought he'd gotten to her in time, but her head might have caught the edge of the building. Well, she sure took Jimmy's death hard, which was in her favor. It was a natural reaction to very bad news. Just when he thought he should take her to the hospital, her head moved slightly, and she rubbed her eyes as if she'd been asleep. Suddenly, she jumped up like a shot, as her mind went to work, and she remembered the sheriff's last words. Jimmy Collins was dead.

Her wail was so loud and so shrill, Sheriff Pierce was afraid she'd bring all the store clerks out into the street. Luckily, she was screaming Jimmy's name. "Jimmy … Jimmy …Jimmy." Over and over. He finally had to put his hand over her mouth to hush her cries. Taking her wrist, he helped her get out of the patrol car.

She struggled with him as he led her into the station. It didn't take long for her to weaken and stop resisting. He could tell from her blank stare that he wouldn't get much out of her. After settling her into a chair, he asked Nelda to get her a soda.

"I know this was a shock for you, Santha, but we have to get some information. We need to know everything, everything you know, so we can catch Jimmy's killer."

"I'll bet his wife did it." The young woman scowled, and just the mention of Debbie brought out a deep seated anger in her that flashed in her stormy blue eyes.

"Why do you say that?"

"She hated Jimmy."

"Why? What do you know?"

"Well, I know Jimmy didn't love her."

"Go on."

Santha looked around the room as if she was looking for a way to escape. "I've said too much. I should have kept my mouth shut." She pouted first, then pursed her bright red lips. "I don't want to hurt Jimmy, but if Jimmy is … dead, Debbie has to be the one."

Santha stood, smoothed down her black skirt, and adjusted her white blouse. She started to pace. "Jimmy was in love with me. He loved me. That's why he bought the Dew Drop Inn. To be with me. He's …." She stopped and looked deeply into Sheriff Pierce's eyes. He knew that look. She was trying to decide how much she should tell him and not sound hateful or guilty. And yet, she was hateful … and maybe guilty. "Debbie knew all about us and was jealous beyond words."

"Jealous enough to kill her own children?"

Santha dropped into the chair looking confused.

"The kids were murdered, too." Sheriff Pierce was blunt.

Santha let out a guttural cry. "The kids were murdered, too?" She thought a minute and when she answered, she looked crazed, like a wild animal. "Could Debbie kill her own kids? Sure, she could. Why not? Isn't it called a jealous rage?"

Santha had him there. Killing was insanity in the worst form. In this case it was not possible, since Debbie's body was found under Jimmy's … shot between the eyes. But Santha didn't know the details, and he'd leave it at that. Let her wonder, stew, maybe make a slip up. Maybe confess. She had motive, and it looked like she had a little bit of her own insanity.

"You can go to work, Santha. I think I have all I need for now, but I may have some other questions in a day or two. Don't leave town just yet."

Santha started toward the door.

"Oh. One more thing. Is Jimmy the Father of your daughter?"

Santha turned back, a look of surprise on her face. "I thought everyone knew that he was Raina's father. Absolutely he is." Her expression was now defiant.

"Is there someone else that could be your daughter's father? Someone that might be jealous of your … love for Jimmy?"

Santha's response was immediate. She held nothing back. "Billy Nelson. He owned the Dew Drop before Jimmy bought it, pennies on the dollar, Jimmy said. That disgusting creep pulled me into his car a few times after work. Said I owed him, it was one of his perks for giving me a job. After Jimmy bought the Dew, I'd see Billy hanging around the back door after I got off work. He tried to talk to me a few times, but I told him we were never going 'there' again."

Santha made it to the reception room, but stopped when the sheriff spoke again. "One more quick question, Santha. Do you smoke?"

She smiled sadly at him just before she shut the door. "Joints. And sometimes Marlboros."

Now he had several suspects, none strong, but all still possible. Tomorrow he'd check in with Billy Nelson. The man was crazy insane and a real possibility. The investigator, Bob Green, had given them enough dirt on Billy to bury him, deep beneath Iowa's fine, black soil.

Chapter Thirty-Nine

Sheriff Pierce tidied up his desk. It had been a long day, with no real target to aim for. As he looked out his single window, he shivered. Gray daylight had turned into a foggy, moisture-laden dusk. That's how he'd describe his thoughts. Foggy with a chance of tears. It was a hodgepodge investigation, with so many angles and opinions. Nelda was sure it was Santha. Deputy Neal thought it was Billy, just from what he'd heard. And the sheriff was afraid they hadn't found the guilty one yet. The majority of those on the long list had an alibi and a corroborating witness. It only took a few phone calls to verify their stories. Sadly, most of them added, without him asking, that they would have murdered Jim if they'd had the guts. Not the wife and kids, though. That took extra vengeance. They all said pretty much the same thing about Jim Collins. "Good riddance."

The day was over. Nelda was home, probably fixing her own TV dinner. Sometimes, he wished she was a decade younger. They had so much in common. They could have a lot of fun together. But she was fast approaching fifty, or had made that hurdle already, and it was showing. She was just too old to be Mother to a toddler. And it was probably better to keep their relationship a working one.

Sheriff Pierce tucked the early copy of the *Pine Falls News* under his arm and turned off the last light, the one in the reception room. As he locked the door, he made a mental list of the few stragglers left to interview in the morning, one of them a prime suspect, Billy Nelson. He'd vowed to keep an open mind until he'd interviewed everybody. That was a promise he'd made to himself when he realized the scope of the investigation. It would be unfair to pick Billy as a front runner without even talking to him. Finding the Collins family murderer was going to be difficult, if not impossible.

He unfolded the newspaper as he walked to his car, glancing at the family pictures on the front page. The one in the upper left hand corner caught his eye. Big Jim glared at the camera with malice, and Bernice smiled uncomfortably. Poor Bernice. She looked ravished, used up, dead. Her thin lips attempted a slight smile, but her eyes weren't anywhere close. They were empty, like shades had been pulled down on them long ago.

Ron Pierce turned over the engine and shifted his pick-up into gear. He loved the old Sixty-Four Ford. It purred and belched all the way down the street. He could never surprise a burglar. They'd be long gone before he actually arrived.

In minutes, he was cruising down Division Street. Bernice Collins had moved to the newer section of town, in a small bungalow in a row of identical houses built just for the elderly, most of them women. He'd decided earlier in the day to stop in and visit with her, see how she was doing. If he was lucky, she wouldn't have any new names for him.

He thought company might be just the thing she needed, take her mind off the murders of her son and family. Talking about a loved one's death was always a good thing, to help the heart heal. She'd have to talk non-stop for the rest of her life.

He didn't have to knock on her door. Bernice was already there. She'd probably sat by the window, staring out all day long, and had seen him coming. She wore an apron over her best Sunday suit, looking as if she expected company.

"Ronnie," she said, with a nod. "I thought you might drop by. I made a little casserole for my dinner, but there's more than enough for you, too."

Sheriff Pierce became Ron after hours. He insisted. "I figured you might like a visitor, a friend to talk to, Bernice."

"I hoped you might come by to check on me. I know you go by here on your way home after work. And I know you eat Hungry-Man dinners every night."

Ron nodded with a smile. She knew a lot. "You're right, Bernice. And I'd love a home cooked meal."

"It's not much, but I do so miss cooking for my …." The sheriff saw tears threatening in her deep-set darkened eyes, but she blinked a few times and must have willed them away. "I'm glad you're here," she said, before turning away.

"You know, Bernice, it's okay to talk about Jimmy and Debbie and the kids. They are still your family."

"Thanks. You're probably right." She pulled her sagging shoulders back. "I know you're right."

She went to the kitchen, straight to the oven, and pulled out a hot casserole dish with two oven mitts. "Sit down," she ordered.

She'd set the table for two, with her best dishes, white with blue edging and a big blue tulip in the center. A big glass of milk sat by one plate, and a coffee cup sat by the other. He hadn't had a glass of milk in years, yet he knew that was his place. "Smells wonderful."

"It's your favorite, or at least it was, well, years ago." She smiled. "Do you remember? Macaroni and cheese with shallots and bacon, and the home-made bread you loved?"

Ron nodded. "I can't wait. I ate like a pig at your house. But I knew it was okay because you had a giant, iron pan filled to the top." The crunchy, buttery cracker topping was hanging off the edges of the iron casserole dish like he remembered from years ago, and Bernice scooped out three big ladles full onto his plate.

"Help yourself to more," she suggested when he quickly cleaned his plate.

Ron took over half of the casserole with Bernice's blessing. "When's Jerry coming?"

"I don't know. I called him yesterday several times, but he wasn't home. I finally called his emergency number and got a neighbor. I don't think they're close, he and his neighbor. He didn't seem to know who Jerry was at first. I hope he gave the message to Jerry. But I haven't heard from him yet, so I'm not sure."

She took a few small bites. "I suspect I'll get a call later, after he gets home from work. Maybe as late as ten, our time."

Ron finished his macaroni and cheese. Bernice ate a few more bites. He was glad to see her eating. As he gulped down his milk, Bernice offered him the last of the macaroni, but he shook his head and patted his stomach. She took the plates to the counter.

"I don't suppose you have room for a piece of home-made apple pie?" she asked, her back to him.

Ron folded his arms across his softening belly.

"Only if you let me help with the dishes."

"I suppose," she said, sighing.

His piece was nearly a fourth of pie. Bernice had a sliver. "I always eat a sliver. And then maybe another sliver later." She looked up, and Ron could tell she really appreciated the visit.

The pie went down as fast as the macaroni and cheese had, and suddenly they were standing at the sink, she with her hands all sudsy, he with a crisp, white linen towel. They were both quiet. They were both comfortable.

"Bernice," Ron started, clearing his throat while he thought of something to say. "It's going to get better. This is the worst thing that can happen to you, to anyone. Nothing now can ever be worse than this."

Bernice nodded, a frozen look on her face.

Then she stammered, "Can I show you some pictures? I just got the albums unpacked. I didn't see any hurry in doing it. But now ...." She turned slowly from the kitchen counter and took a few steps into the living room. She flipped a light on near the couch and sat down next to a cardboard box. It was the first time Ron had seen the room in bright light. The gray tones of night had muted it when he'd arrived near supper time. The thick, gray November air hung over everything in the natural light of dusk. But now, with the lamps on, the walls were actually a light blue, like the sky, the carpet green shag like grass on a warm summer day. Bernice was sitting on a green and blue striped couch, bright yellow flowers popping out all over it. It was a happy room, filled with a lifetime of collections. A large Hummel on the top shelf of a new curio cabinet caught his eye, a boy with a brown school bag slung over his shoulder.

"Big Jim bought that for me when Jimmy was born. He said Hummels were a good investment, so he bought it from a man in town who had to sell all his possessions after he went bankrupt." She looked lovingly at it. "It's ... Jimmy."

Ron took a seat next to Bernice, and she began to open up her life to him, one page at a time. In each picture there were two boys, one in the forefront, one behind. The book could have been titled, "Jimmy."

One picture grabbed his attention, a group picture. Several boys were playing ball in the back yard by the pond. At the edge of the picture, there was a table with a cake on it. Balloons were taped to the chairs. He recognized himself and pointed excitedly. "That me?" His parents had very few pictures of him, his dad not into gadgets.

Bernice nodded. "I have many more in a box, if you'd like them. I took so many when you boys were young." She sighed.

"Is that Jerry behind the tree?"

"Yes. He wanted to see what was going on and happened into the picture. He was always jumping into pictures of Jimmy. He was just curious. But Jim got furious with him."

"Kids do that. Jimmy was testy."

"No, I mean the boys' father, Big Jim. He said Jerry could ruin just about everything. Always poking his nose in."

Ron turned the page. A professional family picture stared back, three sullen faces. It was hard to say about Jerry. He was peeking around his mother's skirt. Jimmy was in the center, between his parents. A pattern was becoming clear.

"Jerry was never in the picture," Bernice said. "Never. We'd call him, and he'd ignore us, wrapped up in something. When he did come, you'd just see him in motion, lunging into the picture. Big Jim said it was just as well. Said Jerry's time here was fleeting. Figured he'd probably run off someday to follow his rainbow."

Ron nodded, not surprised.

"Time for me to go Bernice." He added, "Remember. Nothing bad can happen now. You've been dealt all your bad cards."

Bernice nodded, letting Ron embrace her. She patted his back softly. He could tell she was holding back a sob. He shut the door slowly and waited until he heard the click of the lock. And then he heard her cry. He left her reluctantly, with a heavy heart.

Chapter Forty

Jerry stumbled through the long, warm day. His sleepless, bloodshot eyes burned like hot coals, and he thought he was going to collapse. He was physically and emotionally drained. Sweat seeped from his pores until his face glistened. San Diego was almost always on climate control, but today felt unusually hot. Maybe he was coming down with something. It had been a whirlwind weekend, and he was exhausted. What was he thinking, going all that way for just a few days?

Every day, windows in his office building were opened up in the morning and left open all day. Most days it was comfortable. But today Jerry felt stifled by the heat and finally closed the blinds to keep the sun out. He was dog-tired.

Meetings lasted most of the day, and the droning voices of self-absorbed clients became maddening after eight hours. Finally, he got a few free minutes and went to the break room for coffee. His secretary, Barb, had scheduled three more clients, all looking for tax shelters, and he was the firm's tax specialist. His boss incessantly called him the tax man, followed by him strumming an imaginary guitar and mouthing the words to the George Harrison song.

The weekend was a bad memory. He was beginning to feel like he'd been dreaming through it all. But it had been a real life, awake nightmare, going all that way in one weekend. He didn't even want to think about what happened after he got there. It was too painful. He hadn't thought it through.

Jerry laid his head down on the break table. He could just fall asleep right now. Maybe his next three appointments wouldn't show, and he'd get some rest. With a tap at the door, the dream faded.

"Jerry."

"Barb." His secretary glared at him. He glared back.

They didn't like each other, so words were brief, to the point. She was a single Mom of two teenagers. Although she was his secretary, and he was her boss, she let it be known that she considered herself superior to him. She chided him constantly about his playboy ways. Most of her carelessly chosen words were to tell him to grow up. He resented that. Someday she'd pay, when he could fire her.

"Your four o'clock is here. And I gotta go home, make my kids some supper, do the laundry, pay some bills."

Jerry frowned, and she shook her head. "You'll have one more appointment after that, and then you're free to go. Seven-thirty canceled."

Jerry perked up. He'd be home before seven o'clock, have time to eat some supper before he called his mom. His evening was looking up. Two clients, one quick stop at the boss's office to drop off some suggestions, and then he was gone.

His bike seat felt like a magic carpet as it whisked him toward his apartment, a place he sometimes called Shangri-La. It wasn't that he had any crazy good times there exactly. It was that he didn't have any bad times there, any bad memories. His apartment was just as he hoped it would be ... free of emotion, free of stress. He had a cleaning lady come in once a month, and he stayed on top of things the rest of the time.

He made his way through the traffic as if he were in a trance. They called it threading the needle, but it was more like basting. In, out, in, out. You just had to make sure you were in the right lane to turn when the time came. He had to cut a guy off to get in the southbound lane, and the angry honking made him more alert. He'd been daydreaming again, the same dream he had every night when he left the office … that he had a wife and two kids waiting for him and a home-cooked dinner in the oven, ready to be served. They'd all watch television in bed, then lights out. His wife never had a face, but she had long dark hair, and occasionally, when they were wrapped in each other's arms, he'd see her beautiful, big brown eyes, filled with love.

He arrived home, his nerves shot. He struggled with his apartment key, jabbing and twisting it, flipping it over and over until it finally slid in, slick as could be. His mom's note was still on the floor, and he stepped over it. He'd read it the night before while standing over it and just left it there. It said, "Call mother. Now." Always now. Drop everything and call now. He'd made up his mind this weekend that he would no longer dance or jump for anyone. He would be in charge, no matter what.

He picked up the note and set it down on his kitchen table. After fumbling through the stack of frozen dinners a few times, he picked out the Hungry Man fried chicken. An imitation Bernice family special would put him more in the mood to talk to her. In minutes he was sitting at his table … paper napkin, fork, foil plate, knife, then spoon, just like his mother taught him. He'd set the table at home for years before he left. Some social skills never leave you. Sitting down at the table did make the meal more satisfying. If he had a family, he'd sit at a table every night, not in front of the TV.

Hunger took over, and he gobbled up two pieces of chicken, before drinking a few swallows of water. Two more pieces of chicken were followed by big spoons-full of potatoes and vegetables, until the tin plate was empty.

He tossed his silverware in the sink, his plate and napkin in the garbage basket, wiped his table, and picked up the note again. No more excuses. He'd have to make the call to his mother. Get it over with. And what would she say? He knew it wouldn't be good.

After dialing, he sat down in his brown La-Z-Boy, the only chair in the room. Two rings, and his mother answered.

"Hello."

"Mom?"

"Jerry?" She sounded different, like a child, or like she was talking through a paper towel roll.

"You sound far away. Maybe we have a bad connection. Should I call back?"

"No." This time her voice was strong, bellowing.

"What's up, Mom? Why so urgent?"

"I tried you all day yesterday. Where were you?"

Really? He had to tell her what he'd done on a Sunday? What would he say to her? Make something up, or tell her the truth? "I ... I just went away for a few days. Had to get my head on straight. I ... I went to a concert."

"For two days?"

"Mom, is everything okay?" He knew it wasn't by her voice. He waited.

"Jerry?"

"Yes, Mom."

"Your brother ...." He knew it. It was coming.

"Your brother, Jimmy … Jimmy …." She started to cry, to wail, to sob. Jerry could feel her pain. He could hear her heart pounding, or maybe he could just feel that, too.

His mom took a few deep breaths, and it sounded like she was wiping at her eyes with a Kleenex, her constant companion, an extension of her right arm, always tucked into her sleeve. She cleared her throat. "James Jr. is dead."

"Say again?"

"Jimmy is dead. Murdered in cold blood." Jerry heard nothing after that, as if she'd quit breathing.

"Mom," Jerry shrieked. "Are you okay? Talk to me, Mom. Breathe."

"I need you, Jerry. Can you come home?"

"Yes, I'll be on a flight later tonight or tomorrow, as soon as I can, mom."

He thought for a minute. What should he say? "What about Debbie? Are you staying there with her?"

"The house is a crime scene. No one will ever live there again."

Jerry looked out the window, seeing the farmhouse in his mind, the yard covered in Autumn leaves. The front door would be decorated for Halloween. The house was spooky on an autumn night, with the clouds laying in hazy ribbons across a large moon, corn husks leaning into each other surrounded by bales of hay. Pumpkins would line the front porch.

"Where's Debbie staying?"

"With Jimmy."

"I mean, now, Mom, now that Jimmy's … gone."

"She'll never leave him. They will be together forever."

"What are you saying? Did Debbie commit suicide? Did Jimmy kill her?"

"All of them ... they are all gone. All four of them ... murdered."

Jerry jumped up. "Oh my God. Are you saying someone killed all four of them?"

"Jerry? Come home. Please?"

"Mom, I'll be there, Wednesday, suppertime at the latest. And Mom, I ... love you."

"Good-bye Jerry."

"Bye, Mom."

Jerry sat back down in his chair. He twitched around, thumping his fists on the metal table-top. He jumped onto his feet and paced, going to the kitchen for a drink of water. He nearly choked on it. He couldn't swallow. Had he handled his mother's call right? Did his mom suspect his true feelings? Hopefully, she would never know.

He went into his bedroom and pulled some clothes from his closet. He went back into the kitchen to look out the window. What was going on? What had happened? Had he lost his mind? He didn't intend for this to happen, though he'd wished it and dreamed about it many times over the years. He couldn't hate Jimmy this much, could he?

Debbie, his Debbie. He was supposed to rescue her someday when Jimmy finally failed her for the last time, and she'd had enough. He'd thought about it down to the finest detail. She and the kids would move to San Diego. He'd take care of her, and she'd make paintings in the park while he practiced law at his own firm. She'd have dinner ready for him and make him her special chocolate cake. But he knew deep down in his heart that she would never be his. Never. She belonged to Jimmy. She belonged with him forever. What had gone so terribly wrong in the last few days?

Jerry got on the phone and tried to make airline reservations, but he couldn't speak. He stumbled over his words and felt tears filling his eyes. He couldn't swallow them away and gagged, so he hung up the phone. After he jotted a short note to his law firm, he dropped it in the mail box by his door.

He took a few things out of his travel bag and put a few things in. He would leave before dawn. He was going home, back to Iowa again. It would be a long journey on his bike, but he needed the time to think. And he did his best thinking on his bike, on the open road. When he got tired, he'd find a quiet rest stop and sleep a few hours under the stars. How many times had he done that over the years, slept outside when he was hiding from Jimmy or his father? Out in the woods behind the house, beyond the meadow, he'd find a little nesting area and tuck himself into it ... to hide, to cry, to sleep.

Jimmy was dead. Debbie, Christy, Dougie. All dead. The bleeding tree had gobbled up four more lives, spitting out the bloody remains. Now the land around the tree was saturated with more blood, this time Collins' blood.

Chapter Forty-One

The week seemed to be lasting forever, and it was only Tuesday. Sheriff Pierce had one more person to see. Now the suspect would be prepared, thanks to the newspaper that revealed more of the details than he'd wanted anyone to know. He wondered if Nelda had been a little loose-lipped.

He was about to pick up the phone, when it started ringing … two quick rings, a pause and two quick rings. It was Nelda's signal for an important incoming call.

"Yello," he said, then remembering his little son laughing at that, but it was too late. "Sheriff Pierce. How can I help you?"

"Ronnie?"

The voice was familiar. Very few people called him Ronnie. Bernice Collins was one of them.

"Good morning, ma'am. And, thanks again for dinner last night." He leaned back in his chair. "How can I help you, Mrs. Collins?"

"I just called to tell you Jerry is coming home. He promised me he'd be here by tomorrow at the latest. I thought you'd like to know."

"Yes, ma'am." Sheriff Pierce doodled the name 'Jerry' on his legal pad, then added an underline and a question mark.

"Do you think ... I mean, well, would you ever be able to ... oh, heck, would you and Jerry accompany me to the farm after he's settled in, say, Thursday? One of you might see some things I haven't, you being more knowledgeable about the crime scene. It's all cleaned up, but I would like you to step me through the day to day living ... see if anything else looks odd around there. I know it won't be easy, ma'am."

"Of course, I'll do what I have to. I doubt that Jerry will be much help, though."

"I realize that. But some little thing he notices might lead us to something. It would be a big help."

"I'll talk to Jerry right away when he arrives and get back to you."

"Thanks, Bernice ... ma'am. I can't tell you how much I appreciate it."

"Good-bye, Ronnie."

"Good-bye, Mrs. Collins."

Sheriff Pierce hung up the phone. He was doing some mental math, wondering what took Jerry so long to call his mom back. She said she phoned him to tell him the news early Sunday morning, yet didn't actually talk to him until Monday night. It just seemed odd. But they weren't close. That was for sure.

The sheriff picked up the phone again, hesitated a minute as he fumbled around his desk for a pen, and then dialed the number Nelda had given him for Billy Nelson. He cleared his throat, knowing he had to handle this suspect with kid gloves. If the truth were known, Billy Nelson scared him. He always thought Billy would be involved in some tragedy. He was certainly a suspicious character.

The phone rang several times. The sheriff was about to give up when he heard a click, a bang and then a soft voice saying a very bad word, followed by, "Hello?" The voice was soft, sweet, and definitely not Billy's.

"Miss?"

He could hear sleep in the musky voice. "Melanie Mint."

"Miss Mint." Sheriff Pierce racked his brain. Who was Melanie Mint? Then it came to him. She was the new girl in town, the go-go dancer at the Flashing Light Disco in nearby Dupree, a little town on the Cedar River. One of his friends suggested a while back that he make her acquaintance. Now he was curious, almost forgetting who he'd called and why, but it came back to him quickly.

"Yes, Miss Mint, this is Sheriff Pierce from Pine Falls. Can I speak to Billy Nelson?"

"He's kind of busy right now." The sheriff heard a slap and a man's laugh.

"I really need to talk to him."

The phone changed hands, and he heard a much louder slap. Billy was laughing when he said hello.

"Billy, this is Sheriff Pierce. I need you to come to the station this morning. I have a few questions."

"I'll bet you do."

"So you know why I'm calling?"

"Yes. I expected to hear from you."

"Let's say in an hour?"

"Let's say in two hours."

"Billy, be here in sixty minutes. Bring Miss Mint."

"Sure, sheriff. I guess I can get this done quickly." The phone went dead.

Sheriff Pierce shook his head, scratched his chin, and doodled the name Melanie. Melanie Mint. Nice, fresh name.

Billy and Melanie showed up fifteen minutes late. Not a good way to start a defense for murder. The sheriff watched them play with each other in the waiting area. Nelda was watching, too. She was scowling. Billy winked at her, his hand cupping Melanie's rounded back side. Nelda never flinched. But the sheriff could read her mind. She was thinking, 'You stupid, guilty bastard.' It was as plain as day. You had to love Nelda.

Sheriff Pierce went to his door, pushed it open with his foot, and motioned for Billy Nelson to step in. He put his hand up to signal a stop to Melanie. "In a few minutes, Miss Mint. I need to talk to Mr. Nelson alone."

Billy gave Melanie a kiss and then stepped into the office, brushing his shoulder against the sheriff's elbow. He was clearly several inches shorter.

"So, you've heard then?" Billy asked, his eyes poking in every corner of the room. He took a seat in the chair across from the sheriff, his eyes dropping onto the battered and stained desktop. They landed on the legal pad and the doodles. "Jerry coming home?"

"Yes, he is. You were saying?"

"So, you heard that I get possession of the bar, now that Jimmy is ... deceased."

"Yes," the sheriff lied. "Now tell me how did that come about?"

"Jimmy and I agreed. Until the bar was fully his, fully paid for, it would revert back to me in the event of his untimely ... death. He didn't think Debbie would be wanting ownership of it. So, now it's mine. I own it free and clear. Melanie is going to help me make some changes. It's time this town grew up."

"You do know, that makes you a prime suspect? Pretty damn good motive."

"Wanting men to have a little harmless fun is a motive?"

Sheriff Pierce wanted to wipe that grin right off Billy's face.

"Where were you Saturday night, Mr. Nelson?"

Billy turned and looked out the office window into the waiting area. Melanie was studying her manicured fingers. She stuck one tip in her mouth and started to chew.

"I was in the jungle, hunting wild animals." Melanie looked up and smiled when Billy winked at her. She pressed her open hand over her heart and blew him a kiss. Sheriff Pierce noted a cut on her chin, it looked red and swollen.

"Do you have a witness that can testify to your whereabouts?"

"Yeah." Billy pointed to Melanie. "My prey can verify it. And what do you mean 'testify?'

The sheriff pursed his lips. "As I said, right now you are a prime suspect."

"So you think I'd kill Jimmy, and his wife, and kids to get the Dew Drop back?" Billy stood, and his left fist was balled in his right hand. Left handed? That could be significant, or not.

Billy stepped around the desk and moved up, face to face with Sheriff Pierce. "I don't like what you're insinuating."

"That's why you're here. To change my way of thinking."

Billy smiled. "Talk to Melanie. She can change your mind. She's very persuasive."

Sheriff Pierce looked at Melanie, and she threw him a kiss. The officer's face turned crimson. Billy laughed. "I'm sure you'll enjoy your time with her very much. I'm going to leave her here, and she can walk on down to the bar when you're finished with her."

He left the office without being dismissed. Melanie slipped on her shoes. Billy whispered in her ear and patted her knee, sliding his hand up her thigh. He looked back at the sheriff.

Sheriff Pierce ignored him and offered her a cup of coffee through the open door, which she declined. He needed some time to think before he questioned her. He decided to have Nelda in the room taking dictation, and he called her over. She was lousy at it, but he felt it was best for him to have a witness. He really felt uncomfortable in the room with Billy's girlfriend. She was just dumb enough to be brilliant.

"Dew Drop goes back to Billy if Jimmy dies and the contract is not paid in full …." The sheriff said, softly as he wrote in his legal pad.

Nelda stood in the doorway with him while he wrote, leaving the door slightly open. Melanie looked at both of them, with her head tilted and her shoulders lifted up. Maybe she was playing dumb, the sheriff thought, as he glanced at her and then back at his notepad.

"My money is on Billy," Nelda whispered. "He's mean, angry, and looks like the devil incarnate."

"There's another angle," the sheriff whispered, nodding discreetly toward the girl in the reception area.

"Thought of that, too. I overheard her asking some pertinent questions."

Sheriff Pierce gave his full attention to Nelda. "Like?"

"Can I be the only dancer at the Dew? Can I get tips? If we get married, will I own it, too?"

"How did our suspect answer?"

"No. Yes, if you earn them, and lastly, ha ha ha."

Sheriff Pierce moved out of the doorway and welcomed Melanie in. Nelda had already taken a seat by his desk, leaving the 'witness seat' open. Melanie took it with a flourish, as if she were performing. Her skirt was way too short to be sitting down. She crossed her legs, and began to shake her foot, her toes curling out of the open-toed sandals, an odd choice for a cold November day.

"Miss Mint." The sheriff cleared his throat, and touched the point of his pencil to make sure it was sharp.

"Did you kill Jimmy Collins?" His eyes bore right into hers. She stared right back, as if she was expecting the question.

"Wish."

"So you thought about it?"

"Billy and I thought about it a lot. It was the answer to our prayers. We'd be rich." Her eyebrows shot up. "Come to think of it, we are rich."

"Did you also think about doing away with Billy?"

Melanie Mint shrugged, and her voice lifted to a sing-song. "Sometimes."

Sheriff Pierce got up from his desk and went over to the girl's chair in an effort to intimidate her. He looked down at her, distracted momentarily by her heaving bosom cased like sausage in a tight, stretch-denim tube-top, her shoulders covered in a very prim, white cardigan.

"Where were you on Halloween, say around midnight?"

The girl tilted her head up to look at him. She swallowed several times, and he watched her long, thin neck move slightly.

"Dancing at the club. I had to wear a costume, so I was a lioness. Billy came as a lion tamer. He got into a fight about midnight with a man dressed as a wild game hunter. Over me." She smiled. "The man got a whipping, and so did I, accidentally, when I tried to stop Billy." She touched her nose where the flesh was red. She pulled her top down a little too low, to show another wound. Sheriff Pierce turned away.

"You may go now, Miss Mint. I'll check out your alibi."

"Ask for Hoot."

Nelda opened the door for the tall, willowy girl. "Who's that?"

"She's the owner of the club where I dance. She was a pirate in her younger years." A look of respect and fear flashed in the girl's eyes for a brief moment.

Nelda followed the girl to the reception area and watched her run down the street until she was out of sight. When she came back to the office, she found the sheriff fumbling through a stack of papers, his face still crimson.

"She's a hoot," Nelda said. "You buying her story?"

"Yeah. I suspect she would have been brazen enough to confess to the murders, if she'd done the deed."

He looked up at Nelda, who was smiling. "Don't worry, Ron, I've seen it all before."

His eyebrows shot up, and he just shook his head. "When Deputy Neal gets back, tell him to come see me. I think I'll send him to verify Billy's alibi, her alibi. I've had enough peep for one day."

"He won't like it. He's very religious," Nelda said. "I'll go. Like I said, I've seen it all before. And I really want to meet this Hoot person."

"Thanks, Nelda. Leave early. I'm expecting Jerry Collins sometime tomorrow. I hope he can help us figure this out."

"Yeah. I'm sure he has all kinds of ideas on who would hate his brother enough to do such an awful … just terrible thing." She turned to leave, but stopped. "And why? Why the sweet, innocent kids?" She shook her head and sighed as she left. She'd raised two kids alone, a boy and a girl, so it had to strike a personal chord for her. Nelda had a good heart, and Sheriff Pierce hoped she'd never lose that part of herself, her humanity. It was easy in this business to lose emotion and sympathy, after being exposed to all kinds of law-breakers.

Sheriff Pierce leaned back. The investigation had taken a nasty turn. The town was full of would be, if-the-time-was-right murderers. He might have to rethink that job he was offered in the capital city. Maybe in the big city, the good apples keep the bad apples from stinking. Maybe, just maybe it's safer there.

Chapter Forty-Two

November is not the best month to take a road trip on a motorcycle. It can be warm. It can rain. It can snow. It can be frigid. And it can be all four seasons in one day. Jerry started just after daylight broke along the coast, with comfortable temperatures. After a few hours, the winds picked up, and he was thankful for his goggles. As the sky turned ashen, then dark and starless, his arms started getting tired, and he blinked a lot to keep awake. He was virtually alone on the road.

When morning light was about to creep over the mountains, he'd had enough. Traffic was getting bad, and the roads were begging him to leave them, one way or another. So he chose a stretch of highway that had no life, very little traffic, and he pulled over. To his advantage, the weather had turned unseasonably warm. He walked his bike a few yards into the thicket and found a clearing the size of a large tent. He leaned his bike against a thin pine tree, dropping the kick-stand down for insurance. The sleeping bag he'd brought would be his bed, and his small duffel bag would work as a pillow. He stretched out on the ground for some much needed rest.

But sleep didn't come easy. He kept seeing the crime scene, his brother's bed covered in blood, his brother dead.

And poor Debbie and the kids, innocent victims in a crime of his brother's making. Why hadn't Jimmy been more like their mom? Jimmy hated their dad when he was young. He even swore to Jerry in the early years that if he lived to be a man, he would never be like their father. But at some time in the last decade, Jimmy changed. Somewhere in that time, Jimmy had become their dad, a choice that appeared to have ended his life abruptly, unnaturally.

Mom. Wow, Mom. What was she thinking now, at this moment? Would she ever come to terms with her own part in this? She'd been a caring, doting Mother when they were young. She'd taken many a punch to protect her sons. But when they were teenagers, she'd backed off, letting the monster have his way. She'd left them vulnerable, alone, and went to a place deep in the recesses of her mind where she could survive, never giving them another conscious thought.

Jerry sighed and rolled over, covering his tear-dampened eyes with his hands to block out the searing morning light that had woven its way into the trees and shrubs where he'd taken refuge. He finally slept. It was a deep, disturbing sleep, with his dreams putting him at the crime scene, his hands bloody. And then it was his face that stared up from the confines of a coffin, tears sliding down his cheeks. His mother leaned over him, her face so close, and wiped the tears away with her hanky. Other tears followed. His cheeks would always ache with tears and pain.

He awoke to a fierce scratching nearby. A raccoon turned to look at him, eye-to-eye, as its paws rested on his second pack, the one with the food in it. Jerry jumped up, and for a moment the raccoon stayed, staring at him, sizing him up, and then it retreated slowly into the woods. He couldn't even scare a small animal.

He'd been asleep for several hours and felt rested. He hoped to make it through the rest of Colorado and all of Nebraska by mid-afternoon, if the weather held. It was overcast, a bit humid, not cold yet. But by early afternoon, the skies had turned colorless, and rain drizzled on him for hours, like a form of Chinese torture. He was wet and couldn't get the chill off, so he decided to stop for some warm food. The small town hugged both sides of the highway, and flashing lights from a diner promised the best coffee in Nebraska. A cup of steaming coffee, a bowl of hot chili and a piece of any fruit pie would give him renewed strength.

A pretty, young woman greeted him from the counter, the doorbell still clanging. He took a seat in a front corner booth so he could look out, evaluate the weather, and keep an eye on his bike.

The woman came to his table, looking much older as she approached. At first glance, her small frame and long hair made her look twenty-something. But she was clearly older, or at least looked older, when she got close enough to give him a menu.

"You look tired," she said.

He wanted to return the compliment, but he knew better.

She smiled and her face lit up. Her tired eyes took on a youthful glow. She had been a beauty once.

"I'd like a cup of coffee, please. And do you have chili?"

She shook her head. "No, sorry. But I can get you the coffee."

She took a few steps then turned to look at him. "Lunch crowd ate all the chili, but I just made a pot of beef stew for tomorrow. I could bring you a bowl of that?"

"Great."

Before she could get his coffee, a man stepped out from the swinging kitchen door. He looked Jerry over with a scowl and then came towards him. "Passing through?"

"Yeah, heading home to Iowa."

"Weren't you in here a few days ago?"

"No." Jerry shook his head. "Just passing through." Jerry didn't like the guy, and wished he'd waited for another town to make a stop.

"No. I swear you were here. I never forget a face. You were going to Iowa. Some little town right in the middle of the state."

Jerry thought for a minute. Maybe he should just agree with the man. But Jerry didn't listen to his own reasoning and just shook his head. "Sorry."

The man frowned, and his eyebrows dropped over his squinting eyes.

The waitress stepped around the man and set a cup of coffee and a small carafe by Jerry's hand. The man left, turning to study Jerry one more time before going back into the kitchen.

"Strong," she said, as he sipped. "I just made it, and I put a few more scoops of coffee in for you. Just the way you like it." There was a hint of a smile. There was a hint of new life in her eyes.

"Thanks."

The waitress turned. "You came back. You said you would." She looked hopeful.

Whatever she was thinking now, made her happy. He couldn't take that away from her.

In a few minutes she returned with the stew, and a blueberry muffin. She touched his hand briefly as she set the small plate next to his spoon. He watched her go away, her head a little higher. He'd eat fast and skip the pie.

After gulping down the hot stew and wolfing down the muffin, he was warm, fed and ready to leave. He handed the waitress a five, more than enough to pay the bill, and headed out the door. She watched him from the window, her eyes curious and then fearful as the kitchen door opened. The man walked up and stood right behind her. Jerry couldn't look any longer. He knew the scene by heart, from the many times he'd lived it. The woman was his mother, the man his father. And the nightmare never ended.

Chapter Forty-Three

Jerry pulled into the long farm lane just after the moon crested above the barn on November third. He was tired and not thinking straight. When he saw the crisscross pattern of yellow tape barring entrance to the dusty front door, a Halloween wreath mocking the horror of the situation, he realized then that his mom wouldn't be there. Maybe, subconsciously he wanted to see the place again before he saw his mother.

The tape screamed that it would be trespassing to go into his own boyhood home, the house where he was raised, the house where his brother and family had died less than a week ago. It was now deserted and looked haunted. Maybe it was haunted. There was a possibility that no living person would ever walk the floors again, going about their day-to-day living in this big, old dinosaur of a home.

Jerry stared at the house, willing a face or two to pop into the empty windows. If the house was haunted, it would be a crowded place with Big Jim and Jimmy fighting it out every night in the office or the stairway, Debbie crying on the front porch or in the kitchen, and Christy and little Dougie cowering in their bedroom closets, waiting for the hatred to stop. And then in the morning, the sun would peek over the top of the barn and sweep them all away for a temporary peace. The nightly cycle would never stop for them now. They'd taken all the hatred, agony and pain with them to their deaths, to be replayed every night when the clock strikes midnight. There was no peace for any Collins, living or dead.

Jerry left the house with a sense of dread, his skin crawling. He kept his eyes down as he rode into town, hoping no one would see him, no one would know him. The driver of the first car that he passed honked. Someone called his name from an open window. A woman walking down the street lifted her hand in a somber greeting. He was home, and he wanted to die. But he'd get through it, for his mother.

She was waiting for him on the porch of her new, little house, probably afraid he wouldn't find her. She must have been there all day. He was hours later than he'd told her he would be. She hadn't changed. She was still waiting. Her hours, and days, and weeks, and months, and years were spent waiting. She seemed to be waiting for an eternity … for life eternal. For her sake, Jerry was glad she had her faith to cling to. And cling to it she did. She had a strangle-hold on it. For the first time, he saw his mother for what she was … a little girl in an old woman's body, a frightened child who had been left alone in a never ending nightmare.

"Mom, sorry I'm so late." He followed her into the door of her new home, her little bungalow, she called it, after a quick embrace at the door. He smelled the most wonderful odors coming from the kitchen. She'd made him fried chicken, his favorite as a child. He turned to thank her and found her leaning against the front door, about to slide down it. He got to her in time to keep her on her feet, and he wrapped his arms around her. She let him hold her, her arms tightly at her side. She cried, and his heart leapt to life.

"I've always loved you, Jerry," she said, her tears dampening his jacket. "Just not enough, son. I never let you see it, or feel it, or know it." She pulled away, took a few slow steps, then stopped for a quiet moment as if in prayer, before turning to invite him into the kitchen, like he was a guest. "I made your favorite."

They ate in silence, but she kept looking at him, staring at him, and her eyes said so much more than words could say. It was as plain as if she were yelling it out loud, over and over again. She wished she was dead.

"Thank-you for coming so quickly, son. I know it must be hard to get away from work." She dropped her eyes to her food and finally took a small bite. "How long can you stay?"

"As long as you need me, Mom. I've taken a leave of absence."

She nodded and a thin smile swept across her face. Her eyes lifted into her heavy lids as if she were saying another silent prayer, a thank-you.

His mother needed him for the first time that he could remember, and he needed her. She'd laid out a blanket and a pillow on the long couch, and left him to clean up and get ready for bed. He washed his hands and face until the flesh was raw. The hot water felt good. And the make-shift bed felt like a cloud as he turned to face the wall. But sleep did not come for some time, the memory of his old home haunting him, with faces at every window, all screaming and crying in torture.

Chapter Forty-Four

The morning sun bore into the big picture window and jabbed at Jerry's eyes. He awoke slowly, disoriented. He sighed and stretched. The kitchen clock struck eight times before he rubbed his eyes and looked around. His mother was sitting in her small recliner across from him. She was rocking, and holding her Bible, but she was staring at him. He sat up.

"Mom, how long have you been there?"

"Most of the night. I'm just so glad to have you here, Son. So glad."

He could see tears in her eyes but only briefly. She pushed them away with the back of her hands and got up. "I'll have breakfast ready in a jiffy. You go, shower and get ready. We have an appointment at nine."

Jerry struggled to sit up. He was covered in an extra blanket that his mother must have laid on him. "An appointment? Where, Mom?"

"Sheriff Pierce, Ronnie, is picking us up. He's going to take us out to the farm today. He thinks maybe you might know something that will help find the … the …." She swallowed hard and closed her eyes.

"The perpetrators," Jerry finished for her. "I'm sure I'll be of no use. And do you really think you should go out there?"

His mother took a deep breath and lifted her shoulders. "Yes," she said, with a resolute voice. "I need to go out there, at least once more. I need to ... say good-bye."

"Yes. Me, too." Jerry looked at his mom and wondered how much truth she could really stand. "I went out there last night, before I came here. I was tired and kind of forgot that you wouldn't be there."

His mother moved her head forward and looked into his eyes. "Did you see anything?"

"Nothing, Mom. Only memories."

"Yes. Memories. The old house is full of memories." Her mouth formed the stoic Collins lips. "We should just burn it down."

Jerry couldn't believe what he was hearing. That same thought had crossed his mind, and now he remembered, he'd dreamed about it. The flames reached high up into the night sky, clouds billowing in anger. And all the lost, innocent souls that were still hanging from the tree branch spiraled up and into heaven in the smoke fury. At the end of the dream, when the fire flickered and sputtered, the house was a pile of rubble. When the fire went out, the embers gray, all that remained was a big black stain of shrieking agony. Yes, Mom was right. He'd wait until she was gone, but some day, when he had possession of the place, he'd burn it down, down to the ground it stood on, the bleeding tree and all.

"Ronnie will be here soon. Bacon and eggs on the table in ten."

Jerry showered, again trying to scrub away the flesh that made him a Collins, the cursed flesh of generations. From the living room, he could see his mother at the stove, stirring a pan of scrambled eggs. She was dressed in her navy blue church suit. The small table was set for three.

Jerry answered the knock at the front door and found Ron Pierce, in his official uniform, standing on the other side. The sheriff thrust his hand out, before grabbing Jerry in a quick embrace.

"So very sorry for your loss, Jerry. I know this is going to be really hard for you, both of you." He took off his cap, and nodded toward Jerry's mom. "Mrs. Collins."

"Sit down boys. You'll have breakfast first."

"Just coffee for me, ma'am."

"And eggs and bacon, Sheriff." Bernice added.

"Yes, ma'am."

They all took a place at the table, and Jerry's mom dished up the food. She pushed her eggs around, nibbled on her bacon, and watched the boys clean their plates.

"I hope you don't mind going out to the old place, Jerry. I just think you might be able to shed some light on things," Sheriff Pierce said, shrugging. "I don't have any questions, really. Just don't have any answers. I'm truly baffled."

Jerry nodded. "Sure, Ron. Something might come to mind."

As the patrol car pulled into Collins Lane, Sheriff Pierce looked in his rearview mirror. Jerry was focusing on the tree. The bleeding tree. Until now, all the deaths associated with the farmstead were right there, tied to the old oak tree … dozens of bodies, all sexes, sizes, nationalities, skin color. The tree did not discriminate. In the early days, Jerry's mom hung sheet ghosts on the tree. Sheriff Pierce remembered Jerry felt it was an insult to the people who lost their lives hanging from the long, thick branch. Jimmy said his brother was a sissy for thinking that. Now that the leaves were off the tree, the hanging limb stood out like a giant claw.

"When was the last time you were here?" Ron attempted to make conversation again. Each time he tried, he got yes or no answers. The Collins were a silent pair. He wondered if it was always that way. Neither had been given permission to speak on this ground, Big Jim's kingdom. Only one person talked. And it wasn't either of them.

"Last night."

The sheriff stopped the car, put it in park, and turned to look over his shoulder at Jerry. "You came here last night?"

"I know it sounds crazy, but after riding my bike for so many hours, I was on auto-pilot. I came here without thinking."

"Did you see anything, think anything?"

Jerry shook his head. "It was creepy. I mean without Buster running out to greet me and Debbie standing at the door waving the dish towel in her hand. The barn door was closed. It's never closed."

That was the most he'd gotten out of Jerry. Maybe he would think of something else.

They went around to the back and entered the house through the kitchen. The sheriff thought it would be easier for Bernice. They were unable to completely clean the blood stain where Buster died, so they'd laid a braided rug on the spot. The older woman took a chair at the kitchen table, and Jerry waited at the door while the sheriff turned on all the lights. He thought that would make the scene a little less macabre. He was wrong. The stain from the dog's blood seeped out from under the rug, and Bernice noticed.

"Debbie just got this new kitchen carpet. The latest thing, harvest gold and lime green plaid. Jimmy always tried to please her. She could be demanding."

Jerry looked at Ron, and they both shook their heads.

"Did … Jimmy die here?" Jerry asked.

Sheriff Pierce stepped over the stain. "No. Buster did. His last resting place, poor old guy."

"The dog was killed, too?"

"Yeah, a down-right nasty, heartless bastard." The sheriff looked at Bernice. "Sorry, ma'am." He glanced in the dining room and then back at Jerry's mom. "Why don't you stay here, Mrs. Collins. I'll show Jerry the crime scenes."

She nodded.

The men walked into the dining room. "This is where the witness was found."

Jerry stopped in his tracks. His eyes shot open, as if he'd been slapped. "There was a witness?"

"Yeah, a young girl. Maybe you know her. Sally Munson, I mean Stoddard? She's the daughter of …."

"Abby. Yeah. No, I don't know her, but I know Abby."

Yes, you do. You all did at one time or another, the sheriff thought, studying Jerry's face for any clues that he knew who Sally's father was. There was the Collins' lip curl. Jerry knew.

The steps seemed never ending as they made their way to the second floor. The linen closet door was open slightly, and Jerry opened it fully to look inside. He slipped his hand under the pile of folded sheets, looking for something. "They used Jimmy's gun?"

Sheriff Pierce nodded. So Jerry knew about the gun. "Did Jimmy always keep it there?"

"Dad always kept it there. I assume Jimmy did, too. But no bullets. It was always unloaded."

"Where did they keep the bullets?" Sheriff Pierce asked.

"I don't know. I guess Dad thought it would be a smart thing not to tell us. It kept him alive a lot of times, when Jimmy and I'd had enough."

The sheriff scratched his chin. If it wasn't loaded, then how did the killer pump bullets into Jimmy and Debbie?

Jerry followed his old friend into the children's bedrooms. The beds were still there, blood stains making the bare mattresses look rusty.

"So much blood," Sheriff Pierce said. "They started with the girl, then the boy."

"They?" Jerry asked.

The sheriff smiled for the first time, and Jerry took his first deep breath.

"I keep seeing a pair of thugs doing this, like *In Cold Blood*."

They stepped into the master bedroom. Jerry shivered, as if a chill was creeping into his bones. It was his first time at the crime scene so it probably did shake him up a bit, seeing the room for the first time. His mom and dad's room. His brother's room. Debbie's room. Debbie's blood on the bed. The sheriff knew Jerry had carried a torch for Debbie for years. His face said he was still carrying it.

"Wow." Jerry picked up a small framed picture from the nightstand. "That would mean that it was a random killing ... not planned for weeks, months, years, like I thought."

Jerry stared at the family picture for a long time, and Sheriff Pierce pretended to study the view from the window. He noted that Jerry hadn't shed a tear yet. It seemed unnatural to the sheriff, but probably not for this family, a family void of emotion. It had been beaten out of them for years, decades. Jerry finally put the picture down and closed his eyes.

"Never thought I'd be here in Jimmy's bedroom, and Jimmy would be … gone. I never dared come in here when Dad was alive. And of course, I had no reason to come in here after Jimmy and Debbie moved in." He opened his eyes and looked at the furniture, touching the carved indentations of rosebuds and petals on the headboard, a wedding present to his mom from his dad. "It's the same as I remembered it, only smaller." He touched the top of the little stool in front of the dainty dressing table. "I wonder if Debbie ever used this. I can't remember Mom ever sitting in front of the mirror. She quit wearing make-up and stopped fixing her hair pretty when I was young."

The men left the room in silence. They found Bernice leaning against the front door. The sheriff noted that Jerry was clearly overwhelmed, and Bernice didn't look at all well.

"Why don't you take your mother out for some fresh air," the sheriff suggested. "I'm going to check the barn again and the back yard. It might be best if you wait in the car with your mom. I won't be long."

At the bottom of the porch steps, the sheriff left them and went around to the back of the house, toward the barn. Jerry stopped, pulled out a pack of cigarettes, and lit one. He took a few puffs, then dropped the cigarette butt near the tree.

"Jerry?"

"Yeah, Mom?"

"Can we go up to the attic? I'd love to get my Jane Austen collection. Your dad made me pack them up years ago. You know, he hated seeing me read them over and over again when there was so much work to do."

"Sure, Mom."

The attic steps were tucked into a small closet in Jerry's old room. The old wooden floor creaked as they made their way across it, past his bed and nightstand. The picture of a naked woman was still taped on the inside of the attic door, and Jerry put himself between it and his mother. If she saw it, she didn't let on.

At the top of the attic steps, she stopped to catch her breath. She hadn't turned sixty, yet she was old. At forty she was young. What had happened? In a span of twenty years, she went from a young, vibrant woman, to a lifeless, wrinkled, old lady. He took pity on her and touched her hand. She didn't pull away like he expected, until she saw the large, Norwegian trunk. The ornate, blackened key hung out of sight on one of the rafter boards, and she went right to it and thrust it into the keyhole. He'd never seen the contents of the softly painted floral trunk … rosemaling his mother called it. He and Jimmy had assumed the key was lost, and never even tried to break in.

When his mother lifted the heavy, rounded lid, her eyes lit up, and she had a hint of a smile. Her Jane Austen collection was on top, each book wrapped in tissue paper and all encased in a brown leather satchel. The next item she pulled out was a tape-recorder. She plugged it in to the nearby socket, pressed the 'play' button, and Jerry heard music, soft piano music.

"I was something of a virtuoso," she said, her fingers flying over an imaginary keyboard. With nimble fingers, she lifted a very used pair of ballerina slippers up and held them to her cheek before putting them into the leather satchel with her books. As the music went on, she began to hum. In the recesses of his mind, Jerry remembered that song. When he was a boy, they were words that he loved to hear.

"Sing the words, Mom," he begged.

She shook her head, her eyelids heavy over her death-filled eyes. And then a word came out, and then another, and then she was singing. It was a silly song, a song that had no real meaning except to the two of them. "Snug as a bug in a rug, whenever I steal a kiss, talk about love, love was never like this."

"I know the song, Mom. I remember the words."

"You always loved that song at night, when I tucked you in." Where did all that time go, Jerry? Where did my life go?"

"It's still here, Mom. It's still here."

When the contents of the trunk were laid out, they made a collage of his mother's life. She showed him pictures of her sister, his aunt, who only visited the farm once. "Is she still alive?"

"No, Jerry. She was older, and she died young. My parents died soon after my sister, leaving me all alone." She took a deep breath and lifted her chin, just a little. "You were just a young boy."

His mother's entire adult life revolved around one man and his life … Jim Collins. The only happy childhood memories Jerry had were when his grandpa Collins was giving his dad, Big Jim, hell. In earlier years, he remembered one time when they had threatened each other with guns. His grandma Collins called them two peas in a pod. When he was older, she had brandished her own gun from time to time, stopping the bloodshed on a few family holidays. With a stern face, she had said she wouldn't be afraid to use it, and his dad and grandpa must have believed her. As much grit as his grandpa and dad had, his grandma had more.

Jerry was still bent over the trunk, putting things back for his mother, when she called from across the dusty attic, "Where's the sock, Jerry? It's gone."

Chapter Forty-Five

Sheriff Pierce was waiting in the patrol car when Jerry and his mom left the house, both looking curiously refreshed. He knew they'd been in the attic, and it looked like they'd found something worth retrieving. Bernice smiled when he asked what she'd found, and she showed him her ballet slippers. Jerry was carrying a bag full of her mementos.

"So, Jimmy kept the murder weapon in the hall closet, the linen closet?" Sheriff Pierce asked, as he steered the patrol car in a wide circle and headed away from the house. He was going to get to the bottom of this. It was an important piece of evidence.

"No," Bernice shook her head. He never kept it there. The kids might get to it. He kept it locked up in his office, same place Big Jim did."

The sun was high in the sky, a deep blue color, making the scenery, the leafless trees and white farm houses, look drab and colorless in comparison. Nothing, not even a clear blue sky dotted with cotton ball clouds, could rescue an Iowa November day. It all looked the same, day after day, month after month, until the first trees began to bud in April, and the rich farm lands became vibrant again with color and the sweet smells of new life.

The patrol car was warm, and Jerry unzipped his jacket. He felt he had to tell what he knew. What his mother didn't know.

"Mom … Dad, and most likely Jimmy, kept the gun in the linen closet so they could get to it in a hurry if they needed to. The bullets were hidden safely away so no one could find them. That's how Dad justified the gun being so close to all of us. I never knew where he kept the bullets, and he probably only told Jimmy when you were moving to town. But really, Mom, what good would a gun be, locked in the office?"

"No, Jerry, you're wrong." His mom was insistent.

The sheriff could see it was going to be a stalemate argument, so he changed the subject. "Say, Jerry, when did you start smoking? I didn't think you smoked at your dad's funeral."

Jerry smiled. "Probably had my first cigarette in the barn with Dad. He offered one to Jimmy and me when he was feeling generous. It was his way of breaking Mom's rules without her knowing." He seemed to be waiting for Bernice to complain, but she was quiet, probably still contemplating the gun's proximity to her bedroom.

"Everybody smokes in California. We call our law office the blue room." Jerry lifted out of the back seat to look at the sheriff. "Don't smoke, Ron?"

"Not too often. Too busy. Can't do it in front of people when I'm working. Can't leave any traces that might compromise a crime scene. We catch a lot of bad guys with cigarette butts." Sheriff Pierce did not divulge that he was carrying two of Jerry's cigarette butts in a plastic bag in his pocket. He'd picked them up when he'd come back to the house after checking around the barn.

"I don't know if you heard me, Jerry," Bernice said, in a shrill voice that could wake the dead. "But that sock, the one I showed you in the attic, you know the one I filled with gold coins for you? Well, it wasn't there today. And I know you didn't take it when you left a few weeks ago. I checked after you left, thinking maybe you would take it. It's worth a lot of money, you know."

"Don't know what happened to it, Mom, unless one of the kids found it. I was hoping you'd add a few more coins to the collection before I took it away." He patted his mother's shoulder. "It meant a lot to me, that you did that, that you were thinking of me." He sat back. "The old man never wanted me to have anything, Ron. Dad, and Jimmy, too, thought he deserved it all, every single penny. I guess Mom didn't."

"Jimmy," Bernice sighed, and then she was sobbing. Sheriff Pierce thought Jerry should have been more considerate. He must have forgotten that Jimmy was dead.

"Where did you keep the sock, Bernice? Anywhere that someone might find it?" the sheriff asked, his mental notes getting pretty filled up with small, yet consequential tidbits.

"Heaven's no. It was in the attic, behind the rafters, hooked on a nail. If you go back, I can show you."

"No, that won't be necessary. I'm just curious, is all."

Sheriff Pierce tossed a glance over his shoulder at Jerry. "Now that you've been there, anything curious to you, Jerry? You know at the house?"

"Well, to tell you the truth, Ron, it's all pretty damn curious. I can't imagine anyone in town doing this. I know Jimmy, and Dad too, had a lot of, well, I wouldn't exactly call them enemies but folks who took a respectful dislike to them." Jerry shook his head. "But this crime, well, we're talking crazy, or real, honest-to-goodness hatred here."

Bernice brought out her hanky. Jerry sat back in silence. And the sheriff took it all in. A month ago, he was directing the funeral traffic for the patriarch of this family. Today, he was escorting the remnants of it, the family all but obliterated. He had so many questions and no answers, but he did have some road signs. When he got back, he was going to send Deputy Neal on a little road trip.

Chapter Forty-Six

It was a bleak day, the day of the Collins family funeral. But suddenly, the sun pierced the clouds over the little Lutheran church, sending rays of light down just above the church steeple, giving a pearl sheen to the white clapboard building.

Debbie's family was Lutheran, very religious and committed, Jimmy had told Jerry years ago. Jerry knew from what Jimmy had said, that they would be a united front and very formidable. In the car on the way to the church, Jerry's mom said she had acquiesced to their wishes to have a Lutheran service, giving her blessing for the funeral to be in their church. She'd added that she'd had more than her share of Debbie's time.

Jerry and Bernice stepped into the church vestibule just minutes after Debbie's family had arrived. No one noticed them. Debbie's mother remained inconsolable from the first moment. She was a fine lady who obviously loved her daughter and grandchildren very much, evident in her deep blue eyes swimming in never-ending tears. Debbie's dad stood strong and proud beside his wife, his grieving more subtle, bellowing silently from deep within his eyes and the crevices along his trembling mouth.

Jerry sat in the front pew with his mother, on the opposite side of the sanctuary from Debbie's family. It reminded him of the day Jimmy and Debbie had been married in the same church ... Jimmy's family on one side, Debbie's on the other. It was not a happy memory.

He listened to some of the sermon ... almost exactly the same words he'd heard just weeks before at his father's funeral from the Methodist preacher. But the Lutheran pastor was more dramatic, like a performer. He drew you into his mind and thoughts with well-chosen words and sweeping hand gestures. He made Jerry want to believe.

Some of his words were profound. He said that grief never leaves the mourner's face, but joy returns from time to time in the eyes of the believer. "Faith reaches out from the soul with enduring hope. Grief is easily sustainable," the pastor said. "Yet I encourage life to go on for those who are deeply saddened by a devastating loss." He continued, "The bereaved must live a life outside themselves to find the sanctuary of peace."

As Jerry looked at his mother, he could see that she had found that sanctuary in her own way. He saw her differently that day, strong, not a victim anymore. The pastor concluded with the words, "A peace that passes all understanding." And with that, Jerry had to agree. How could you ever understand someone accepting this tragic loss with a sense of peace?

The church was filled to capacity ... standing room only ... and the pews were surrounded by reporters, all holding notebooks discreetly. An occasional click of a small tape-recorder broke the silence throughout the service. No picture taking was allowed inside, but lots of cameras were outside, set up on tri-pods at a respectful distance from the mourners. Camera men nodded when they caught Jerry's eye as he and his mother left the church steps. And then the camera bulbs started flashing, and the news reporters came rushing toward them. Some had come from as far away as Chicago and St. Louis and really wanted this story. He understood their interest. The Collins murders came on the heels of the newly published book, *In Cold Blood*. Some suggested it was a copycat crime. But Jerry had nothing to say to them. Nothing they could print.

The funeral home had taken great care to line up the cars to make a circular route for the processional to the family cemetery and back to the church. Jerry would be with his mother in the sixth car, right behind the four hearses and the limousine for Debbie's family. Jerry was driving his mother's new Ford Galaxy 500. She bought the four-door sedan just days after his father's death. It was a yellow-gold, a lady's color. It was perfect for her.

Flower arrangements lined the cemetery drive. Lavish floral tributes surrounded the gravesites. But the caskets were each topped with one small bouquet of wild roses, the state flower. It was Debbie's request, made to her mother once and honored. She wanted her last bouquet to be what God would have provided. Debbie believed in dust to dust, according to the preacher.

There they were, the perfect little family all lined up for one last time together. Two large caskets, two smaller ones. Four deep holes in rich, dark Iowa soil. The newest family portrait stood on a brass easel behind the caskets. And when Jerry heard the words, "gone forever from this world," he let out a shriek, like the harsh, searing cry of a wounded animal. But it wasn't for the woman he thought that he loved, Debbie. It was for his brother, Jimmy. Jimmy was gone forever. Jimmy, the boy that Jerry clung to all those dark, scary nights when evil overpowered both of them. Jerry broke down and cried like the child he'd been years ago. Jimmy had protected him in the early years. He'd been there for him, first in line to take their father's wrath, trembling, yet defiant, as he was subdued. "If you cry like a baby," he whispered, "it only gets worse." He'd been right. Maybe Jimmy had loved Jerry once, all those years ago, when two boys stood side by side against the world, Jimmy's arm slung over Jerry's shoulder, the younger boy's head tilted slightly up to gaze at his brother's face.

"Good-bye, Jimmy," Jerry whispered. "Good-bye, Jimmy," he repeated louder, his eyes filled with the tears of a lifetime of pain, a life sentence that they had shared.

Chapter Forty-Seven

Sheriff Pierce was touched by Jerry's first open display of any real emotion since he'd returned to Pine Falls for the funerals. The younger brother stood in front of a crowd of nearly a thousand people, with reporters watching, camera bulbs snapping, and had given his older brother unconditional love for all to see.

His picture of anguish made the front page of the next day's newspapers, along with the story. But none of it sat right with the sheriff. There was a piece of the puzzle missing. He was scratching his day-old beard when Deputy Neal walked into the station. The young deputy looked tired from his long trip, but his eyes were bright with emotion, as if he were going to explode. It was clear he'd found the missing piece.

"Yeah, Neally, and good morning, by the way. Coffee?"

The deputy nodded, and the sheriff tapped the button on the intercom. No words were needed. Nelda had already poured three cups of coffee and set them down on the sheriff's desk. She took her usual seat.

"What did you find out?" Sheriff Pierce tilted his chair back and took a big gulp of hot, black coffee.

Deputy Neal sipped once, then pushed his cup aside and leaned forward.

"Yeah, it's what we thought. He went through twice."

Sheriff Pierce was angry at himself for overlooking the matchbook from the roadside diner during the first investigation. He'd seen it but hadn't considered it important. Thankfully, Neally had dropped it in the evidence box. When he'd found the same match box on the ground, tossed near new cigarette butts … A light-bulb went off. He'd seen Jerry toss a cigarette down atop another just before they left the farm a few days ago. Both cigarettes were partially smoked, like the butts they'd found the day of the murders. They were the same brand.

"This doesn't look good for Jerry," Nelda commented.

"And I have one more nail to hammer into the coffin." The sheriff looked at his doodle pad where he'd written the word 'bullets' at least ten times and circled most of them a few times. He checked the top one off again. "Got a call last night from a guy in a gun shop in San Diego."

Deputy Neal and Nelda put down their cups. Their faces said they knew this was it, the smoking gun.

"Anyway, the clerk, a guy who graduated from Pine Falls High, well, he called because he said he sold Jerry a box of ammunition for a rare gun, a 38 caliber long colt, the murder weapon." The sheriff took a big gulp of his coffee and let it swirl down his throat before he continued. "While they were making small talk, Jerry mentioned he was from Iowa. They discovered they were both from Pine Falls, different graduating classes. The guy said it happens all the time. He said, 'Everybody leaves Iowa, Everybody leaves Pine Falls.'"

Nelda begged to differ, defending their little town and how safe it was to the sheriff and the deputy, but she stopped right in the middle of her sentence. The Collins' murders had changed all that forever.

"How did he know about the murder weapon?" Deputy Neal asked.

"The clerk's mom sent him the clippings about the murders from the *Pine Falls Sun*, and the guy felt he had information relevant to the case, so he called me. I agreed with him."

They all sipped their coffee as they contemplated the implications of the new information. Three cups hit the desk like a drum beat, a cadence.

"Now what?"

"I have one more lead to follow, and then I guess we bring him in. See what he has to say."

Nelda and the deputy left the room in silence. This was not what anyone expected. This was not what anyone wanted. Small towns are like families. They love, they hate, they fight, they care. The town would be affected by this forever, Bernice Collins most of all.

Sheriff Pierce picked up the phone and dialed the number that was doodled under the word 'bullets,' at the bottom of the sheet. The man that called about the bullets also learned in his chit-chat with Jerry that he was seeing a married woman, a woman named Peggy Baxter. Jerry had even written her name down on a receipt pad and left it, the store clerk said. The sheriff was able to get a telephone number from the operator.

"Hello?" The woman's voice was soft.

"Peggy Baxter, is this Mrs. Baxter, Mrs. Phillip Baxter?"

"Yes."

"My name is Ron Pierce. I'm the sheriff of Lake County in Iowa, and we're following up on the murders of Jimmy and Debbie Collins. You do know Jerry Collins, correct? He tells me you're his friend."

"Yes. My husband, Phil, and Jerry are … good friends." Her voice sounded frightened now.

"When was the last time you saw or talked to Jerry?"

"Is he okay?"

"Yes, ma'am. He's fine."

There was a pause, and it sounded like the woman put the phone down briefly. "It's been a while. I was living with my mother in Coarsegold for a few weeks. She's not well and … I was taking care of her. So, it's been a few weeks." The woman took a deep breath, and the sheriff gave her some time to think. He always got more information if he waited and didn't distract them with another question.

"But he did call me collect last week. It was a bad connection, and I couldn't hear what he was saying." The woman on the other end of the phone-line sighed. "I've been worried about him. Are you sure he's okay?"

"He's fine. He's staying here with his mother."

"Tell him … well, tell him hello."

"I'll give him the message." The sheriff cleared his throat, pursed his lips, then dropped his eyes to the doodle pad, pen poised to write.

"Oh, one more thing. Why would he call you collect?"

"I don't know. He usually just calls me … to see how I am. We don't talk long. But I did accept the call because I was worried about him." She thought for another moment before adding, "Maybe he wasn't at home?"

"Yes, that's it. He probably wasn't at home." Sheriff Pierce jotted a few lines on his pad. "Thank-you, Mrs. Baxter. I'll keep in touch."

"Yes, and please tell Jerry hello."

"Will do."

The sheriff hung up the phone and shook his head. He let out the big, deep breath he'd taken in little spurts. "She was not shocked or surprised, so she must have known about the deaths." He thought about asking her how she knew about the murders if she hadn't talked to Jerry, but he'd be talking to her again in the next few days. He was beginning to hate his job.

Chapter Forty-Eight

Sheriff Pierce leaned back in his desk chair and closed his eyes. Deputy Neal sat at the edge of his chair at the same desk, studying his notes. It was becoming the longest day for both men who were trying to make sense of all the new information. With one unsolicited phone call, they probably had their man, but that concept did not sit well with either of them.

"Bernice called," Deputy Neal said. "Jerry is planning on going back to California later this week. She said he's thinking of coming back home to live after he gets his affairs settled there."

"Yeah, he probably won't get that chance, right, Neally?"

"I'll tell you what I have, boss. I have the brotherly hatred angle. I have a lot of money to be inherited for motive. I have bullets bought by Jerry in San Diego for a unique gun that Jimmy owned, and Jerry knew about. I have a diner waitress and short-order cook in Nebraska who saw him twice in one week. I have a collect-call Jerry made to his girlfriend, er I mean Mrs. Baxter. I have cigarette butts of the same brand and a matchbook from a diner, found a week apart."

"All circumstantial." Sheriff Pierce looked less than happy.

"All good enough to tie this guy up in a big fluffy bow and send him to State prison for a good, long time ... maybe life, Sheriff."

"I'd still like more, Neally. This is Jerry we're talking about. He's the little kid that hung out with Jimmy and me. He's Bernice's last hope. She'll be devastated." The sheriff stood up, pulled his shoulders back, picked up his notepad, and flipped the doodled page to a clean one.

Nelda came in with a fresh cup of coffee for each of them. "Should have bought coffee stock instead of McDonalds. I'd be rich when I retired," she mumbled.

"Eat more hamburgers," Sheriff Pierce said, as she sat down in her chair.

"What now, boss?" Deputy Neal asked.

"Bring him in, Neally. We'll talk, tell him a little of what we suspect. I won't give it all to him just yet. I'm hoping he can lift this burden from my shoulders and get us back on track to find the real killer."

Deputy Neal left, glancing back briefly when the phone rang. Nelda stood up to answer it. "Forgot," she said to the sheriff, with an inclusive glance at the deputy. "Abby Stoddard's bringing the girl, Sally, in like you asked. She's on her way."

"Thanks." Sheriff Pierce hadn't talked to Sally since the day they found her. He needed to see if time had cleared her mind a bit and eased her terror. He was anxious to see if she remembered anything else. And he'd been worried about her.

Sally and Abby sat quietly in reception, listening to Nelda chat about the dog that Deputy Neal had chased around the town earlier in the morning. They both seemed distracted but polite as Sheriff Pierce watched and listened. They'd come in a little earlier than he had planned, and Jerry was late. He'd been with his mother when Deputy Neal had attempted to bring him in for a few questions, but promised he'd come as soon as he got his mother settled in front of the television for her afternoon soap opera.

They could hear the roar of the motorcycle engine long before they saw it. It purred into town, becoming a growl as it approached the station. The sheriff was glad most of the town's citizens did not own a motorcycle. The sound was irritating and disruptive. Even the child, Sally, turned her head toward the sound. She was staring at the door when Jerry walked in. Her eyes dilated to saucers when she saw him, his helmet still on his head, his gloves in his hands. But she was staring at his boots, clearly agitated. When Jerry pulled off his helmet and turned toward the room, she screamed. Her mother tried to console her, but wasn't able to settle her down. The girl ran out the front door and down the street without a coat. Abby grabbed the coats, shot Sheriff Pierce a helpless look, and then followed her daughter until they were both out of sight.

Jerry turned toward the door and watched them leave. He looked curiously at Sheriff Pierce, who was in his office doorway. "Was it me?"

"Sorry, Jerry. That was the little girl who witnessed the murders."

Jerry nodded, and his face contorted into a grimace. He hadn't seen them until he turned around. He knew right away who she was.

"I'm so sorry if I scared her," he offered. "She must be a mess."

"Yes. She is. At first we didn't think we'd get anything out of her, so we thought we'd just wait, give her some time to calm down. She's so young and the experience so awful, so life changing." The room became uncomfortably quiet. Sheriff Pierce finally asked Jerry to come in and take a seat.

"You can smoke if you like."

Jerry shook his head. "I don't really have a habit."

"You said everyone in California smoked, and I see a pack of Marlboros in your pocket."

Jerry smiled. "Just in case. Sometimes I get nervous. Or if I go to a bar and have a drink."

"So you smoke when you're nervous? But ...." Sheriff Pierce stood and took a few steps toward the window. "You're not ... nervous now?"

"No. Not really. I'm too absorbed about making the trip out West again."

"When were you planning to go?"

"Tomorrow. I think, tomorrow."

Sheriff Pierce sat down in his chair and looked at his doodle pad. He took a few short breaths. "I think you should wait. We have had some leads, and I think we might need you here for the next few days."

Jerry leaned over the desk toward his old friend. "You know who did this, Ron?" He looked clearly emotional. "Do you have him locked up yet?"

"No. Working on it. There's a lot of paperwork."

The sheriff scratched his ear. It always itched when he was nervous.

"Why did you call your girlfriend, Mrs. Baxter, collect a few weeks ago?"

Jerry turned his head and looked out the window. "I called Peggy but not collect."

"Were you at home?"

Jerry thought for a minute, trying to remember the last few calls to Peggy. "I ... I think I called her before I left town. I really don't remember what day."

"You left town? Where did you go?"

Jerry lifted his eyebrows. "I rode my bike to San Francisco. I had a ticket to the Rolling Stones final concert tour. It was a long drive, too long, and the concert was, well, a waste of time. I couldn't even see half of it, girls on guys shoulders. Dumb kids."

"Did you call Mrs. Baxter recently?"

"No. The night I got back, I got a call from my mom. I left right away to come home, and frankly, I haven't even thought about Peggy this week."

"How did Mrs. Baxter know about your brother's death?"

Jerry stood. "Ron, I really don't know." He was shaking his head. "What's this all about? Is Peggy a suspect?"

"No, no. I'm just following up on some questions I had. I know they seem irrelevant, but in a murder case, every tiny speck of information is important."

Jerry smoothed his hair back. "Can I go now? I told Mom I'd be home to help her move some furniture."

"Sure, Jerry. But don't head out of town just yet. I might have a few more questions." He watched Jerry put on his helmet. "Say, why don't you leave your bike here in Pine Falls and fly back to California. You're coming back later anyway, right?"

Jerry nodded. "Think so."

"You'll probably have to get a moving van?"

Jerry put on his gloves. "Yeah, I guess."

"New gloves?"

"Yeah, lost the old ones."

"Talk to you later, Jerry."

Sheriff Pierce watched Jerry lift onto his bike seat and start it up. The bike roared to life and moved into traffic. No wonder Sally looked afraid. Jerry's appearance could be frightening to a child. He looked like a space man in his biking gear, and the bike's engine was deafening. But there was no doubt, Sally had been terrified.

Chapter Forty-Nine

Day six at his mom's bungalow. Jerry had now been sleeping there for five nights, and the couch was getting uncomfortably short. It worked well at first, when he wasn't sleeping at all. But now he needed sleep. He was desperate for sleep. He awoke every morning to the smell of bacon frying in the skillet and coffee brewing in the old drip pot. He could get used to this. He could almost taste the bacon and coffee through his nose.

His mother was warming up to him, and that made him happy. He let her wake him, like she did when he was a child. It was silly but it meant a lot to her. She'd tap him on the shoulder gently and say in her motherly voice, "Rise and shine."

All her life she'd been a slave and a martyr. No one ever thought about her needs. And Jerry couldn't remember her ever having anything brand-new. She'd bought all her clothes at the church bazaar or a garage sale, even her dress shoes. She'd taken great pride in finding matching shoes and purses at second-hand stores. And now, after this tragedy, her sanity depended on the busywork, on taking care of him. When Jerry had lifted the laundry basket to haul it downstairs, his mother had slapped his hand away. When he'd tried to help her fold the clothes, she'd given him a stern look.

"I like them folded my way. Go read the paper."

But breakfast every morning, a big country breakfast, was a little more than his California health indoctrination could absorb. He'd taken to sticking a few of the delicious bacon strips into his pajama pants pockets and tossing them out the bathroom window. He wondered if his mother ever noticed all the dogs that came to the door. After the stray dogs started their day with breakfast at her bathroom window, they probably made their way to her backdoor for lunch and dinner. When he left her, he wouldn't be leaving her alone. He'd leave a legacy of four-legged companionship to fill her days.

And just as quickly as he thought it, Buster came to mind. Poor, sweet Buster. Jimmy never liked that dog, said he was stupid. And he was stupid for liking Jimmy. Every day he'd tried to get Jimmy's attention, going in for a lick if Jimmy ever let him get close enough. Buster was gone, dead. The final bloody deed done on a cold, ghoulish night in October. The darkness would always be with Jerry, his mother, and the town. Jerry thought about the house. How could anyone live there now? Yet his mom had mentioned moving back there several times in the last few days.

"We'll go back home, you and me," she said more than once, waiting for his agreement. He could never agree to that. "You'll farm," she added, hopefully. His look told her that that was never going to happen. "You'll open a law office in Pine Falls then, and oversee the running of the farm. You can hire that Tim Buckly to do the farm work. He can get a crew together."

Yeah, it didn't surprise him that his mother would think it would take a crew to do Jimmy's work. Jimmy the super hero. "I'm coming back eventually, Mom, but not to farm. You're right. We'll have to hire someone, a renter, to do the work. I don't really know anything about farming. And I won't live in that house and neither will you."

"You can learn to farm. It's in your blood." She lifted her chin to look into his face. "And the house didn't kill my Jimmy, Son. Some monster did."

Jerry ignored her comment about the house, but he had to make it clear to her that he was not a farmer. "No, it's not in my blood." Jerry took a deep breath in an effort to remain calm. "It was never in my blood, Mom. I have your blood. I have none of my father's blood." He was thankful for that. "Let's take a drive today. We'll go to *Bishop's Cafeteria* and get some French silk pie. We both need a break."

"But Jerry, I have my laundry to do ... and dusting."

"I don't see any dust, Mom. And besides, I need to get away. We'll drive to Des Moines."

"No, not that far. Waterloo has a very nice *Bishop's*."

Jerry smiled. If he started with the worst choice, he knew that she would take the lesser of the two evils.

It was a cold November day, but the sun was shining. They would start with a drive around the countryside and count the cows. They'd look for farmers clearing their fields and burning the debris. They both loved the smell of bonfires. They both loved the music they played on the AM radio ... sweet, old tunes sung by real men and women, not kids with accents. They both loved French silk pie. Yes, he was his mother's son. He'd never been his father's. Never. And that was okay with him.

They put on their jackets. He carried a blanket and a box of Kleenex out to the car. His mother brought a canvas bag filled with home-made peanut butter cookies and some potato chips, in case they got stranded. They'd actually shared a smile, the first smile he'd seen on his mother's face in all this time, when they both agreed that they'd love to be stranded someplace far away. Just the two of them.

Before the car was running, before they could make their escape, Sheriff Pierce's patrol car pulled into the driveway behind them. Jerry looked in his rear-view mirror and watched Ron slip on his cap, speak into the radio mike, and then stare out the window for a second before opening his door. Another officer was with him, stepping out of the passenger side. Jerry rolled down the window.

"Jerry Collins. Step out of the car please."

'We were just heading out for a drive, Ron. Can we talk later?"

"Jerry, step out of the car."

Jerry opened the car door slowly, aware that the other officer was helping his mother out of her car door.

"Jerry Collins. You are under arrest for the murder of your brother, James Collins, your brother's wife, Deborah Collins, your niece, Christine Collins, your nephew, Douglas Collins … and the dog, Buster Collins."

Chapter Fifty

Jerry sat still as death in the back seat of the patrol car and watched his life go by in slow motion. His mother stood by her car, refusing the arm of the officer who stayed to take care of her. He could see them arguing with each other, until the patrol car turned at the corner, and they were out of his vision.

What was happening? Ron said they'd talk at his office, and he refused to answer any questions. For starters, "What the hell?" Ron was Sheriff Pierce now, and he kept his eyes tucked under the bill of his cap. Jerry almost asked if it was a joke, but he thought better of it. He could tell by Ron's demeanor that it was no joke.

They passed people in the street going to work or to the shops on Main Street. Everybody stared, their eyes penetrating the car windows to see who was being hauled in. Some looked surprised, but most expressions were slight nods, as if they expected to see him. Jerry was surprised.

Ron helped him out of the car. "I'm sorry Jerry." Ron patted his shoulder, then turned him around. "I should have put hand-cuffs on you, but I just couldn't do that in front of your mom."

"Thanks, Ron. I appreciate it. It would have been too much for her. She's very fragile right now."

"We'll go in the back room. I have a few questions for you."

"Yeah, let's clear this up. I guess I hadn't thought about me being a suspect, since I was in California at the time and all."

Sheriff Pierce led Jerry past reception, past his office, and down the narrow hall. Nelda was waiting there, sitting at the end of a long table.

"Did Deputy Neal read you your rights?"

Jerry looked around the room. No windows. Two jail cells were at the far end, each with a small window, like a basement window. Bars covered them. He couldn't catch his breath. "Yeah," he whispered.

Sheriff Pierce took his cap off and set it on one of the chairs. "Is there anybody Nelda can call … an attorney?"

"Don't know any, Ron. Do I really need one?"

"Yeah, Jerry. I think it would be wise."

"I guess I'll have to do for now. I know a little bit about the law. If that's okay?"

"If that's what you want."

Nelda lifted her pen and began to jot in shorthand.

Deputy Neal stepped into the room. "Mrs. Collins told me to leave her alone after I explained what was happening. Her neighbor gave me a lift back here. They said they'd see to her."

"Good, then we can begin." Sheriff Pierce offered Jerry a seat and took the chair across from him. "Jerry, that morning, after we discovered the bodies, we found these in the barn. Are they yours?"

Jerry took the gloves and studied them. "They look like the gloves I use when I ride my bike. I've been missing them for a while. Had to get a new pair."

"We noticed they had your initials inside them. At first, we thought they were Jimmy's."

"Yeah, those are mine."

Sheriff Pierce slipped the gloves back in the plastic bag. "You said you went to San Francisco that weekend, the weekend of the murders, yet you were seen in Nebraska at a roadside diner. How is that possible?"

"I don't know. I was absolutely in San Francisco."

"Can you confirm that?"

Jerry thought for a moment. He'd taken cash to spend on everything, since he hadn't been able to find his credit card. He'd paid for the motel with cash, the clerk just pocketing the twenties, so his name was probably not on any ledger, and he didn't recall giving his name ... no record there. He'd been pretty much alone. He couldn't even entice a young lady to have a late night drink with him, after they met at the concert. Even when he'd agreed to pay for her friend, too.

"No. I guess I was pretty much alone that weekend, Ron."

"We have witnesses that say you were eating in the Brady Diner in Brady, Nebraska."

"I did eat there a few days ago." Jerry remembered that the waitress and the cook both thought he was a return customer. Yet that wasn't possible. They must have been thinking of someone else. "I look like a lot of guys. They were wrong. It wasn't me."

"They talked about your bike, your helmet, your hair." Jerry listened closely. He knew each word had a clear meaning. "We found the diner's matchbook at the murder scene."

Jerry's scalp erupted in prickly heat, like he'd been set on fire. And in a way he had been. He was being cooked slowly by circumstantial evidence. Good, strong, but circumstantial evidence.

"You were also identified as a customer in a gun shop a week before the murders, buying a box of bullets for a special gun, like the gun your brother kept in a secret place, a place you knew about, the linen closet. You used your credit card there." Sheriff Pierce watched for his reaction.

"That sounds highly suspicious, Ron. Someone in the gun shop knew me?"

"Yeah, went to our high school, graduated a few years after you did. His mom sent him the news clippings about the murders and the gun found at the scene. He called us right away, thought it might be important. He said you were there. You exchanged names when you discovered you came from the same state and town."

Jerry dropped his head and tried to focus his eyes on the jagged pattern etched into the wooden table-top. He tried to stay conscious. "Ron, I think I need a lawyer. Can you recommend someone?"

"Hey, Sheriff Pierce to you, Mr. Collins," the deputy said. "He's Sheriff Pierce back here." Deputy Neal thrust his chin out and gave Jerry the very chilling news in those few words. He was under arrest. He was being interrogated for murder. This was not a nightmare like most of his life had been. This was for real, a real life never-ending nightmare. He looked at Ron again, remembering the days they'd been together fishing or hiking in the woods that dissected the farmland, or just hanging out in the barn. Ron his friend or really, Ron, Jimmy's friend. Now Ron was Sheriff Pierce. Now Jerry was nobody.

Chapter Fifty-One

Jerry spent the afternoon in jail, pacing the eight feet to the wall of bars and back again. He counted two hundred passes, finally giving up and dropping to the cot. He thought his mother would come right away to bail him out. He hoped a lawyer would come and get him released. He prayed someone would come, someone would listen to him. He felt a scream building inside with no place to go. The spattering of stains on the walls and floor were like a macabre painting of the end of life, his life. Daylight faded into gray and then black. He stared out of the small, barred window and nibbled on a cold hamburger and French fries from the Dew Drop Inn.

When the deputy brought him his meal, the young man was somewhat sympathetic, at least his eyes were. He said that Jerry was his first prisoner. Prisoner sounded like such a cold word to Jerry, inhumane. The young officer brought him an extra blanket, saying it was going to be cold … like winter. "It might snow in the morning," he said, before leaving Jerry alone.

Jerry stayed awake to see if the deputy was right. And sure enough, about two in the morning, the snow began to fall like little cotton puffs. Jerry never thought snow would

look so wonderful. But on this night, in his cell in the back
of the sheriff's office, it reminded him of Christmas, the first
Christmas he could remember, the only Christmas he wanted
to remember.

His mom, a pretty woman in her thirties, had put up the
tree alone, struggling with the big, fresh pine tree until she had
it ramrod straight. She'd poured a bucket of water in the tin pan
that secured the trunk while Jimmy and Jerry sat on the couch
and watched. It had been a thrill to see and smell the pungent
pine tree in their living room ... right there in front of the big
picture window that framed the winter wonderland that was
their farmyard.

After the tree was up, his mom had brought out a big
cardboard box. It was full of family treasures she'd said,
ornaments from the Collins family and her family, the Gibsons.
She'd let the boys unwrap them and line them up on the coffee
table. Of course they'd broken a few, but she said never-mind,
and she'd smiled. Before she started decorating the tree, she'd
turned on her record player, and they'd listened to "Frosty the
Snowman," "Jingle Bells," and her favorite "Silent Night," sung
by a choir of angels, she'd said.

And then their dad had come in early because of the snow
and gusting winds. He'd yelled some obscenities and said he
couldn't work in a blizzard. He'd looked at the goings on with
disgust and told Jerry's mom to pick up the mess. He'd said
he was hungry and wanted dinner early. She'd showed the
boys how to put the ornaments on and let them do the lower
branches while she went to fix their supper. She'd told them
that she would do the upper part of the tree later and string
some garlands around the branches after they went to bed.

By the next morning, when they'd gotten up, his mom
had finished decorating the tree. It had been lit up with large

colorful bulbs and sparkled with gold tinsel garlands and silver icicles. She'd put presents under the tree, all of them wrapped in bright patterned paper and shiny ribbons.

And then a miracle had happened. A Christmas miracle. Their dad had taken a bad fall while he was clearing the road, and he had to go to the hospital. He'd shattered his pelvis when the blade came down on his side, after he slipped under it. He'd be at the hospital for a week, maybe more, his mom had said, with joy in her voice. Since Grandma Collins had gone to her sister's home for Christmas, Grandma Gibson came to stay with them. She'd told them stories about the baby Jesus that they'd never heard, stories they needed to know, she'd insisted, before they could celebrate the wonder that was Christmas.

On Christmas morning, the tree had been ablaze with color and unwrapped toys had circled the other packages. Christmas carols played softly on the record player, and his mom and grandma were singing. Jerry thought he'd died, and he was in Grandma Gibson's heaven. He and Jimmy had hugged each other and even danced when the music changed to a more modern Christmas tune.

Jerry turned his face toward the wall. For the first time, some of his grandma's teachings made sense. He felt so helpless. He needed to find strength. He knew that if he didn't find peace, he'd lose his mind. And for the first time in years, in his memory, he prayed. In the confines of a jail cell, he finally went to sleep with hope. He hoped that someone would save him. He knew he couldn't save himself.

Chapter Fifty-Two

Jerry was deeply disappointed when a lawyer of his mother's choosing arrived the next day. She'd hired a man who'd been at the job a little too long and was clearly over the hill. He should have retired a decade ago. Jerry remembered hearing the name when he was young, but he didn't recall any more about the guy.

"Name's Harry Ledder, son." The man thrust out his fleshy hand, and his class ring stuck out like a beacon. Jerry couldn't tell exactly what college he'd attended, but it had to be Ivy League, or he wouldn't be wearing the ring. Nobody around the Midwest wore a class ring fifty years after getting their law degree.

Jerry gripped the man's hand hard, even when he felt the old man trying to break free. Hand shaking was for idiots. It didn't mean anything anymore, not like it did years ago. A handshake was a man's word in the old days. But today, promises were meant to be broken. So Jerry's feelings of abandonment exploded. He was a dead man. His mother had done her duty and gotten him someone respectable, but Jerry could read the truth in the man's watery, blue eyes. This lawyer thought he was guilty.

"Your mother tells me we have a lot of work to do."

That didn't sound like his mother. She would have told the man to do his job and get Jerry out of jail... today. Yes, his mother wouldn't want this shame to fall on him or her.

"I really don't know why this is happening, Mr. Ledder. I don't know for sure what they have, but it's all circumstantial evidence." Jerry looked a little closer at the ring, still unable to see the insignia clearly. He looked back into the man's eyes. "When can you get me out of here? I'm sure my mom is worried sick, and I need to be with her. My brother and his family just died a week ago."

"Ten days ago," the lawyer corrected him. "It is quite amazing that the Pine Falls Sheriff's department put this all together so soon. They are good investigators."

Jerry stood up. "What the hell? They suspect me. They have the wrong man. How much worse can they be?"

"Sit down Jerry. We have a list of evidence here that we have to go over. Let's not waste time, son."

Jerry listened to the list with a lawyer's ear. Like he thought, nothing substantial. Even the witness was shaky, just a child. He shook his head with every item and repeated, "Not me." He bit his lips until they were bleeding. After hearing the list a second time, he dropped his head on the table. He didn't want to cry. He hadn't planned on crying, but tears washed over his tired eyes anyway. "You don't believe me, do you?"

The old, yet oddly energetic man, thick in the waist, bald on the head, stood up. "Son, I don't have to believe you. I have to make the jury believe you." He tapped on the table with his fingers and looked up at the ceiling. "I think I can make you a sympathetic defendant with a little help. You seem like a wounded, young man." He touched Jerry's hand briefly. "Think about your past, give me something, anything that I can take to the jury. I'll do the best I can for you. For your mom."

"How do you know my mom?"

The older man scooped papers into a manila file, and the file slipped neatly into his briefcase. "I'm married to her high school friend."

Jerry looked confused. "But she went to school out east, in Massachusetts. You came all the way from there?"

"No. We moved to Chicago years ago. The girls have kept in touch. My Mary got the news about your brother just hours after it happened. And then when you were arrested, your mom called my wife, said there was no one to help you. She asked me if I would consider representing you. When I heard you have a law degree and practice in California, well, I was curious. So I decided to come and meet you, see if there is anything I can do."

"And can you?"

"I'm pretty good at what I do. But my biggest fear is that the jury will see me as a big time lawyer from a corrupt city. If I don't feel I can do the job, I'll find someone local to take the case. I can't make any promises."

"So when can you get me out of here?"

The lawyer tapped on the bars, then turned to Jerry. "I can't. They'll be moving you soon to Waterloo, to the county jail." The older man pulled out a hanky and wiped at his own eyes. "Son, I have to be perfectly honest with you. I don't think you'll ever get out. Ever. It would take a miracle."

Deputy Neal unlocked the cell door, and the old lawyer walked away. Jerry saw the deputy shake his head before he disappeared into the reception area, and the cell room door closed with a shattering bang. He was alone. He was a prisoner, maybe forever.

Chapter Fifty-Three

Another day, another slow, agonizing step closer to death, rotting in a jail cell. Ron came in with lunch, a hot roast beef sandwich that his mother brought to the station. After Jerry had eaten what he could, Ron sat down with Jerry and repeated what the attorney had said. He would be going to a county jail, where he'd stay until after the trial.

"You have a visitor," he added.

Jerry stood up, smoothed his hair down, and looked for his mother.

"I thought she'd come. I was hoping she'd make it here before they moved me."

"It's not your mother, Jerry."

Jerry turned to look at Ron. "Who is it?"

"It's Santha Mason. She says she'd like to visit with you."

"Okay, I guess. But why?"

"Let's find out." The sheriff went to the door and called Santha in.

Santha was dressed in a navy woolen jumper over a blue-flowered blouse. Her shoes were high with thick soles, making her legs look long and thin. Her reddish-blonde hair was tied up in a bun, and she wore wire-rim glasses. Jerry hardly recognized her. She looked like a nice young woman, a mother, not a bar-maid.

He took the hand she offered through the bars. Her skin was soft and warm, her handshake firm. A human touch was something quite nice, and he'd remember it long after her perfume scent disappeared.

Santha sat down in the chair that the sheriff put beside the cell door. She looked a little uncomfortable until the sheriff left them alone.

"Hi."

Jerry answered back, "Hi," his voice tentative. "What can I do for you, Santha?" He didn't know what else to say. She must have had a reason for the visit.

"Well, I just wanted to say thank-you. Your brother being gone has changed a lot of lives. I didn't think I could ever break free from him. Don't get me wrong, he did help me keep my job, and he did help out from time to time, but he always dangled the extra money like a carrot. I felt like I was always one miss-step away from hell."

"Yeah, I know the feeling. Jimmy learned that technique to perfection at our father's knee." Jerry shook his head. "But I didn't do it, Santha. I could never kill my brother."

"It doesn't matter, Jerry. I just wanted to let you know, your mom has offered to help me out with expenses and stuff. She knows the baby is Jimmy's. She said she can't be a part of the baby's life, but she'll help. She said you told her to."

Jerry scratched his head. He never really talked to his mother about Santha's baby, but he wasn't surprised that she believed Jimmy was the father. And he was sure that his mom also knew about Abby's daughter. Jimmy still had two kids, and it looked like Jerry would never have any. He was just realizing his list of regrets, and kids were at the top, right after marriage, and growing old.

"I'm glad for you, Santha. You seem like a nice enough girl." He didn't know what else to say. "So, if so many people's lives have changed for the better, why am I the only suspect?"

Santha shook her head. "The papers haven't said much, just that they have a lot of circumstantial evidence against you. What does that mean, exactly?"

Jerry was impressed with her question. That was a sign of intelligence to him. Anybody could get a college degree, but only bright people were curious. "It means they have evidence that puts me in a place I never was, doing something I never did. It means I'm screwed." Jerry looked into Santha's eyes and saw that she understood. "I can't believe that circumstances against me fell into place so easily. I feel like I've been set-up."

"Jerry, you don't have to feel guilty, if you didn't do it. I didn't come here to upset you. I just wanted to see you." She stood to go. "I'll visit you again, if you want. I'll bring pictures of the baby so you can get to know your niece." Santha laughed a short, soft laugh. "She looks like you, blonde hair, no eyebrows, piercing blue-gray eyes."

Jerry smiled. "I'm going to get out of here, Santha. I have a great attorney and he'll figure this out. He'll get me off. I'm innocent."

"Sure, Jerry. I believe you."

Jerry knew that look, the one that Peggy always used with Phil when he said something totally unbelievable. "No, you don't, Santha. I guess I shouldn't expect you to. You don't really know me." He stood, when she stood. The door to the cell area opened when she tapped three times.

"I'll come to the trial," she offered. "You're right, Jerry. I don't know you at all. But everybody in town says they weren't surprised when you were arrested. They said you put up with a lot from your pa and Jimmy your whole life." She stepped through the door, turning to look at him one last time. "Good-luck, Jerry."

Jerry watched her until the door shut. She was a sweet girl. How did his brother have such dumb good luck? Well, at least it was good luck until he was killed. It seemed like he was the golden boy. And in a matter of a few minutes that early October morning, the gold turned to dust.

Jerry dropped to his cot and punched his pillow before curling up. He covered his face with his blanket and thrust himself into a daydream where he was out in the cold November winds, the blistering northerly winds that he could hear howling through his jail cell window. If he could escape right now, he'd run into the woods, just tuck himself into an open space in a thicket of trees, and lay down to sleep … to die. Or maybe he'd climb a tree, settling into the crook of a tree branch, praying for death. He just wanted to fall asleep and never wake up.

Chapter Fifty-Four

Sheriff Pierce came for Jerry first thing in the morning to take him to the county jail in Waterloo. Nobody could fathom how alone he felt. His mother didn't come to see him. Maybe she was afraid that she'd see guilt in his eyes. He had no friends in the area, having moved thousands of miles away from home years ago. And now, with 'suspected murderer' written on his back, he'd have a lot of trouble making new friends. Who would befriend a brother killer, a child killer, a dog killer?

The drive out of Pine Falls lasted forever as the car moved in slow motion down the familiar streets. The sky was angry gray, and bursts of wind slapped the patrol car from side to side like it was a toy. It was so early, they were about the only car on the road. The sheriff stopped at the edge of town, at the Junction Diner, in spite of Deputy Neal's four objections made in as many minutes. Sheriff Pierce announced that they were having breakfast.

"He's a suspect, innocent until proven guilty. I know him, I'll vouch for him." He looked at Jerry sternly. "Just to be perfectly clear, though, I'll shoot you dead if you try to make a run for it."

Jerry felt like he'd been given a gift. For one more time, maybe his last, he'd be out in society, a free person, having eggs and bacon with an old friend. "Thanks, Sheriff."

Sheriff Pierce nodded. "You can call me Ron from now on, Jerry. That is, out of the courtroom."

Jerry made his breakfast last as long as he could. He even ordered pancakes after he'd eaten scrambled eggs and bacon. But they had to leave sometime. As he headed for the car, he thought about making a break for it and letting Ron end his life with a bullet in his back. It would save them all the trouble of a trial, and everyone could get on with their lives. But then Ron would have to live with the memory of killing him, and Jerry couldn't do that to Ron, the one person who had compassion for him.

The paperwork didn't take long at the prison, most of it was sent earlier. The transfer of the prisoner was just a formality. Deputy Neal signed the papers while Jerry and Ron said their good-byes.

"I didn't kill Jimmy, Ron." Jerry said softly, looking at his childhood friend.

"I find it hard to believe you did it, Jerry. But the path to your guilt was so deeply cleared, so overwhelming, I just …."

"I understand." Jerry dropped his eyes to the floor. "Take care of my mom, Ron."

"I will … as much as she'll let me." They both smiled knowing that would be difficult. "Do the best you can."

"Good-bye, Jerry. Guess next time I see you, I'll be a witness for the prosecution. I'm sorry for that."

Jerry sighed. "I'm sorry, too, Ron. But do what you have to do. Just keep your eyes open for the real killer. He'll be out there... free. And he might kill again."

Chapter Fifty-Five
April 1976

Glowing white snow packed the roads, and tracks from car tires left a zipper pattern on the streets, as the official transport van moved slowly along the route to the county courthouse. Tree limbs, frosted in soft, fresh, late-season snow made an icy canopy above them, and Jerry shivered with cold and fear. He wiggled his feet and knees to keep warm and blew hot breath on his bare fingers. His attorney said the trial would be short, and that scared him. Easy trials were always short. He had almost accepted his fate, knowing in his heart that he was condemned the day Sheriff Pierce arrested him and took him to jail. But he still held onto a small thread of hope.

Witnesses came from around the country. He studied each one, not like a defendant, but like a lawyer. They were all strong and believable to him, and the look on each juror's face confirmed his fear.

The gun shop clerk had come back to Iowa from California to testify. He looked 'Iowa' ... scrubbed face, well-fed, polite. The young man's mother came to court with him like it was a family outing. He'd pointed to Jerry without hesitation, followed by an admission that he'd looked up Jerry's picture in the high school annual after he'd gotten the news article about the murders. He said he wanted to verify the face before he called the sheriff's office. He'd testified that Jerry had introduced himself, and the name was well known to him from his high school days.

Peggy had come for a day. Her eyes had never left his face as she'd testified. They were damp, and shiny, and love-filled. She'd worn a bright yellow dress, his favorite color. On the stand, she'd confessed to their affair and confirmed Jerry's fascination with guns and knives. She said he'd called her the night of the murders, but they never talked. She'd accepted the collect call from him and said hello, but no one answered. After her testimony, she'd stayed the rest of the day in the courtroom. At the end of the day, she'd hugged him and kissed his neck before an officer pulled her away. Later, she'd told the *Des Moines Register's* reporter that she would always love Jerry, that he was a good man and could not have committed this crime. Her interview and picture had made the front page news.

The Nebraska waitress and cook had testified the day after Peggy. They both identified Jerry as the man in question. "He looks a little different than the first time he came to the diner. He had a mustache and beard stubble then, as if he wanted to hide his face. But that's him," the man had said, pointing a thick finger at Jerry. "He was quiet, just a few words about his family in Iowa and his girlfriend in San Diego." The waitress had also confirmed Jerry's identity, but she couldn't look at him without tearing up. It was obvious that she'd tried not to incriminate him.

Sheriff Pierce walked reluctantly to the witness stand. He'd talked about the crime scene, the bodies, the gun. "Jerry knew where the gun was hidden. And he bought the correct bullets for the unusual weapon." The sheriff had explained that Jerry's credit card was used at the gun shop and on one stop that he'd made on the way back from the killing spree. "The cigarette butts we found at the crime scene were the same brand that Jerry smoked when I took him to the house to help me find a lead."

Sheriff Pierce had looked tired as he finished his testimony. He took a deep breath, looked at Jerry briefly, and sighed. "We kept the name of the eye-witness out of the papers to protect the young girl. But she identified him, in a fashion, at the police station." The sheriff had stood slowly and shuffled his way back to his seat.

When the Prosecutor had called the eye-witness, Jerry knew that her testimony would be the most damning. It was probably what they were hanging the entire case on. Jerry had not been prepared to hear any of it. When the young witness had taken a seat, Jerry's heart sank. Little Sally Stoddard, Abby's girl. He didn't think a child should have to testify in open court. And he hated the prosecutor for putting her through the nightmare all over again.

The young, newly minted prosecutor was efficient and had been cold-hearted about the killings until the girl came to the witness stand and got settled in the big wooden seat. He smiled at her and told her in soft, kind voice that he was sorry.

"So, you are, er were friends with Christy Collins. Is that correct?" The pre-teen girl looked up, way higher than the lawyer's head. Her lips were hidden inside her mouth.

"Yes," she whispered.

"Speak louder, please Miss Stoddard, Sally."

"Yes, sir."

"How old are you?"

Now Sally's eyes were downcast, as if she were counting on her fingers. "Twelve."

"Why were you at the Collins farm that night?"

"Christy invited me to spend the night. She had a new Monkees album and we were going to memorize the songs."

"Did you get to play the record?"

The girl lifted her eyebrows and smiled ever so lightly. "Yes. Over and over."

"Did you go to bed late?"

"No. We went to bed on time, since we had Sunday School the next day. But we did talk after lights out."

"Now, let's go to the next day. Deputy Neal said they found you under a library table in the dining room. Is that correct?"

Sally's eyes closed and squinted tightly shut. She started to take little breaths in rapid succession.

"I heard him come in and go upstairs. I heard gunshots." She started to cry.

The attorney waited while her mother comforted her. When she stopped crying, he continued. "I know this is really hard. But, why weren't you in the bedroom with Christy?"

"I was hungry. I went down for a cookie. I was just going to have one...."

"When did you know someone had come into the house?"

"I heard the front door open, and I got scared, so I hid in the dining room. I didn't think he would see me there."

"Why do you say he? What did you think when you heard the door open?"

"At first I thought maybe Christy's dad had gone out and come home late like my dad does."

"Where did you think he went?"

"I thought he went to the Dew Drop Inn."

"And that would be what?"

"A beer joint. The place that has red and blue and yellow flashing lights."

"How would you know about that?"

"Once, me and my mom followed my dad to see where he was going. The lights over the door flash on and off."

"Yes. Well, when you thought it was Jimmy Collins, why didn't you come out?"

"I was waiting till he went to bed. When it was quiet, I figured I could go back to Christy's room. And then I heard a bang, like a gun shot." Before the attorney could ask, the girl added, "I shoot pheasants with my dad, so I know the sound of a gun."

"Good." The attorney smiled and nodded. "How many shots did you hear?"

"One, two, I think three? No, two." She put her hands over her ears as if she were hearing the sounds again. "I hid under the table."

"What do you remember next?"

"I think I heard him say Piggy or something like that."

"Could it have been Debbie?"

"Maybe." She scratched her head. "But, no, it was Piggy. I'm pretty sure."

"Then what did you think?"

"I thought he was going to hurt me." The girl broke down and cried. The attorney handed her a few tissues.

"You thought he'd found you under the table where you were hiding?"

After a few deep breaths and her mother nodding for her to go on, she added, "Christie painted my toenails. Bright red. They were sticking out from under the table and I was afraid to move."

"Did you hear anything else?"

"I thought I heard a car engine. Loud."

"Have you heard a car that sounds like that?"

"Uh huh, I mean yes."

"Where?"

"The drag strip. My dad takes me sometimes."

"Do you have any brothers, Sally?"

The girl scowled and looked at him curiously. "No."

"I didn't think so," the attorney said, lifting his left eyebrow slightly.

"When you heard it again, at the sheriff's office, that engine sound, you recognized it, didn't you?"

"Yeah."

"You knew right away what made that sound. Right?"

"Yes. It was loud. Louder than a car."

"It was a motorcycle. Correct?"

"Yes. A big one. I think they call it a hog."

The attorney smiled. "You're a very clever girl. Good memory."

"Did you hear anything else?"

"I remember he was eating in the kitchen, then the dog growled. Buster." Now her tears were flowing. The attorney gave her a few more minutes.

"Did you see anything clearly? Anything at all?"

"Yes. I saw boots. They were black."

"Did they look like this?" The attorney held up a boot in a plastic bag. It was well-worn and had a metal bar across the heel.

"Yes. That's it!" Sally exclaimed. "That's what I saw from under the table."

"Anything else?"

"I saw light hair, not dark." Sally shifted her eyes towards the defendant and then back. "Like his hair," she said, pointing. She started to tremble.

The attorney nodded his head. "That's all. Let this courageous girl go back to her seat, back to her mom. The Prosecution rests."

When Sally had finished her testimony, even Jerry believed that he was guilty.

Chapter Fifty-Six

The defense calls Jerald Collins to the stand. All eyes focused on him. He felt awkward in his black pin-stripe suit. His burgundy tie felt like a noose. And he didn't know if his legs would hold him as he tried to stand. Peggy's yellow plastic barrette was in his pocket for good luck. She'd pushed it into his hand when she hugged him briefly before the guards took him away. It was all he had of her, of his past life.

He looked over at his mother, who sat at the back of the courtroom, staring at the ceiling. He studied her outfit, a navy blue suit with a white blouse, as colorless as her life had been. She was balling up a fancy, lace edged hanky in her fist instead of a Kleenex, her only extravagance. He knew she was trying to be strong, but maybe if she cried, he'd look better, like a loved son. She'd lost almost everything, and now she was about to lose the only thing she had left. Him.

Jerry leaned on the railing that set the witness chair apart from the rest of the room. He'd been there for practice in law classes. Today it felt like a pyre, about to be lit on fire and consumed by flames. He felt guilty just sitting in the over-large chair.

"Jerry Collins, brother of Jim Collins, correct?"

"Yes."

"Did you love your brother?"

"Yes."

"Did you like your brother?"

"No. He was a brute. He was like my dad."

Did you love your sister-in-law, Debbie?"

"Yes. I thought she was ... wonderful."

"You were in love with her?"

"Yes, I guess. I could never hurt her or the kids."

"Could you hurt your brother?"

"No. I didn't like him. But I could never be ... like him."

"Where were you the night of the killings?"

"I went to San Francisco, to a concert. I needed to get away."

"And your credit card, what happened to that?"

"I couldn't find it when I was packing my duffel, so I had to take cash, pay for everything with cash. I was going to call *American Express* on Monday and tell them it was missing, but I was busy at work all day, and then I got a call from my mom about Jimmy."

"So you didn't buy gas in Nebraska on October thirty-first?"

"No, sir."

"Did you buy bullets at a gun shop earlier that week? On October twenty-fifth?"

"No. I've never been in that gun-shop."

"What about the gloves they found, the biking gloves?"

"They were mine, but they were missing when I went on my trip, so I stopped and bought new ones."

"How did the gloves that they have in evidence get into your brother's house?"

"Maybe I left them when I was back for my dad's funeral. Maybe Jimmy found them and used them in the barn. I really don't know."

"Do you smoke Marlboro cigarettes?"

"Yes, but usually just a few puffs. I've never finished a whole cigarette. It's my way of cutting back."

"Did you kill your brother, Mr. Collins?"

Jerry took a minute and reflected on his life. Jimmy had been a thorn in his side, but Jimmy had saved him plenty of times. Life with Jimmy was better by far than this life without him.

"My brother was the only person in the world that knew exactly where I was coming from. He was my brother … and I … I …."

"Yes, Mr. Collins?"

"I loved my brother, Jimmy." Jerry broke down and sobbed. He felt like sobbing, so he sobbed. He could feel the tears rush down his face, down to his chin. He didn't care. He felt his face contort in excruciating pain, it felt ugly, yet it felt good. The pent up emotion was released, and he was finally free. His lawyer handed him a box of Kleenex, and he used them liberally.

"That will be all, Mr. Collins."

Jerry stood up to leave, but his lawyer nodded for him to return to the chair.

The prosecuting attorney was on his feet, and he thrust his face close to Jerry's.

"So you were in San Francisco the weekend of the murders. Did anybody see you?"

"No. I got some gas, food, and then stayed in a motel outside of town. The night clerk took my cash and put it in his pocket."

"The credit card, the one in question, what happened to it?"

"I don't know. When I was getting ready for the weekend it was missing from my wallet."

"It was used that weekend in Nebraska. How is that possible?"

"I don't know."

"You don't know how to explain it? You used it, didn't you, Mr. Collins? In Nebraska?"

"I was not in Nebraska."

"Your credit card and telephone records say differently. Your girlfriend, Peggy, says she got a call from you that Saturday night."

"No, I didn't call her. I was at a concert in San Francisco."

"But the records show that she received a collect call from you, from a gas station in Nebraska. How could that be?"

"Again, I don't know."

"And what about the sock that your mother filled for you with old coins. She testified in depositions that she showed it to you, gave it to you the day of your dad's funeral. She stated that it was still there after you'd gone back to California. And yet, it was missing when the detectives went to search for it. Where is that money, Mr. Collins?"

Jerry hadn't thought about the sock after his mother's brief inquiry. It seemed so irrelevant at the time, and she never brought it up to him again. "I don't know."

"I understand that this is really all just circumstantial evidence. Pretty damning, though, wouldn't you agree?"

The prosecutor had Jerry there. Jerry nodded, then remembered the basic instruction to make his answer audible. "Yes. Yes, it is."

"And finally, Mr. Collins, how do you explain the eye-witness account, that little Sally Stoddard saw you at the house the night of the murders?"

Jerry glanced at Abby and her husband, and he shook his head. "I really don't understand, and I certainly can't explain it, unless she saw someone who looked like me."

"And had a motorcycle like yours, and boots, and a leather coat like yours?"

"Most bikers have those same things."

"But they don't look like you. She picked you out of six pictures. She pointed her tiny finger at you, Mr. Collins."

The courtroom was getting stuffy, and people were shuffling around as Jerry left the witness stand. Some were leaving and more were coming in. Jerry walked slowly back to his seat at the defendant's table next to his lawyer, who was doodling. He was writing the name Bernice and then crossing it out, and then writing it again.

"The defense calls Mrs. Bernice Collins to the stand."

Jerry watched his mom make her way slowly to the witness chair. Her back was as straight as a board, her head tilted up, so that her eyes never landed on anyone's face. She was a pro at staying private. He thanked her for that today. No matter what the prosecutor asked her, after the soft-ball questioning by the defense, they'd get nothing damning from his mother. At least nothing that she didn't want to give them. He just wished she'd look at him.

"Mrs. Collins ...."

"Yes. My name is Mrs. James Collins."

"I'm sorry, ma'am. That wasn't a question."

"Then what is your question, Mr. Ledder?"

"You've known Jerry since he was born ...."

"I am his mother. Yes, we've been acquainted these nearly thirty years."

"You've heard all the evidence. Is your son capable of this horrible act?"

"No. Jerry is not the kind of boy who would do such a thing."

"But the Prosecutor just painted him as a monster. What do you say?"

His mother took a few moments, and he could see tears dampen her lashes. "There are any number of monsters, sir. We try to be civil and humane, but some basic animal instincts dwell in all of us." She looked at Jerry as if she were seeing her dead husband, Big Jim. "Some more than others."

Jerry could tell that his attorney was not pleased with his mother's answer. It would be a good time to end on a good note. "Do you love your son, Mrs. Collins?"

She took another moment, pulling her hanky from her sleeve where she'd tucked it away. "I loved him once, when I thought I knew what love was." She stared off into the crowd, disappearing into it. "How do I love now? When everything I loved has been taken away? I'm left with nothing, don't you see? Love is dead to me." She looked up at Jerry for the first time. "And, Jerry, where are the coins? I know you didn't take them with you after your dad's funeral. So … when did you take them?"

Jerry's lawyer stood next to her, debating his next question, but he had none. "That is all, Mrs. Collins."

When Jerry's lawyer took his seat, the prosecutor stood, a small yet visible smile on his face.

"I rest my case, your honor."

Bernice Collins, Jerry Collins' mother left the witness stand and the courtroom slowly, in a hushed silence. And with her went all of Jerry's hope. She'd pounded the last nail in his coffin. The overflow crowd erupted from the benches and followed Jerry's mother from the room. A din of voices could be heard in the hallway ... some gasps, some cries, some laughter.

Jerry's mother had lost all hope the day that her beloved Jimmy died, and therefore, had none to share with her only living son. His fate was sealed.

Chapter Fifty-Seven

The courtroom was filled beyond capacity the day that the jury came back with the verdict. Jerry could feel all eyes boring into his back, like fingers poking him. His mother was not there. He didn't even have to look to know that.

He knew it would be a suspenseful moment, a heart-stopping moment, and he thought he was prepared for the worst. But when he heard that first sound from the jury foreman, the guttural sound that he'd learned to recognize in other trials, g ... guilty, he cried out, all the oxygen leaving his body. His lawyer kept him from falling sideways. He never heard the other three guilty verdicts.

The Waterloo sheriff and deputy-sheriff had Jerry in handcuffs and out the side door before he could focus. In a blur of sounds, he heard the judge concluding that the Iowa State Penitentiary would be his new home for the rest of his life.

He was clearly agitated while he waited for the patrol car to pick him up, anxiety exploding in all his nerve endings. And then his attorney stepped out of another door with his mother. He calmed down. She was there. His mother had been there when the verdict was read. She'd come to say good-bye, to tell

him that she loved him, would always love him. He waited for
her, desperate to have her arms around him, wondering what
he could say to make this moment easier for her. She looked
deeply into his face from a distance as if for the last time, said
good-bye softly, and turned away.

He watched her until the patrol car pulled up between
them. He knew he'd probably never see her again. The gray
Iowa sky opened up a crack, and a sliver of blue leaked
through. The soft rumble of the car engine filled his senses
and helped him let go of his last image of his mother, a heart-
broken and hopeless old woman.

He was surprised when Sheriff Pierce stepped out of the
vehicle. Deputy Neal was with him. "A professional courtesy,"
Sheriff Pierce said to Jerry, as he helped him into the back seat.
"I've asked to do the honors of taking you to Fort Madison. I
explained that your brother was an old friend." Just before he
shut the door he added, "I'm Ron from here on out, Jerry."

Jerry sat back and stretched his legs. He'd kept himself
so tightly wound up that his muscles were aching. The fear
was over now. The reality was setting in. As they approached
the highway, Ron made a left turn, going the wrong way, and
Jerry was puzzled. At first, he thought maybe Ron was going
to spring him, but after a moment, he knew where they were
headed.

"You may never see the old place again, Jerry. I know
how I'd feel, let's say if I didn't do something I was going to
prison for."

Jerry's pent up emotions flooded his body. He trembled and
cried out loud like a baby. With no hands to wipe at his eyes,
his face became a mess of bodily fluids. He was still shedding
tears when they pulled into the farmyard. Ron stopped
the patrol car close to the big oak tree. The tree held real

significance to Jerry on this day, the day of his condemnation. His own blood now dripped down the ragged bark that cloaked the tree, mingling with all the others. But oddly, he felt at peace as he studied the tree and the branch, committing it to memory. He wanted to thank Ron for his thoughtfulness, but there were no words, so he just nodded his thanks.

The house looked old and tired like Jerry felt. It needed paint, so sadly obvious in the late afternoon sun.

"Let's just walk around, Jer, down to the pond and back around the barn," Ron offered, taking the lead.

Jerry followed his old friend, thankful that Deputy Neal had chosen to stay in the patrol car.

"This is really, I mean, I don't know how to thank you, Ron. But you were always good to me, like a real brother."

Ron smiled. "I did save your butt a time or two. I don't think Jimmy knew his own strength."

They were both quiet when they got to the edge of the pond. Layer upon layer of ice glistened around the edges, but the center was silky smooth, black ice. It was about ready to go out and melt into a brand new Spring. "I think I even pulled you out of that water a few times. Jimmy thought you could breathe like a fish." Jerry nodded, looking out to the center of the pond where movement caught his eye. The life under the surface was renewing in preparation for the warmer months ahead. He was remembering good times when they fished along the grassy shore.

Ron turned to look at Jerry. "You were always different, Jerry. Different than Jimmy and your dad."

Jerry looked up at the snow-laden sky, wishing that he'd had a brother like Ron, wishing he could go back in time and do things differently. He had so many regrets, so many unfulfilled dreams.

"Jerry, I just want you to know, I'm not convinced that you're guilty. And I'm going to keep investigating. I think there's something out there that we missed. And if anything new comes to light, I'll see to it that you get a new day in court."

Jerry tried to speak, but he didn't know what to say. Ron had said it all. Life sucked. "I never thought Jimmy deserved a friend like you, Ron. You were different, too."

"Yes. You and I were more alike than you probably know." Ron stopped. "I'll confess to you now, and it has to stay here … I like ballet."

Jerry laughed, a haunting, aching laugh that filled his belly, and Ron joined him. Deputy Neal was out of the car when they returned. He looked baffled but asked no questions. When Ron helped Jerry back into the car, he patted his shoulder with affection and spoke in his ear. "I'll come to visit you sometimes, Jer."

Jerry was now on his way to the Iowa State Penitentiary. He'd never been to the town of Fort Madison in all the years he'd lived in Iowa. It was not a destination for law-abiding citizens. Criminals went there, most to spend only a few years of their sentence before getting out for good behavior. There were a few capital offenders in the state, but not many. Now he was one of them, condemned to a life of confinement. He would spend the rest of his days hiding in the recesses of his troubled and lonely mind.

As they turned from the drive to the gravel road, Jerry took one more look at the old farmhouse, at the tree they called the bleeding tree, and the colorless land around it. And in his artist's vision, blood seeped up from all corners of the house and dripped from the limbs of the ancient, hanging tree. People died in the tree. People died in the house. And their life blood would mingle and linger with his for all eternity.

Chapter Fifty-Eight
1995
Iowa State Penitentiary

Jerry took a seat in the nearly empty visitation room, the only furniture a few tables, each flanked by two chairs. He had been in this place often, every time Ron Pierce paid a visit. The walls were cold, as if they were frosted in ice. The chairs were small and hard. The room was colorless, like the rest of his life. Names and symbols had been scratched into the surface of the small metal tables and had rusted over the years. As bad as his cell was, this was far worse. His cell had his books, his notepads, his pillow, the pillow that he used to cover his ears at night. If he held it tightly to his head, he could imagine that he was in his own place, his own bed, a California moon beaming light and life into his bedroom window.

He'd been in prison for almost twenty years now, but he still remembered vividly his San Diego apartment as if he'd just left it ... the floor creaking occasionally, the windows rattling on a windy, stormy night, the smell of soap rinsed down by a recent hot shower, a bit of fragrant grass clinging to his tennis shoes days after walking on a freshly mowed lawn. Here inside the walls of the ancient prison, he smelled sweat, and defecation, and garlic permeating from the bodies of all the men that slept around him, side by side, inches away. The only sounds were natural, human sounds of bodily functions.

The girl walked in, just after he felt drowsy and laid his head on his hands on the desk. He looked up, but didn't lift his head. Another, college student, ho hum. Law students all wanted to interview him, interrogate him, study him … the monster. The boys and girls alike asked the same questions, listened inattentively, scribbled in notebooks, then left. He felt like an experimental rat. He must have looked and sounded like one, too. Nobody came back for more, for clarification, for anything. They left and reported back to their class on the murderer who could kill his own brother and two small children. Everyone left out Debbie, the one who really mattered.

"Hi."

Wow, she was really talkative. This should go well. "Hello, yourself. Law?"

"Yup," she said, as she pulled out the chair across from him and sat down.

The girl wore her blonde hair tied up in a ponytail, with pompadour bangs. "First year?"

"Nope."

"Hmmm. Do you live in an apartment?"

"Sure." The girl looked confused. She studied him with bright blue eyes covered in the obligatory thick glasses that all law students wore to appear older, more intelligent. This time it wasn't working. She looked too pretty to be smart. He appreciated that she had on colorful clothes … a neon green sweater and striped pants. She wore tennis shoes.

"They say you still claim you're innocent."

Jerry lifted his head, turned in his chair, and stared at the wall. If she was going to get an interview, she'd have to earn it.

"I am." He nodded, his back to her. "I am innocent."

"So, who do you think did it? Who killed your brother, Debbie, the kids?"

Jerry stood up. She said the magic word. Debbie. She would be the first to get his true thoughts. She would get her interview, be the first to know what was in his heart. She would get the prize. This young law student remembered that Debbie was a victim, too. Debbie was slaughtered that night, too.

"I don't know. I've gone to bed thinking about it every night for all these years. Lots of people hated my brother. Most of the women he fooled around with had husbands. Maybe a biker guy just happened to ride by, a complete stranger, a coincidence. My brother kept his gun near his bedroom, easy enough to find. I hadn't had time to hate him with that much passion ... yet."

"Did you love your brother?"

"Are you going to be a defense lawyer or prosecutor?"

"Dunno."

"You are a girl of few words."

"Yup."

"What's your name?"

"Sandra."

They looked at each other for a long moment before he spoke. "I didn't love my brother, Sandra. I wasn't raised to love my brother."

The girl lifted her brows and scribbled.

"I was raised to hate ... but not to kill." The girl put down her pen and tilted her head. Her eyes were kind and sad.

"Where are you from?" he asked her, taking his chair again and turning it towards her, this time fully engaged in the conversation.

"San Diego."

"So, are you connected to my old law firm?" She shook her head. "Are you an intern?"

"No." The girl sighed. She reached down in her book bag and brought out a piece of paper, folded into a square.

"My mom wanted me to give you this if something happened to her. She mentioned you the last time I talked to her. She died almost a year ago now. I didn't get a chance to say good-bye."

Jerry opened up the paper and studied it. It was signed, Peggy. It was a love letter. The post script said, take care of our girl. He took a deep breath, so deep he couldn't exhale. He felt like he might explode or pass out.

"Your mother?"

"Yes, Peggy Baxter."

"I don't think I know her," he lied.

"She was married to Phil."

"Phil." He hadn't heard that name in years. At one time, briefly, he'd considered Phil as a suspect. They looked a little alike, and he knew almost all the details of Jerry's pathetic past. But he never told anyone that he suspected Phil. It was absurd.

"So, you're Peggy and Phil's girl. I remember now that she was pregnant."

"Phil's not my dad."

"But she was married to Phil. You look like him."

"No I don't. Look at me." The girl stood up and took a few steps toward Jerry, forcing him to face her. "Look at me. I look like you."

"Why do you want to go there?"

"Mom told me everything. She knew that I was curious, and I had a right to know. She said that you were my dad, not Phil. She ... loved you very much." Sandra took a deep breath. "When she thought I was ready, she told me where you were and what had happened. She thought that you were innocent." The young law student paused just when he was getting curious. "I've studied the case and your appeals. I think you're innocent, too. I want to help you."

Jerry laughed. It started small, an awkward, ugly sound. He hadn't laughed in years. It wasn't that what she said was so funny. It wasn't funny to him at all. It was that she, this young girl from nowhere, a stranger ... she believed him. She was the only person besides Ron Pierce, in all these years, that ever said that. Not even his mother had considered, or put into words the idea that he might be innocent. He felt giddy.

The girl got up and went to the door looking for help. She was baffled and a little bit afraid. Maybe she'd set off the sleeping monster within the quiet man. Jerry couldn't stop laughing, laughing so hard that tears streamed down his face. He reached out to her from his chair. He touched her arm softly. The only time he'd touched another human being since he'd been in prison had been the handshakes he'd gotten from Ron and the parting hug.

"Thank-you ... Sandra," he sputtered out. He was crying now, like a baby. It all came up and out, all the emotion, all the fear, all the hope, and then the hopelessness. He died every day in this place, and right now, he felt young and alive for the first time. It was a moment he would cherish for the rest of his days.

The girl had tears, too. She sat back down across from him and touched his hand, patting it with a genuine affection.

"I have something else," she said. "I found this in my mom's things. It had your name on it."

She reached into her bag and pulled out a manila envelope. He stared at it for some time before he took it from her. He opened the flap and fumbled inside, inching out a small piece of corrugated cardboard. He turned it over and gasped. It was the picture he'd painted in oil years ago, when his mind was fresh, and young, and full of ideas. The year before his father did his last bit of sculpting, to take out his heart, stomp on it, and seal him up … heartless, forever. The painting was his rendering of the pond at the farm. He couldn't remember the last time he'd seen it, and now like a miracle it reappeared. How?

"I never told your mother about this. How did she get it?"

"Dunno."

"I haven't seen it, well, since I painted it. I wonder where she got it?" Jerry was crazed, trying to remember anything about the painting. "I only told one person. I only shared the story with … Phil." He took a deep, hissing breath. "Phil."

His mind went deep, deep into his memory, to a time just before his father died when in a drunken state, he told the story to Phil.

"Phil," he said, angrily.

"Phil!" He dropped the word like it was a bomb.

"It was Phil." Jerry bit his lip, until it was bleeding. He trembled, deep in his thoughts, forgetting the girl who sat across from him. He almost felt hopeful, a feeling he barely recognized. It was Phil! It had to be Phil. He did it out of revenge. A case could be made! This young college girl could get him off, get him out. She could be his savior. He lifted his eyes to look at her, really look at her. Yes, she could be his daughter. He prayed she was his daughter.

Jerry stood and paced, looking out the window and then back at the girl. "You have to tell Ron Pierce. He's the sheriff in Pine Falls." Jerry felt hope exploding in his mind and his heart. After all this time, Ron would still help him. Ron made a promise years ago, that if new evidence was found, he'd get the case back in court. Ron and Sandra would find the truth and set him free.

"Where is Phil, Sandra? Where is Phil, now?"

"Dead. He's dead. Cremated and tossed into hell where he belongs."

Hope dropped like a lead ball for both of them. A dead man could not defend himself. A cremated body left no DNA.

Chapter Fifty-Nine

Sandra came to visit Jerry every day during her Spring break, and they forged a unique bond, two minds identical in so many ways.

"Tell me about your mother, about Peggy. How did she get away from Phil?"

Sandra leaned toward Jerry and tilted her head. "We did live with him for a long time. I thought he was my dad. He wasn't around much. Mom was always anxious and drank when he was around. She made me stay in my room. I believed her when she told me I'd be safer." Sandra leaned back and closed her eyes. She rubbed at them a few times and then continued.

"One night he came home really drunk and really mad. He said he was horny, and he hit her. I heard her cry. I snuck out of my room and watched from the hall. He pushed her down on the floor and punched her nose. It started to bleed and I cried out. I saw the look of terror in her eyes when he got off her and came after me. I was only eleven. I thought he was going to hit me too, but he just picked me up and took me to my bedroom, to my bed … and pulled my pajama bottoms off. Said he was glad he wasn't my dad."

Sandra sat back and looked sad and frail like a young child, her memory draining her strength. Jerry felt himself responding like a Dad for the first time. It was a helpless feeling that he couldn't explain, and he swiped at his damp eyes to make the tears go away.

"My mom came into the room," Sandra continued. "He didn't see her. I think she would have killed him if she could. She had a heavy skillet and swung it against his head, once, twice, three times. He was out. Limp. She rolled him over, and lifted the frying pan again, but I pleaded with her to stop." Her voice got stronger as she spoke. "We packed a few things in a small suitcase, and she took all the money from his wallet. We left town, went to where grandma lived before she died."

Sandra leaned in toward Jerry again. "Mom waitressed and went to night school. She graduated as a paralegal the same month I graduated from high school. She said my real dad was a lawyer, and he encouraged her to find a career. Mom was smart. She got a job right away, and I got her waitress job."

Sandra stopped and turned away from Jerry. She cleared her throat, yet her voice was ragged with emotion. "Mom died a year ago, my first year of law school. She was hit by a car when she was crossing the street by our apartment. I always wondered if, well, if it was Phil. It was a hit-and-run."

She looked deep into the cracks on the holding room wall, as if she were seeing her past on a television screen. "We didn't have much money, but all my gifts from Mom were gifts of an experience. She took me to a play, and a ballet. But most of the time, we just made popcorn and watched old movies. Or had picnics in the park."

Jerry nodded. "She always loved picnics."

Sandra was anxious to share more. "She found books for me at the second-hand store. We'd both read them and then talk about them."

That surprised Jerry. He wished he'd known that Peggy, the thinking Peggy. He only knew the pretty girl who loved to kiss.

Sandra continued, "When I went off to college, she convinced me that I would do well if I followed in …." She looked at Jerry with the saddest smile. "In my father's footsteps. She wanted me to become a lawyer."

Jerry smiled and reached out to touch her hand in his first fatherly gesture. And then his smile became a curious frown. "I always wondered, Sandra, how did your mother find out about the murders? Sheriff Pierce said she knew about them when he called her for information. I never talked to her after that."

"I don't know for sure, maybe Phil told her. I know she hated being a witness for the prosecution. She was convinced that you didn't do it. You were too kind, too good. That's why I'm here."

Jerry nodded, tears in his eyes. Peggy would have said that because she only saw the good in people. That's how she ended up with Phil, and Phil took her life. Phil got even with both of them.

Chapter Sixty
1998

For all his years in prison, for all the years that he'd lost in the real world, fifty-two year old Jerry Collins was a happy man. Peggy, the woman who had loved him when he was lovable, before he became the convicted monster, had given him a daughter. He cried tears of joy for days after Sandra's first visit. She truly cared about him and visited him three days in a row before going back to school. She was smart, attractive, funny, and loveable. She promised to write to him when she said good-bye their last day together. He received her first letter two weeks later, and one every month after that.

At first, he had moments of doubt that she might not be his daughter. But two years after their first visit, when he never thought he'd see her again, she showed up with a paternity test. They were a perfect match as Father and Daughter.

"How did you get my DNA?" he asked.

She smiled ... his smile. "I went to your mom."

"My mother talked to you? Let you in?"

Sandra nodded. "We have a lot in common. We both love ballet. We both sing high soprano. We both love Paul Anka." She looked directly at him. "And we both love you."

"Well, now I know you're lying. I haven't seen my mother in years." He turned away from her so she wouldn't see his eyes. "I never knew any of that about her. Paul Anka?"

"Yup. We had a little drink together, too. We had a shot of Vodka. She wanted to make me a martini, but she only had a small bottle of vodka, so she closed her eyes and waved her hand over the small glasses like a magic wand and said, 'vermouth, olives.'"

Jerry turned around and laughed out loud, which made his daughter smile. It was preposterous that this young woman could tell him so much about his own mother. It was glorious.

The next time Sandra arrived, she brought his mother. His mother! The woman who had looked at him with no emotion and had said good-bye as he was being led out of the courthouse on his way to prison. He hadn't seen her in over twenty years.

"Mother." He did not smile, but his voice spoke of his emotion and his love.

"Jerry." His mother studied him and reached out to touch his hand. Tears fell from his mother's eyes and landed on top of their grasping hands. "I'm sorry," she whispered. "I'm so very sorry," she said, louder. "Sandra is ... she came to me, knowing I'd need proof."

Jerry nodded. "I understand."

"She's my ... she's your daughter." His mother was smiling. How old was the frail woman now, his mother? Fifty-five at the time of the trial. She was seventy-six. But her eyes looked much older, buried deep in the folds of her sagging eyelids. She'd been condemned to a living death with him for the last two decades. They'd both been condemned to hell long before that.

"I'm sorry, mom. I'm sorry that I couldn't prove my innocence."

"Don't worry, son. Sandra will prove it. She won't give up."

Chapter Sixty-One
2014

Sixty-seven year old Jerry rested in his new cell. A few weeks before, the state had opened a new prison. They'd moved the prisoners in after correcting an engineering problem, months after it was completed and slated to open. He didn't want to move, and he'd never get used to the new cell. The bed was hard. The mattress hadn't molded around his body, and it felt like a board. The old familiar smells were gone, human smells, his smells. It was a sterile room and even colder than his old room, if possible.

There was a time, at the beginning, when he'd hated the long, endless afternoons. That's when he'd most wanted to be free. But now he was older. He'd learned to escape into vivid daydreams where he could do anything he wanted. Freedom was a state of mind.

Today was another day. Just before he closed his eyes to rest, he studied the picture that he'd painted and hung at the foot of his new cot. He created it from memory. After several attempts, he'd finally gotten it right. It wasn't large, just eight inches by ten inches on a paper-backed canvas board. The old oak tree was bare, its knobby branches reaching up. The few leaves on the tips of the branches shined golden, as if all of them were on fire. The sky was several shades of red. A deep, dark shade at the edges eased into a golden red center. The tree was being consumed by the blood of so many sacrifices. He called the rendering, 'The Bleeding Tree.'

He would be alone now until supper, so he let himself sink into the picture, be absorbed by it. He closed his eyes. For him, every day was the same, a routine severely adhered to. His cell was the last one along the cement wall, so no one ever walked by it. He was asleep when the guard came to get him.

"Visitor."

It couldn't be his mother. She had died a few months ago. That was the last time he'd seen Ron Pierce. He'd come to tell Jerry the news, and he had a bit of bad news himself. He had cancer, and at the age of seventy-two, he didn't see a good outcome. They'd hugged one last time and Ron said, "See you on the other side, friend." Ron had never given up on Jerry's innocence. He'd just given up on trying to prove it.

A month later, Jerry read the week old newspaper from Pine Falls. Ron was dead, died just like he said he would. Ron had never lied to him. He envied Ron.

Maybe his visitor was Sandra but why? She usually only came on his birthday or hers.

The guard saw his curiosity. "Lawyer."

"I don't have a lawyer."

"Yup, you do."

"Why?"

"Ask him." The guard shrugged his shoulder.

Jerry moved into the conference room, the nice one, the one you got before you were found guilty of a crime. After that, you got the small cubicles to discuss your case. He'd never actually been in the room except for the brief tour some of the older inmates got in the first few days after the move. He didn't like it much either. The lights were too bright. A thin, older man was sitting in a chair. His hands were atop a very expensive briefcase. He smiled.

"What's going on?" Jerry took a seat across from the well-dressed man.

"I'm getting you out of here."

Jerry's head snapped back as if he'd been sucker-punched. "What?"

"Your daughter brought me some new evidence a few months ago. Some DNA from a guy named Phil."

"Yeah, Phil." Jerry rubbed his forehead and his eyes. And then it struck him hard. He knew Phil had to be the murderer, but he never thought they'd prove it. Phil had been cremated and his ashes had been scattered. So Jerry had given up.

"Your daughter received a package from her aunt's estate, Peggy's sister. All these years, she'd kept a box of Peggy's old mementos ... a necklace, a fancy comb, some hair ...."

The attorney pulled out a report. It was a DNA test. "The hair belonged to Phil.

He handed a small white envelope to Jerry. Inside, there were two pictures and a small lock of hair. He pulled out the pictures. In the first picture, Peggy was leaning over a very young looking Phil. He was straddling a kitchen chair, his eyes burning into the camera lens. He had a beard, and his hair was long and scraggly, down to his shoulders and beyond. Peggy had a pair of scissors in one hand and was holding a lock of hair in the other. She only had eyes for Phil. In the second picture, they were standing side by side. Phil's face and head were clean shaven, and he was wearing army fatigues. He was dressed for battle. His arm was draped across her shoulder, his hand dropping casually atop her breast. After Jerry studied the pictures again, he reached in and pulled out the snip of hair, tied in a white ribbon.

"Your freedom has been stored in a cardboard box in a basement all these years. Imagine that." The attorney tapped the papers. "The DNA in the hair is a nearly perfect match to the DNA on the cigarette butts found at the crime scene. As near as it can be, this many years later."

"Is that enough? Is that enough to prove I'm innocent?" Jerry's heart was racing.

"Yeah, probably. But there was more evidence in the box from the crime scene. There was a pillowcase full of towels. Apparently Phil dried his hands off … lots of blood. He must have cut himself on his knife, the one he used on the little ones and the dog. Sandra convinced me that Phil had a reason to kill your brother and his family. Revenge."

Phil had killed them. Jimmy, Debbie, Christy, Dougie, and Buster. It was Phil. Jerry couldn't take it all in. He felt a sharp pain in his chest, and then he fell into blackness.

Chapter Sixty-Two

After a few weeks and some intense rest, Jerry was able to get around his cell again. They thought he'd suffered a heart attack, but really he'd just gone into shock. He was pacing. The news going around the cells, like the game of telephone, concerned him, and he was anxious. Maybe they were going to give him bad news about his health.

When the guard came to get him, he called him Mr. Collins with a polite nod, and escorted him to the conference room where he found Sandra with the lawyer. She was carrying a back-pack.

Hi Jerry … Dad. We're going home."

"There is no home. Didn't Mom sell the farm?"

"Well … Dad … there is justice." She stopped to take a breath. This was the first time she'd called him Dad. "Grandma Collins did sell the farm, but she also set up a trust fund for me before she died, with the stipulation that we would share it when you were set free. She believed it would happen. She believed in you. You can go anywhere you want. You can make your home anywhere in the world. You're a free man. But before you make any decisions, I want you to meet my husband, John, and your grandsons. They are all waiting outside."

Jerry felt as if he knew them already. Sandra had sent pictures of her wedding and pictures and videos of the boys since the time they were born. Parker, Holden and Carson. Sandra had three boys, ages eight, nine and eleven.

"Did Mom ever meet them?"

Sandra nodded. "The last time I came. She was sick, remember? But she held each boy's hand and welcomed them into her family, into her heart."

Jerry nodded, imagining that emotional moment in his mind's eye, and then his eyes glazed over with anxiety and fear of being free for the first time in forty years. He never thought he'd be leaving this place, his home for most of his life. He was terrified.

"My guys are waiting outside. If you choose to come back to California with us, we'll be a family. It's up to you."

She thrust the back-pack at him. It held a sweater, a pair of jeans, some tennis shoes, and a brown bomber jacket, similar to the one he wore all those years ago.

Jerry thought of his mother as he walked out of the prison for the first time. She'd finally believed in his innocence thanks to Sandra. The last time he'd seen her, she'd brought him a small prayer book, the book of John. After she'd left, he'd read it, then tucked it under his mattress. Every night before lights went out, he'd reached for it, reading it over and over, until he'd memorized each word. He stopped and took a deep breath of fresh, cool air, his eyes searching the clouds. This was it, the peace that passes all understanding. At the funeral, the preacher had gotten it right.

It was a warm Autumn day, awash with sunshine. An artist's palette of burnished colors exploded before him, almost blinding him. He looked down at his new tennis shoes. They were moving along a tree-lined sidewalk. They were taking him toward a small pond and a park bench. They were turning toward a parking lot and a bright yellow car he'd only seen in pictures. They moved faster toward three boys who were huddled together, watching for him.

He was free. His daughter, Sandra, had proven his innocence. All these years later, he was really free. She had found proof without doubt that he was innocent. Proof that a man named Phil hated him so much that he'd taken the worst kind of revenge on him. He'd learned a bitterly hard, heart-breaking lesson. Actions have consequences. He'd paid the highest possible price for his indiscretion, but as he looked at the boys waiting near the car, it was all worth it.

Jerry's grandsons gave him a welcome like none he'd ever known. In their innocence, he regained his own. It was almost as if he'd never been in prison, like he'd been on a long, lonely journey that was over. His daughter's husband thrust his hand out and shook Jerry's hand with a gentle respect. His eyes were kind. He knew everything, the whole story, and yet he was there, welcoming Jerry into his family.

The new world he was entering was so different than the one he'd known. He'd seen it change over the years on television, but he was not prepared for the real life experience. He felt like he'd been born again as an adult. Nothing he'd seen or read prepared him for the first meal outside of prison. The lack of notoriety at the local diner put him at ease. No one knew him. No one cared.

The look on his daughter's face said it all as she smiled and laughed. This is what love felt like. This is what love looked like. He'd never really known love before, with the exception of a few months with Peggy. And yet, here he was at the age of sixty-nine bursting with love for a woman, his daughter, and her three sons, his grandsons. He had a family.

"So, when do we leave for San Diego?" Jerry asked, his eyes tearing up, but his smile full of hope. He'd be going back, back to where the air was neither cold nor hot. Fresh air, clean air, free air. A place he knew and loved, where he could live his life in peace ... a life he thought he'd lost forever, a life now suddenly found.

He was an old man. His life had been tragic. And yet, he was filled with joy.

Thank-You:

To Gregory Moser for my beautiful book cover.

To God for my awesome grandsons:

Carson, Parker, and Holden